CROOKED Crows

BOYS OF BRIAR HALL
BOOK ONE

Petal
& THORN

GROOKED Crows

BOYS OF BRIAR HALL
BOOK ONE

Petal and Thorn Books is an imprint of Thorn House Publishing Inc

Copyright © 2021 Elena Lawson
ISBN-13: 978-1-989723-11-1

Cover design & formatting: Pretty In Ink Creations

Edited by: Jennifer Jones @ Bookends Editing

To all the cuntnuggets who think it's all right to raise a hand to your child or your partner, your spectacular deaths are folded between the pages of this book. May you rot in hell.

And to my fiancée, for being the good man I get to come home to after fantasizing about bad men all day: thank you for not being a cuntnugget.

Corvus

ONE

Randy's body hadn't begun to smell yet, and judging by the still-tacky smears of blood around the carving on his chest, I'd say he'd only been dead an hour. Maybe less.

"*You idiot,*" I seethed, glaring at his prone form as I drew my blade, giving a short, sharp whistle to alert the others that we may not be alone.

Rook and Grey's quiet footfalls sounded behind me as they jogged down the alley, slowing to a walk as they approached.

Rook cursed, rocking back on his heels when he saw the body half-laying, half-sitting against the side of a rusted green dumpster. He scrubbed a wide palm over his jaw. "The tip was legit."

No shit.

A chick from the after-hours stocking crew at the Valley-Mart was the one who tipped off the Saints about the body. Damn near the whole town knew better than to call the cops first, and the ones who didn't...they'd learn.

If there's blood in the streets, you don't want the useless rent-a-cops from Thorn Valley PD on the case. They don't care about you. They won't protect you. The Saints will.

I knelt to drag my red-stained fingertips over Randy's eyelids and bowed my head. Grey crouched next to me, reaching two digits to the hollow beneath Randy's chin, feeling for a pulse. As if someone this pale, this *still* could possibly be living.

His hand dropped not two seconds later, his head with it.

"I'll call it in," Grey said, dutifully drawing out his phone and rising from his crouch.

"Stay close," I growled when he moved to walk away.

"He was supposed to be made a full member at the next meeting," Rook mused aloud, biting on his lip ring. A habit he knew annoyed the absolute fuck out of me.

I stood, pushing off from my knees. "Not anymore." I held out a hand for the bag slung over Rook's shoulder. "Give me the tarp. Let's get this shit over with. I need a fucking shower."

Rook tossed me the bag, and I pulled out the folded blue square, wincing when the sound of it crinkling echoed back to us from the tall brick walls of the alley. The whole place smelled like trash, but there was an undercurrent of something out of place, too. Cologne. Or just some really terrible aftershave. Like a pinecone got ass fucked by a lime. My nose wrinkled at the reek of it.

"Keep an eye out."

Rook nodded, drawing his blade and hissing at Grey to get off the damned phone and help me.

"The carving," Grey stated as he ended the call, helping me lay out the tarp to roll the poor bastard's body onto it. "It was the Aces?"

The letter 'A' brutally carved into the pale flesh of Randy's chest would make anyone think so, but I wasn't convinced.

"We haven't had beef with the Iron Aces in months," I hissed. "There's no reason for this. Doesn't make sense."

"But the carving—"

"I know what it looks like, Winters."

At that, both of my brothers fell silent, and we wrapped Randy's body tightly in the tarp, binding him like a fucking sausage with half a roll of duct tape.

He was only twenty-four. Didn't have a family. No kids. Not even a girlfriend. Without any of those things, Randy would be given a whiskey-fueled farewell by the Thorn Valley Saints and then sent to a watery grave. It was the best many of us could hope for.

"Diesel's orders are to bring him to the Crow's Nest

for now. Said he'd deal with it later," Grey told me as we finished, and I stuffed the rest of the duct tape back into the bag and tossed it to Rook.

When I didn't reply, still trying to work through the puzzle that was Randy's mangled corpse, Rook stepped to my side. "Want me to bring the Rover 'round?"

I nodded, jerking my chin for Grey to follow. "Go with him."

At least it was a cool night for early October in Northern Cali. Hopefully, his corpse wouldn't stink up the Rover too much before Diesel sent the cleaners to deal with it. Nothing worse than the smell of dead guy in the morning.

They turned to leave, but the roar of an engine coming to a stuttering, screeching stop at the mouth of the alley had me throwing an arm out to shield them, gun drawn, finger resting next to the trigger.

The sleek black sedan hadn't even come to a full stop before a body jumped out of the backseat.

I took aim.

Air rushed from my lungs in a heavy exhale. I relaxed as I took in long legs, a mane of dark brown hair, and an ass so fine it made my cock twitch beneath my jeans.

"Move the body," I hissed. Grey and Rook each took an end, pulling Randy with us into the shadows behind the trash bin and out of sight.

A driver exited the sedan as the girl pounded white-knuckled fists on its trunk. The bitch could hit. I'd be surprised if she hadn't left at least one dent in the thing.

"Miss," the driver pleaded. "Miss, the school is another mile *uphill*. Miss, please—"

"Open the fucking trunk," she snapped back at him, her voice carrying. It was laced with warning, and the pinhead driver must've sensed it because he lifted his hands in a placating gesture I knew well and retreated to the open driver's side door to pop the trunk.

"Ava Jade," came a woman's willowy voice from the darkened backseat as a window rolled lazily down. "You get back in the car this instant."

The girl, Ava Jade, I presumed, ignored the older woman's plea, hauling a massive suitcase and satchel from the trunk. When the damn thing fell over, it nearly took her with it, but she righted the suitcase, and herself, and took off in a huff, lugging all of her things up the road.

"*Ava Jade!*"

The girl paused, an audible growl tearing from her lips as she spun. A dark simpering fury in the set of her jaw. "I'd rather be at some bullshit elitist academy than spend a single night at your fucking *museum*."

She didn't spare another second for the old woman. She turned on her heel and left, upper lip curled with distaste.

Both Grey and Rook craned their necks to get a better look, and I suppressed a groan.

"Is that Old-lady Humphrey?" Rook asked.

The bitch was rich; her dead husband came from old money. She lived in the big mansion over at Waverly Place all alone with, rumor had it, at least nine cats and a parrot that squawked all hours of the day and night.

"Looks like it," Grey replied, and I strained to hear the distant hum of more civilized conversation as the old bat instructed the driver to *leave the girl and take her home for Christ's sake*.

The car drove off after a minute, and we were left listening to the distant echo of the suitcase wheels bumping noisily over the pavement as the girl made her way down Main Street and up toward Briar Hall.

Both the guys darted forward after the red glow of the sedan's tail lights vanished, peering around the edge of the alley wall to get a better look at the chick.

"Should we…" Rook trailed off, a mischievous grin tipping up one corner of his lips, Randy forgotten for the moment.

"*No.*"

"The fucker who killed Randy could still be around," Grey added. "We should at least warn her if not give her a ri—"

"I said *no*," I repeated, leveling the full weight of my glare on them both. Rook was quick to shrug it off, but Grey, he still didn't get it. He would though, even if I had to pound it into him.

I tucked my gun into the back of my waistband. "She isn't our fucking problem."

We weren't about to go out of our way for some spoiled rich brat who was going to be in the nurse's office all day tomorrow sobbing about all the blisters from her brand new heels. Not a fucking chance.

Grey stared after her a moment longer, and I didn't like the way his eyes followed her movements. Hell, even Rook still seemed bent out of shape that I wasn't going to let him loose on her. Turning his lip ring round and round with his teeth, his dark eyes gleamed with malice even though he was clearly trying to play it off like he didn't give a shit.

"There are finer asses than that in Thorn Valley," I said to Grey, attempting another tactic. "In fact, I'm pretty sure you left one in your bed an hour ago."

Grey tipped his head to one side, snorting a laugh.

We both knew I wasn't wrong about that last part, but fuck if I didn't know the first bit was total horseshit. I'd never seen a piece of ass that was worth wasting more than a night on. But *that ass*—that ass was trouble if I'd ever seen it.

It was in both of my brothers' curious stares as they took one last look at her before turning back to me for orders. I was going to have to do something about this *Ava Jade*. Fast.

"Get the Rover," I told them. "Looks like tomorrow we have a new student to welcome to Briar Hall."

Ava Jade

TWO

"*Stupid motherfucking bullshit wheels*," I cursed, kicking the suitcase back onto its front. The damned thing was overpacked, old as hell, and I lost one of the wheels about a quarter mile back. I tugged it along anyway, balancing it as it teetered precariously on the one wheel that was still working.

Everything I owned was in this bag. One way or another, I was going to get it up this hill.

As though in answer to my prayers, a break in the clouds allowed the moon to illuminate what was unmistakably a building taking shape amid the trees around the next bend.

A weathered brick exterior covered in young ivy came into view in bits and pieces. Darkened windows on the main floor were framed in black metal to match the large door set into the shadowy maw of a front stoop. Above the door in a bold pewter serif read *Briar Hall,* and below in shining silver cursive were the words *as the crow flies.*

What? No Latin inscription? How very modern.

I chuckled darkly to myself, wincing as the strain to my shoulders began to reach a breaking point. The damn suitcase chose *that* moment to catch a loose stone on the curving driveway and the case went down hard, nearly ripping my fucking arm from its socket.

I whirled around and kicked the thing as hard as I dared, cursing under my breath.

"What did that poor suitcase ever do to you?"

I had a blade out in half a second, letting the suitcase fall with a thud at my feet.

A girl emerged from the gloom beneath the front stoop, her shining brown eyes wide as she took in the slim blade gripped in my left hand.

"*Uh,* sweetie, I'm not here to hurt you. I'm just the welcoming committee."

That was when I noticed the haze of smoke in the air around her and how the heel of her knee-high black boot was stubbing out the remnants of a joint.

Not a heartbeat later the smell of pot-smoke wafted toward me on the cool breeze. I relaxed.

"Weapons aren't allowed on school property," she

added, clearing her throat as I slipped the blade back into the garter belt beneath the hem of my skirt.

"I won't tell if you don't," I replied, inclining my head toward her foot and the stomped out joint hidden beneath it.

She laughed, bending to retrieve what was left of her midnight puff. I guessed that meant it was a deal. "I assume my aunt called ahead?"

The girl nodded, pushing long black hair back from her face. "Yup. Apparently, Mrs. June couldn't be bothered to welcome you herself since it's the middle of the night and all, so you get me."

"And you are?"

"Becca. Becca Hart. You'll be rooming with me."

She didn't sound too thrilled about that. Her smile tight.

"I was told I'd have my own room," I argued, a prickle of unease going through me at the idea of sharing with a total stranger.

If I'd learned anything, it was that people could not be trusted. And having a safe space to plop your ass down at the end of a hard day to sleep was paramount to survival.

A shudder ran through me, and it wasn't from the chill of the late hour. I shook off the imposing memories. This wasn't the time.

The girl, Becca, came down to the bottom of the stoop

and reached out to help me lift my suitcase from the ground, showing off fingernails that were polished a perfect pearlescent black. Not a single chip.

Mine were a similar color, a deep plum, but shorter, chipped, and with all the color peeled off the right pinkie. She definitely noticed but said nothing.

"You do have your own. We share the floor as in: you have your own room, I have my own room, but we share the common living space. Most of the other students share at least four to an apartment. And on some floors, it's six. No one at Briar Hall has their own apartment except Bri. Well, and me, I guess, until *you* came."

"Shitty," I muttered as Becca helped me get the suitcase to the top step.

She made no comment to the contrary, but I felt her gaze roving over me as she shouldered the heavy metal door open and ushered me inside.

"The elevators are usually reserved for the Crows, but since they aren't here and it's the middle of the night, I think we're safe."

Becca walked across a wide marble foyer toward the single elevator against the far wall. To my left was a hallway twice as wide as the ones at my old school, a wooden sign on a wrought iron hook hanging from the ceiling farther down indicated the main office. Opposite that hallway on the other side of the foyer was a curved staircase leading up to where I imagined the classrooms to be.

The whole place smelled of oiled wood and old paper with an undertone of chemical cleaning product.

A loud *ding* in the dim foyer brought me back to reality, and I saw Becca striding into the elevator, throwing out an arm to keep the door open.

"Hurry up, would you? Before someone sees."

I did as she said, not because I was afraid of some mysterious *Crows* but because if there were any way I could avoid lugging this fucking thing up all those stairs, I was taking it.

Painfully aware of the trail of dirt and bits of gravel I was leaving in my wake on the waxed marble, I strode into the elevator and Becca released the doors.

"Who are the Crows?" I asked, my curiosity getting the better of me as Becca jabbed a button, careful to wipe it with her sleeve when she was finished.

Better to know in advance who to be on the lookout for.

I had to get through this last year of school, and then I would be home fucking free. Nothing was going to get in the way of that freedom. Not if I could help it.

Like Pops always said, *head down, eyes open, Ava Jade, that's how people like us make it in this world.* I'd never been very good at the *head down* part, but a girl could change.

Becca cut a sidelong stare my way, arching a brow. "You really aren't from around here, are you?"

"Is it that obvious?"

She bit her lower lip, thinking something through before she responded. "Tomorrow afternoon," she said finally as the doors opened again, letting us out in a long, dark hall.

"Tomorrow afternoon *what*?"

She shushed me, indicating the doors as we passed them, and I got the picture that these were the dormitories. The doors were too close together for them to be the larger rooms. At almost two in the morning, all of the students would be asleep.

Once we were clear of the corridor, Becca led me through a set of double doors and around a steep turn in the hallway. A sign in the same pewter serif as the front door of the building read, *East Wing*.

"At lunch," she continued as the door closed behind us. "I'll explain everything you need to know."

She took out a handful of keys from her pocket and separated two rings, handing me one. On it were two silver keys. Though I noticed there were not two, but three keys on hers. "We're just through here."

Becca unlocked the wooden door with the number 3 on it and pushed it open, flicking on a light switch as she stepped inside.

And holy motherfucking shitballs.

Equal parts stupefied, ecstatic, and disgusted, I strode past the wide foyer where a row of neat iron hooks held several jackets and hats and into a fully furnished living room. A black sectional U-shaped couch hugged a polished black square of a coffee table. On the gray stone wall across from it, a fire licked lazily at its chimney.

Behind the couch was a kitchen made up of a long bank of cabinets with a fridge at one end and a stove near the other.

Not like a cooktop or something. No, this was a monstrosity of polished chrome and black glass. With at least six burners. Matching cherry wood doors stood opposite one another to either side of the main living space. One sealed shut, the other slightly ajar.

"Holy shit."

I didn't realize I'd spoken aloud until Becca stepped up beside me, making me jolt. "Yeah. I like black. It just kinda matches everything."

When I didn't reply to her right away, she pursed her lips. "I mean, I can live with some color if you wanted to change anything—"

"It's fine," I hurried to say, picking my jaw up off the floor.

The living room and kitchen alone were damn near the size of mine and Dad's basement apartment back home. Definitely bigger than the trailer we lived in before that.

A painful jab in my chest made my lips tighten.

"I like black. But I thought we weren't allowed to

change anything in the rooms anyway? My aunt drilled me on all the rules on the way here."

After she tried to convince me to stay with her and have Jarvis, or whatever the hell that dickwad driver's name was, drive me to school every day. Until I shut her the fuck up by literally jumping from the moving vehicle. No way in hell that was happening.

Becca shrugged. "My dad donated a new library to the school and has promised them a new gym, too."

She paused.

"*After* I graduate."

I cocked my head at her. Did she just say what I thought she'd just said? That her dad was literally blackmailing the school with fancy new shit so his daughter could do what she liked? Fucking rich people. But even I had to admit, that was pretty ballsy. He could just as easily have gotten her kicked out pulling shit like that.

"Sounds like an upstanding citizen of Thorn Valley."

She barked a laugh.

"As if. The formidable Mr. Hart doesn't live here. He just shipped *my* ass here so he wouldn't have to worry about me doing drugs or riding dick. Don't think he realized there are drugs and dick in every nook and cranny of this country, and I have my way with both no matter where I'm at."

She shrugged.

"I don't mind him feeling guilty though. His guilt got me this room. Oh, and my Audi. So I can '*drive home for the holidays.*' "

I narrowed my eyes at her, still a little taken aback at her drug and dick comment. I expected goody-two-shoes. I expected brown-nosers and posers and assholes. I didn't expect…

Whatever the hell Becca Hart was.

We might just get along after all.

"Fair enough," I nodded. "I'm assuming that's my room?"

I gestured to the door that was slightly ajar. Becca didn't strike me as an open-door sort of chick.

"That's the one," she trilled, capping off the sentence with a yawn as she dragged herself to the kitchen and rifled in one of the cupboards for a bag of peanut M&M's.

She stopped with a hand on her door handle. "Find me in the cafeteria at lunch," she added before leaving me alone in the living room. "I'm bagged, and you won't see me in the morning. I have somewhere I need to be."

"All right," I replied, hefting my suitcase over the hardwood, afraid to let the mangled wheels rub against the polished surface.

Huffing as I leaned my bag against the wall inside the room, I felt around on the cool bumpy surface for a light switch, cursing when I stubbed my toe on something.

I flipped it on, and the overhead light flashed to life,

bright enough that I damn near turned it right back off. But in the end, curiosity won out.

The bed was the first thing to catch my eye. It was covered in a frilly purple monstrosity, with matching pillows. Who the fuck needed eight pillows anyway? I was lucky to have one at all half the time.

I cringed inwardly, making a mental note to get a new set the first chance I got. The rest of the space wasn't really that bad, though. The wall with the light switch was covered in a textured pearl wallpaper, and the deep purple color of the other walls looked pretty good with it.

The thing I'd stubbed my toe on had been a long dark wood desk with one of those fancy brass lamps on top of it. There was what looked like a walk-in closet to the left of the bed, and to the right, another door led to what I *prayed* was a bathroom.

Nearly tripping in my haste, I rushed to check it out, finding the light switch more easily this time. Fuck yes.

The room had its own en suite. Complete with a glass encased shower and removable shower head. Double sinks because...*rich people*. And a bright band of light embedded in the mirror. Stepping closer, I noticed there was a blurry bit and reached out to touch it.

The light brightened.

I touched it again, and the light changed from an orange hue to a blue one, making the dark pink circles beneath my dull eyes pop.

Jabbing the mirror again to darken my reflection, I tried to remember where I'd stuffed those big t-shirts in my suitcase. I could feel the tackiness of my own sweat drying against my skin beneath my clothes. A shower was absolutely mandatory before I crawled into bed and stuffed my blade beneath the pillow.

I noted the panel of shower buttons and my lips fell open.

It was official. Ava Jade was *not* in the Lennox ghetto anymore.

Sighing, I tore myself away from the awaiting spa experience and surveyed the room, checking the vents and every nook of the walk-in closet before I found what I was looking for. A loose board in the wood paneling beneath a shelf and hanging bar. I used a blade to carefully pry it free and peered into the dark hollow within.

It would have to do for now.

I upended the contents of my suitcase on the bed and pulled back the lining. The wrinkled Manila envelope filled with cash from my last job came free with a sharp tug, and I set it into my new hidey hole, notching the small panel back in place.

Chances were I wouldn't need it anymore. Not with a rent-free roof over my head and three square meals a day provided by my aunt's tuition payment, but if I couldn't do what she expected, I'd wind up right back where she found me on the streets of Lennox. Not fucking happening. I'd die before I went back to that shithole.

I set my blades right outside the door to the shower and stepped inside, hoping I wouldn't need a manual to work the thing. I jammed a few buttons, cursing when nothing happened.

"Come on," I groused, hitting the up arrow to increase the heat. "Let me simmer in my hell water you stupid fucking—"

I gasped as water sprayed from not one but five different places. Cool at first, but growing in temp until my skin flushed red. Just how I liked it.

Ava Jade

THREE

I rushed to the bathroom, the sound of sirens in the distance getting closer by the second. My pulse pounded in my ears, drowning out all other sound as I crashed through the door, hands scrambling to turn on the rusted faucets, smearing them with blood.

"Come on," I urged, as though by sheer force of will I could make the plumbing in our tiny trailer cooperate just this once. *"Come on!"*

My entire body trembled as the first flickers of red and blue lights swept into the trailer.

No.

If I could just get it off, they wouldn't know. I just had to get it off.

I scrubbed at my hands until they were raw,

ripping the tips of my nails off when I couldn't get the blood out from beneath them and prodding them down the drain.

Fists pounded on the front door. If they hit it any harder it would collapse and they would come inside. They would find me. They would see what I'd done.

Hot tears pricked at my eyes as I shut off the faucet, ready to strip the crimson-soaked t-shirt off next, but not knowing where I could possibly hide it in the closet-sized bathroom.

The pounding began again, and I heard a muffled groan from next to the bathroom that could only be Mom waking up.

"Get fucked!" she slurred in a drugged stupor, groaning. Something shattered in the room as the mattress springs groaned beneath her. "Now look what you made me do!"

I turned off the taps and whirled, vision blurring at the edges enough that I had to slap myself back into the present. But something sticky and wet was left behind on my cheek, and I knew what would come next. I knew because it was what happened every time. A hopelessness filled my bones, weighing them down, and I sank heavily to my knees.

My hands were coated in his blood again, and I let them rest against my dirt-streaked jeans, giving in to the nightmare. I couldn't beat it; I'd tried so many times before. It didn't matter if I washed it away again, it would come back as if I never even fucking tried.

I clenched my shaking hands to fists and set my jaw, waiting for the officers to come and take me away like they always did. But I wasn't shaking because I felt guilty. My breaths weren't coming short and sharp because I regretted what I'd done.

No.

It'd been a rush unlike anything I'd ever felt before, and I wasn't sorry. As the darkness had finally taken over, pouring strength into my adrenaline-addled muscles and malice into my mind, I'd smiled. The bastard deserved it.

I'd do it again. *And again*.

I only feared what kind of monster that made me. I only feared a life in a cage.

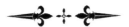

I awoke with a startled gasp, my chest covered in icy sweat as I heaved to get air into my lungs. No matter how deeply I breathed, it was like there would never be enough air to blow away the shadows clinging to my bones.

"Fuck," I muttered, throwing back the covers and rising on shaky legs to strip the bed, tossing the damp sheets and pillowcases into the wash basket. The more I moved, the more the fluttering beneath my ribcage came under control. But only once I pulled on a pair of joggers and a loose hoodie, sliding my sneakers onto my sleep-numbed feet and my earbuds into my ears did I truly feel a sense of calm.

I hesitated before grabbing my blade, hand trembling before I came to my senses and snatched it up, tucking it into my pocket and keeping my fist curled around it.

It didn't matter that it was barely dawn, or that it was cold as all hell as I crept through the room, down the still-vacant halls, and out into the early morning.

My breaths came easier as fresh air finally filled my lungs. I did a quick stretch before taking off toward the back of the old building, thumbing my phone until the haunting tones of Ruelle poured into my ears, singing to me of a game of survival.

A game I would win because I couldn't afford to lose.

I sang along, setting a brisk pace, relieved when I found a trailhead beyond the manicured field and gardens at the rear of Briar Hall. The trees welcomed me into their shaded embrace, and I breathed in the heady scent of petrichor, finding a sense of calm I hadn't had in days.

Had it really only been that?

Days?

Since Dad...

Since what happened.

I shook my head, savoring the burn starting up in my legs. The wind tugging at the ends of my loose ponytail.

What was done was done, and now, because of my father's incredible stupidity, I might just have a chance to do what he couldn't: escape the life I was born into.

Since Mom left a few years back, Aunt Humphrey was now the only person standing between me and the streets. After it happened, I thought I was fucked. Being eighteen meant that I was completely on my own. I'd have made do. Dropped out of my shitty high school and worked as many jobs as I needed to in order to keep a roof over my head.

Hell, I had already been paying most of the rent for Dad anyway. But then she showed up in her fancy town car with her ridiculous hat and an offer of a lifetime.

Aunt Humphrey and Dad didn't get along. I could see why, the woman was completely insufferable, and Dad was...well, *Dad*. About as much her opposite as opposites went.

She offered to take me off his hands when I was practically still in diapers so that he could spend the formula money on gambling. A proposition I bet my left kidney he considered well and good before turning down.

It almost felt like a betrayal taking her up on her offer now, knowing he'd refused her before.

It was too tempting to turn down, though. Only an idiot would.

She offered a comfortable allowance, to pay for my education, and buy me a small flat in the city, but it came with a caveat; I was to spend my final year of high school at Briar Hall, stay out of trouble, and get accepted into a good college by the end of the term.

If I could do that, she would set me up for a whole new life. The escape I'd always dreamed of back in Lennox was within my reach. All I needed to do was follow a few rules and be a good little Ava Jade, and I could have it.

I snorted through heavy breaths as I ran, giving my head a shake. As long as the privileged offspring of the wealthy and famous here at rich bitch academy stayed out of my way, it would be easy as pie. I could act the part of a nice girl and keep my head down for another nine-ish months, right?

Damn right.

A *crack* in the distance made me slow, tugging out an earbud to scan the trees, my free hand in my pocket, curled around the slender metal of my blade. I thought I saw a flicker of movement, but I couldn't be sure it wasn't just a trick of the slow-growing dawn light.

Shit. I needed to be getting back anyway. With one more good look, I decided there was nothing there and turned around. My skin prickled as phantom eyes followed me all the way back to the manicured lawn.

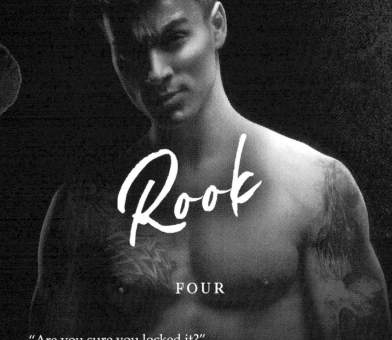

Rook

FOUR

"Are you sure you locked it?"

Mrs. June's voice came out in a rough pant as I shoved her over the edge of the pew, lifting her long skirt and nudging her legs apart with my knees.

"It's locked," I told her, though honestly, I couldn't remember if I had. Didn't really give a shit.

I ran a hand down the line of her thick ass, flicking her skin-tone panties aside to press two fingers against her opening. Her hands lifted to grip the back of the next pew as a stuttering moan left her lips.

She was already so wet for me. She always was.

"You like that, Care?"

"Call me Mrs. June," she cried as I shoved them inside of her, feeling her pussy clench around the digits.

I unbuckled my jeans and let them drop, exposing my hard on to the cool air in the chapel only for a second before I buried it into the heat of her cunt, not bothering to give her time to adjust. Groaning, I slapped her ass, leaving a bright cherry-red handprint behind.

"*Yes,*" she cried out, and I reached forward, clamping a fist around the prim little bun of blonde hair at the nape of her neck.

"*Quiet,*" I hissed. Not because I gave a flying fuck if anyone heard her, but because it ruined it for me when they spoke. She moaned as I eased out, driving back into her hard and fast, pulling so sharply on her hair that a whimper escaped her lips.

Her manicured nails dug into the old wood of the pew as I fucked her like a man starved. Until her little moans turned to startled cries, and she wriggled beneath me, trying to tug her hair free from my grasp.

"Rook!" she croaked between my thrusts, and I bent over her, wrapping my other hand around her dainty little neck as I drove into her from behind. I never really liked blondes, but Mrs. June had the body and the willingness to oblige my *tastes* to make up for that.

"Shut up, *Mrs. June.*"

My hips pounded against her ass, no doubt turning them as red as her pretty neck as I increased my speed, battering her against the pew until the thing started to come loose where it was bolted to the floor. Fucking her until all of my frustration was spent and the image of Randy's pale corpse faded from my mind.

The fucker who killed him was a dead man walking, he just didn't know it yet. I hoped Diesel would let me be the one to do it. It'd been a while. Too long.

I didn't let myself nut until Randy was fully purged from my skull. Not until the haunted memories seeing that carving in his chest brought back were gone, too.

"*Fuck,*" I roared, burying myself in Mrs. June until she found her release, her pussy clenching around my cock in a way that had me groan as I poured into her. Every meticulously crafted muscle in my body tense and writhing beneath my tatted flesh.

I released her throat, and she took a strained, gasping breath. Guess I was squeezing a bit too hard. I'd only meant to apply pressure to her carotid, but like Corvus always liked to remind me...I sometimes got carried away.

My phone went off in my pocket and I pulled out of Mrs. June, slipping my still-damp cock back into my jeans as I yanked them up.

Before I could get the phone out to check the message, Mrs. June whirled around. I saw the slap coming a mile away but didn't bother to stop her as the little slut's open palm cracked across my face.

Mmmm. My skin bristled, and I licked the dribble of blood from where the force of her strike tore at my lip ring, grinning at her.

"What's wrong, Caroline? I thought you liked it rough."

She moved to hit me again, defiance in her haughty stare and curled upper lip, but this time I stopped her. Snatching up her wrist, I yanked her in until she was close enough that her disgusting vanilla musk perfume filled my nose. Even in heels, she seemed so small, so insignificant as I stared down at her. "Hit me again and you will live to regret it."

Her bottom lip trembled for a moment before she got control of herself, snatching her wrist away to attempt to right the mess that was her hair and adjust her shirt to try to cover the marking my hand left behind on her throat.

"*Heathen*," she snarled at me as she stuffed her feet back into her shoes and made her way toward the door. The door that was not locked after all as she opened it without the need to undo the deadbolt.

She growled her frustration, turning back to give me one last blistering glare before leaving.

"You know you love it. The rough fuck. The fear of getting caught. It's what you need to get off, *Mrs. June.*"

She took off into the north wing of Briar Hall, leaving me with only the sting of her slap and the scent of her sweet pussy lingering in the air. She'd be back.

I rolled my shoulders, pressing my thumb to my phone to unlock it.

Grey: New girl is in our homeroom. Hasn't shown her face

yet though.

I had absolutely no doubt Corvus made some midnight phone calls to make that happen. The guy never missed an opportunity to control a situation.

I stuffed my phone into my pocket and pushed my dark hair back, shooting a look at the statue staring down at me from the dais. "What?" I asked Jesus, shrugging as I reached into my other pocket for a cigarette. Lighting it up, I inhaled deeply, tipping my head to the side to work out the kinks in my neck. "We're just going to play with her."

And this time, I had a feeling I was going to enjoy the game.

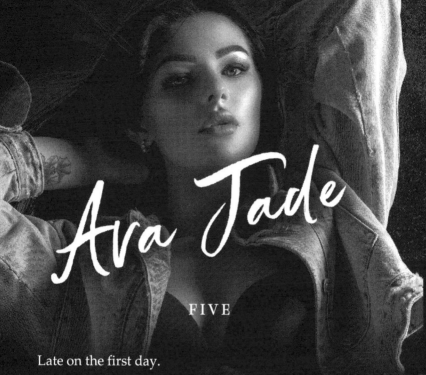

Ava Jade

FIVE

Late on the first day.

Joy.

Even though Becca warned me she wouldn't be there in the morning, I had to admit I was a little disappointed to find the flat empty when I returned from my run.

I wanted to ask her how to get to my homeroom and where I needed to go to wash my sheets. Tucked away in the pamphlet and massive rulebook my aunt gave me before carting me off here had been a map, but I couldn't find either in my things. I was pretty sure I left them in her town car after I hopped out in the middle of the street.

She hadn't called, and I wasn't going to be the one apologizing. She only said I needed to finish the year and be well behaved at Briar Hall. She said nothing about sitting there mutely while she badmouthed my father before he was even cold in his fucking grave.

"Where is it?" I muttered to myself, searching the entryway of the school for any sort of map. Of course, the office was completely vacant even though the bell had rung for first period five minutes ago.

"You look lost."

The voice was deep and gruff but playful. When I spun around in the corridor, I found him leaning against the wall in the mouth of the darkened corridor labeled *North Wing.*

I spluttered for a response, taking in what was surely *not* a high school boy but a combination of my best dream and worst nightmare all wrapped into one.

With lips clearly stolen from a Greek statue and a square jaw sharper than a razor's edge, his allure was undeniable. But painted over his knuckles and poking out from the top of his black shirt were tattoos. I was willing to bet that beneath the jacket concealing his arms, there was even more ink to be found. That, combined with the dark gleam in his eyes spelled trouble in big ass bold letters.

His teeth bit lightly at a lip ring at the edge of his mouth as he watched me curiously. Like one might watch an ant before busting out a magnifying glass to sear it into the pavement.

"Do you know where room 701 is?" I finally managed

around the lump in my throat, lengthening my spine. It didn't matter that in my rush to shower and get to class I'd had to forego my usual five-minute makeup routine in favor of some hastily applied mascara. Or that all my clothes were wrinkled to shit from being stuffed haphazardly in my suitcase. At least I had my baggy black sweater to cover most of it up, though that wasn't exactly pretty either.

It didn't matter one little bit.

"701?" he repeated, making me wonder if he was daft. Someone as gorgeous as he was had to have some sort of flaw. As he slid his tatted fingers through his damp dark hair, I noticed the word inked into his knuckles was, in fact, *ROOK* and that his knuckles were bruised and cut. I also noticed how his left cheek was blooming with a patch of red that looked suspiciously like a handprint.

"That's what I said," I snapped and then remembered myself. *Play nice, Ava Jade.* "Could you tell me where it is?"

"I'll do you one better."

Without another word, he brushed past me, a nasty vanilla scent trailing along with him that made my nose wrinkle. I assumed he meant to show me instead.

I considered saying fuck it and finding the room myself, but in a building this massive, it could take me all day. So, instead, I caught up to the guy, brushing the stray hairs that'd snuck out of my messy bun back behind my ears.

"Won't you get in trouble for being late?"

If the rules were as archaic as the old building, I was willing to bet they beat you with rulers for a tardy.

He seemed amused by my question and his lips tipped up into a crooked grin. "Nah."

We fell back into silence and that suited me just fine. I wasn't about to make friends with a guy who looked like he might be here to stage an attack on the place. Though I did do a sweep over his hand and neck tatts again, checking for any discernible gang ink.

Finding none, I was satisfied for the moment.

We passed several classrooms where teachers prattled on to the whispered drone of student conversation until I noticed the pattern of the numbers.

"I think I can find it from here," I said, eager to leave the guy behind in the hallway. His nearness was setting my teeth on edge, and not least of all because he kept sneaking glances at me when he thought I wasn't looking.

I called back a hasty *thanks* before rushing forward to room 701 which should be...*ah*. Right there. I shoved my way inside, pulse thrumming in my ears. My sigh of relief turned to something entirely different as the teacher halted mid-lecture, his gaze piercing me in place.

My eyes skimmed over the class, searching for one specific face, but not finding it. No Becca. Great.

"I, *uh*, I'm Ava Jade, I just started—"

"You're late," came his sharp reply, and my first

instinct was to snap right back at him with a comment about his Harry Potter wannabe glasses, but I smothered it with a forced nod.

"Sorry, sir, it won't happen again."

"See that it doesn't. Late students aren't welcome in my classroom, is that clear?"

"Yes, sir."

"Well don't just stand there, find a seat."

I bit the inside of my cheek and surveyed the rest of the class, face heating as I realized all eyes were on me. Eyes ringed in false lashes and faces framed in too-perfect hair. Clothes that looked like they were stolen right off the mannequins at Prada or Chanel.

The door bumped into my ass as it reopened at my back, sending me staggering forward toward the two empty seats in the room.

"Sorry," I muttered at whoever's way I was in, gaping when I saw it was the guy from the hall.

"Rook," the teacher said, removing his glasses to pinch the bridge of his nose with a sigh. "Glad you decided to grace us with your presence."

What?

Was he seriously not going to give the guy hell for being late after basically just verbally bitchslapping me for doing the same? Awesome, so the school was sexist as well. Why wasn't I surprised?

"Of course, Mr. Jameson." Rook tipped his head to

the teacher, giving a little salute and absolutely no excuse as to why he was late.

He shouldered past me and took his seat, leaving me only one option: the desk and chair in the absolute center of the classroom.

Rook had taken the seat behind me and to the right, but he wasn't who I couldn't seem to peel my eyes away from.

Directly behind the empty seat was a guy who was staring at me like he was contemplating murder.

If it weren't for the scowl twisting his face, I might have said he was handsome. With a whisper of dark blond scruff on his jaw and menace in his bright baby blue eyes. The guy was big and thick through the shoulders, though not as big as his pal Rook, who was whispering something into his ear.

"Take your seat!"

I shot Mr. Jameson a glare before rushing to sit down. I didn't have to turn around to find out that the guy behind me was still staring. I could feel his eyes on the back of my head as if he were leaning into me, making the hairs on my arms and neck stand on end and my hand twitch toward the blade strapped to my ankle beneath my bootcut jeans.

Mr. Jameson launched back into a lecture on something I had absolutely no hope of absorbing, but at least I could try to take notes for later. I dug into the desk, ignoring the whispers and stares all around me, but my hands came up empty. I thought…

I thought the handbook said I would be provided with textbooks and study materials and supplies on my first day. Entirely unwilling to raise my hand in this den of vipers, I resigned myself to just sitting still, which was a feat of its own.

As Mr. Jameson lifted a piece of chalk to scrawl something in unintelligible handwriting on the blackboard, someone tapped my shoulder.

I glanced back, finding the guy who I'd briefly seen sitting to the other side of the psycho-looking one. He was holding out a few sheets of paper and a pen.

"The fuck you doing Grey?" the one in the middle hissed to the one holding out the shit for me, his voice dripping venom.

"*Umm*," I muttered, glancing back and forth between them. "I'm good. Thanks."

"Just take them," the one called Grey insisted, shoving them at me. He didn't look like he belonged with the other two. Where they were all dark and edgy, he was an All-American stud. With one of those short on the sides and long on top haircuts in a brassy gold too shiny to be dyed.

A winning smile split his face, and he wielded it like a weapon, slashing away any hope of my being able to deny him.

"Okay then." I cleared my throat as I spun around in

my seat, paper and pen in hand. I caught the girl next to me glaring in my direction as I began to try and decipher what Mr. Whatshisface wrote on the board.

I gave her a *the-fuck-do-you-want* look, eyes bugging out of my skull in question until she finally looked away, her barbie pink upper lip curling in distaste. She had long blonde hair flowing in a perfect wave down her back with a solid gold pin keeping it tucked back behind her ear. Her outfit screamed money and her unblemished skin told me she hadn't had to work for a damned thing in her entire life.

There was no way those tits were real, either.

Fake bitch.

She gasped, and I realized I'd muttered the words aloud and clamped my jaw shut, redoubling my efforts to focus on the lesson and not on all the eyes watching the new girl.

Once they got their eyeful and made their judgment, they'd move along.

"Are you just going to let her talk to me like that?" The girl hissed in a low voice. Unable to curb my curiosity, I tilted my head to the side to see her baring her pearly whites at Grey.

His eyes lifted to the ceiling as he leaned back in his chair, looking bored as hell.

"Chill, Bri. You'll smudge your lipstick sneering like that," Rook crooned and an angry flush rose to her cheeks, mostly concealed by the thick layer of makeup she wore. She spun back around, her hands curling into claws atop her desk, practically shaking with rage.

Wow. Bitch really needed to get a grip. It wasn't like I'd called her a cunt or a whore, but judging by her reaction and the way she immediately looked to the nearest dick-bearing human for protection told me she was likely both of those things, too.

I studiously took notes for the next thirty minutes, droning out the whispered conversations around me and the way the asshat behind me kept 'accidentally' kicking my chair leg. Though, when the guy got up to use the bathroom I saw how gigantic he was so, maybe it *was* an accident after all.

Where Rook was all wide shoulders and dense muscle, this guy was tall as fuck. Like, he had to be close to clearing seven feet. Six-five at a minimum. For all I knew he probably couldn't help catching his size thirteens on my chair, but judging by the bitter look he gave me as he passed, he wouldn't have given a shit either way.

The blonde next to me, Bri, had her phone open beneath her desk and a coy smile tugged at the corners of her lips as she thumbed a message. Not more than a few seconds after she sent it, an audible buzzing sounded behind me, and she passed something back to Angry Face

My immediate suspicion was drugs, but then I had to remind myself where I was and amend my suspicions. Not drugs—*designer drugs*. There would be no tic-tacs or cloudy crystal here. It was likely all blow and bath salts at hoity toity prep.

And no search dogs, bag checks, or metal detectors to catch them.

At least I could keep my blade on me in class now. Having it close by almost always settled my nerves, even if in most circumstances I wouldn't need to use it.

Piggybacking on Dom's private self-defense lessons for the last two years back home made me just as lethal without it. Speaking of, I wondered how long it would take her to notice I was gone. It hadn't exactly been a priority to let anyone know I was leaving. Besides, she was sequestered up at her dad's place for the next two weeks while he defended some crime lord in court. Being a lawyer for one of the bigger gangs in California came with certain...risks.

He always made her stay with him in Madison Heights when he was going to trial. There was no telling what his clients might do if he lost on their behalf. Good thing he never did.

It was why he made her take the lessons in the first place. Why he didn't complain when I tagged along with her—since it seemed to be the only way his daughter would go herself.

"Hey," Bri whispered and it took me a full ten seconds to realize she was talking to me.

I squinted at her, checking to make sure the teacher was busy before replying. I didn't want to incur his wrath twice in the same morning. "What do you want?"

Her lips pressed together as she tapped a piece of paper in her glittery pink three-ring binder. Groaning inwardly, I leaned over to look at what she'd written and froze. Burning rage seared through my chest and steamed my cheeks, turning them no doubt a blistery red.

In a deep red ink were the words:

GO BACK TO YOUR TRAILER, LENNOX. YOU DON'T BELONG HERE.

Great, so everyone already knew exactly who I was then. I wondered if they paid off the office admin for the info or if they'd just handed it over with no questions asked. Neither would surprise me.

The darkness I always kept at bay slid up my throat like poison, making me have to choke it back.

I smiled sweetly and slid my middle finger over my lips, pretending to blend imaginary lip balm. *Fuck off,* I mouthed and earned myself a chuckle from Grey, who was at the perfect angle behind us to read my lips.

But Bri's grin only magnified at my slight, a deviant glimmer in her bright green eyes as she turned to the teacher, her expression morphing completely.

"Thief!" she shrieked, standing so sharply that her desk jostled, her perfect row of multicolored pens scattering to the floor. "Mr. Jameson, she stole my bracelet!"

I rolled my eyes. Yep. A cuntnugget for sure.

Mr. Jameson's beady eyes slid to me accusingly, his face in a disgusted pucker. "Now, now, class," he said firmly, making the chatter of the other students lower as he cut between the aisle of desks with his sights set on me.

I put my hands up, knowing the drill, even if Mr. Jameson wasn't an officer of the law. He might as well be here. Plus, if your hands are up, they're less likely to shoot.

Of course, you're still not totally safe even then. Getting one that'd had a bad day almost always ended in at least a few bruises from a baton or a getting tased for 'resisting' even if you were statue-still. At least, that's how it worked in Lennox.

"I didn't take anything," I said preemptively, cutting off the teacher before he could speak. "I don't know what she's talking about."

Mr. Jameson glared between Bri and me, his face growing redder by the second. "Miss Moore, is it possible you simply left your bracelet in your room?"

"No," she whined, pointing her finger in my direction. "Check her pockets."

Jesus fucking Christ.

Sighing, I turned out my right pocket and then my left, knowing the drill and just wanting this bullshittery over with. But something cool brushed my fingers a second before it toppled from the pocket of my baggy sweater. The dainty silver bracelet hit the polished floor with a little tinkle, and the rage I'd been working to squish back into the jar where it belonged began to overflow.

"I did *not* steal that," I said through gritted teeth as Bri crossed her arms over her chest, dignified in her accusation now that it was proven correct. I wasn't an idiot; I knew how this looked. And how weak my rebuttal sounded.

Mr. Jameson collected the bracelet and handed it back to Bri who looked far too pleased with herself for my liking. I wondered if she'd look so damned smug with two black eyes but managed to rein myself in, clasping my hands together beneath the table in a vice.

"Theft is not tolerated at Briar Hall."

Bri shared a conspiratorial look with the guy behind me, and it all made sense. The bitch had set me up. She'd passed the bracelet to the douche canoe behind me, and he'd slipped it into my pocket when she made me lean over to read her stupid note. I'd been played.

Wow. Touché, bitch. *Tou-fucking-ché.*

"Do you have anything to say for yourself?"

I glared up at the teacher, running my tongue over my teeth and half expecting to find fangs. When I didn't give Mr. Jameson the response he wanted, because I'd be damned if I was going to admit to something I didn't do, he shook his head.

"Gather your things and get out of my sight."

With pleasure. There was no sense arguing about it, not when the evidence was right there for everyone in the entire class to see.

"Detention," Mr. Jameson called back over his shoulder without turning to look at me as he made his way to the blackboard. "Every day this week after last period."

Bri grinned gleefully at me as I gathered up my notes, and I got an idea. It wasn't nearly as much as she deserved, but I remembered one of the cardinal rules of Briar Hall from the pamphlet my aunt gave me.

No cell phones in class.

I knocked my hip into Bri's desk as I bent to retrieve the pen I'd purposefully dropped, easily slipping my hand into the darkened mouth of her desk to grab her phone.

"Oh, so sorry about that," I said, my voice dripping sarcasm and growing loud enough that the teacher would be sure to hear me. "I didn't mean to make you drop your phone."

Her eyes went wide.

"Here." I dropped it onto her desk, and she went white as she scrambled to grab it, eyes shifting to Mr. Jameson who looked like he was ready to blow his top.

"Miss Moore, you should know better."

"Mr. Jameson, I didn't—"

"Detention," he shouted over her plea. "And I'll take that for the rest of the day."

I gave her a one-shoulder shrug as she fumed with a

declaration of war clear in her haughty stare. I hadn't waved the white flag like she wanted, like she expected, and I got the feeling she didn't know how to handle someone who stood their ground.

On a whim, I tossed a wink at the asshat who'd colluded with her to set me up, letting him know that I knew exactly what he'd done. That I wouldn't forget it.

His stony blue eyes watched me, never wavering, as I left homeroom. It was me who had to break the connection, my throat going dry as I recognized something in his stare: a darkness that should've terrified me, but instead had me curious to see how deep it ran. My finger aching to press his buttons.

No.

I shook my head, clearing it of any lingering shadows. Freedom was within my reach. One school year away.

Another run before second period sounded like a good idea. If I stayed here, I couldn't guarantee I wouldn't wait around to give that blonde bitch a rude awakening after class.

At Lennox High, I was the girl everyone knew better than to cross. All it took was my curling a fist around the disappointingly small cock of the Lennox Lions' quarterback, and pressing one of my blades firmly against its base. I only drew the tiniest dribble of blood, but it did the trick.

If the jerkoff didn't already think I was insane for

turning down his offer to fuck me in his truck, the blade helped finish the job.

By the next day I was branded a psycho and shunned by the rest of the school. Just how I liked it.

I half wondered if the same trick would work here before remembering the way the guy behind me had been staring. If I got his vibe right, the fucker would probably enjoy that. I sighed, tucking the idea away in a back pocket of my mind just in case I needed to use it.

Ava Jade

By the time lunch rolled around, my legs were stiff from my run and my brain was absolute mush from second period history.

Left with only my baser instincts, I followed the smell of roast chicken like a stray dog, practically panting as I found the entrance to the dining hall.

Dear sweet baby Jesus, I was *starving*. How long had it been since I'd eaten anything? A day at least. Probably more. My stomach burbled loudly as I made for the serving line, eyes saucer wide as I took in the heaps of steaming, glistening goodness along the self-serve counter.

Every kind of salad you could imagine. Not one but *three* different soups. Sandwiches with little toothpick flags sticking out of their tops. Steaming trays of lemon and herb chicken. Seared tofu. Artfully cut fruit that looked too pretty to actually eat. Sushi. There was fucking sushi.

"Drool much?" A girl sneered as I got into line behind her. She abandoned her tray, leaving the line presumably just to get away from me.

Her loss was my gain. She'd already filled one small plate with salad, and not knowing where she'd gotten the tray, I helped myself to hers, adding a bowl of creamy soup and three sandwiches to the pile. I promised myself I'd come back for some sushi after I was finished when I realized there wasn't room on the small black tray for anything else.

I spotted Becca as I turned and blew out a breath, glad to see a face that wasn't staring at me like I might be contagious. She flashed a smile my way, and I slid into the seat next to her, barely getting out a 'hey,' before stuffing the first sandwich in my mouth.

Becca picked at an orange on her plate and watched me with an amused look on her face.

"What?" I managed between mouthfuls.

"Just get out of prison?" she joked, eyeing my plate and mayo coated fingers.

I laughed around the bite in my mouth, swallowing it down with a grimace. "I might as well have."

I winced, realizing I'd said that out loud, but Becca

didn't comment or question, just snagged a grape from the top of one of my salads and plopped it into her mouth.

The girl from this morning strode in a moment later with three other girls strutting behind her. They had to be related, I thought at first. All three were blondes, though after closer inspection it was easy to tell at least one of them wasn't a natural. Her brows were too dark and her roots were beginning to show. I assumed it was a prerequisite to join her clique and snorted, going back to my lunch.

"I heard about this morning," Becca said, drawing my attention back to her.

Why wasn't I surprised?

"People are saying Bri has it out for you."

I rolled my eyes.

"Yeah. She's sort of like the queen of Briar Hall. A legacy student. Her family has been going here for generations."

Woop-de-freakin'-do.

Becca licked her lips and scanned the students in the dining hall like she was considering how she might want to chop all their heads off.

"You look murdery," I commented, wiping my hands on a napkin before swapping out my sandwich for the soup.

Her expression softened, and she smirked, one corner of her deep crimson lacquered lips tipping up as her eyes leveled back on me. "A bad case of resting bitch face," she explained. "Inherited from my mom. I checked and there's no cure. I always look stabby. Probably why bitches like Bri generally steer clear of me."

"Teach me?"

She chuckled. "Maybe. If you're lucky."

I set the spoon down in favor of drinking the rest of the soup straight from the bowl, wondering if it was too soon to go back for seconds. So much fucking food must get wasted here. Enough to feed all the students from Lennox High who couldn't afford a proper lunch. It looked like most of them weren't even eating, going straight for the sparkling water and not much else.

"So, you were going to give me the low down," I said, sitting back in my chair to give my stomach a moment to adjust itself before I attempted to pile anything else into it. "Anyone besides Bri I need to be wary of?"

She jerked her head to the side, gesturing toward the door. The three guys from my homeroom were just entering the cafeteria. The one who'd colluded with Bri to accuse me of theft scanned the student body, making heads spin away from him as though they were afraid to be caught staring.

When his cold stare found me, I stared back, tipping my head to one side, raising a brow.

His jaw twitched as the blond one said something, and the trio went to sit at a table in the back corner of the cafeteria. I didn't miss how it was the one vantage point that would give them an unobstructed view of the entire room, *and* ensure no one could slip behind them undetected. It was where I would have sat. Where I *did* sit when I actually ate in the cafeteria at Lennox High.

"Yeah. Kind of figured. They were in my homeroom," I mused as the blond guy went to pile a plate sky high with food and carry it back to the table. Grey. I thought he was going to share it—the bitch boy going to get everyone's lunches—but he kept the tray to himself, immediately diving in. Demolishing the mountain of food like a starved beast.

The guy was thick with muscle, but if he ate like that all the time, you had to wonder where it all went.

"You shouldn't stare," Becca said. "They're the Crows."

I lifted a brow.

She leaned in, her brown eyes cutting to the table in the corner and back again as though she were afraid they might hear her from this far away. "They're Diesel St. Crow's adopted sons."

I knew that name. Where the hell did I know that name from?

"The Saints," Becca said when she saw I was having trouble catching on. "The Thorn Valley chapter. Diesel's one of the original three. This was ground zero for the gang. Now there are chapters all over Cali. One in

Phoenix, too, I think."

Heat licked up my back, and my appetite for food vanished, replaced with something more savage. Of fucking course they were part of a gang.

I thought I was escaping that bullshit when I agreed to leave Lennox and come here. I should've known better.

"They're members then?"

She nodded, absently picking at the orange on her plate. "What's his deal?" I asked. "The one who keeps staring."

"Corvus? He's kind of their leader, I guess. Hot as fuck, but still a psycho. Totally a Scorpio."

"A what?"

"Scorpio," she repeated, her cat eyes taking in the long line of him before flitting to the guy next to him. The scary sexy one with the dark hair and the lip ring. "And that's Rook. I have him pegged as Aries."

"What about the one eating like he's on his way to death row?" I asked, curious. I never paid much attention to horoscopes or whatever, but clearly Becca lived by them.

"I'm not sure. I go back and forth between Gemini and Taurus for him. He's a hard one to read."

"And me?"

She pursed her lips, considering as she eyed me up and down. "I haven't decided yet."

I opened my mouth to tell her, but she stopped me

with a look. "No, don't tell me. I'll figure it out."

A knot began to form between her brows, and I sensed she had more to say, and it wasn't to do with which star sign I fell under.

"What?" I prodded.

She readjusted herself in her seat, her face pinching as she considered how to say something.

"Thorn Valley can either be the safest place you've ever lived—or the most dangerous."

"Depending on what?"

Her eyes flicked up to meet mine and then zeroed back in on the Crows. "Them."

"So, hypothetically, if I'd already maybe pissed one of them off—"

"*You did what?*"

"Well, I didn't exactly *do* anything. The guy looked like he wanted to erase me from the face of the earth the moment I walked into homeroom, and then he *helped Bri* set me up."

Her eyes widened. "Which one?"

"The tall one with the permanent scowl."

Her cheekbones flared. "Shit, girl. If Corvus James has it out for you, you should just leave."

I barked a laugh, but the sound died in my throat when her stony expression didn't crack.

"I mean it. It isn't worth staying."

My fingers automatically went to my lap, inching

lower toward the blade hidden beneath the hem of my jeans. "I'm not going anywhere."

Her lips quirked up at one side. "Then you're an idiot."

I shrugged. "I've dealt with worse."

"Something tells me you aren't lying."

She inhaled deeply after a moment, biting on her lower lip. "Fine. If you're staying, then it's only fair I give you a proper welcome."

Becca eyed my clothes. "Friday, there's a party. Maybe you can make peace with the vultures…What size are you?"

I looked at her in question.

"We might have to go shopping first," she explained. "There's a place in town here that I love. I'll take you after school."

I cringed even thinking about buying something at a place where she shopped. Not because I wouldn't like it; the price tag and I might have some differences of opinion.

But if they didn't have alarm tags on them then…

"Shit. I can't," I huffed. "I have detention."

Her lips parted in surprise. Clearly the *whole* story hadn't circulated yet.

"On the first day? I mean, I'm impressed. Took me a full week to earn mine."

This girl just kept surprising me.

"Took the queen down with me, too. I have detention

all week, but she has detention today, too."

Her eyes lit up.

"Brianna Moore has detention? That's new. She'll probably find a way out of it, though."

Becca glanced conspiratorially across the table. "Okay, so here's what you do. Ms. Wood runs detention, and she's an ornery fucker, but lucky for you I've learned how to tame that dragon. Listen closely and you'll have her eating out of the palm of your hand by the dinner bell…"

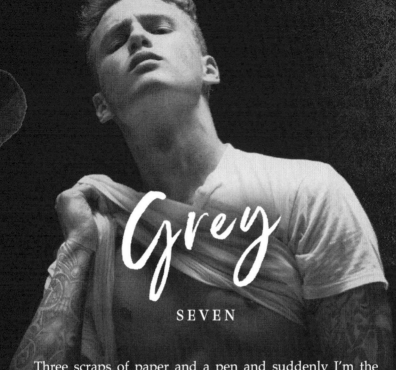

Grey

SEVEN

Three scraps of paper and a pen and suddenly I'm the fucking devil. Corvus got over it, but Bri...

My phone went nuclear at lunch. The instant we entered the cafeteria, she and her little posse turned up their noses and left. She barely waited two minutes to send the first in a slew of bullshit messages.

None of which I replied to.

She knew what we were. I made it clear to her from the start, and she agreed we wouldn't get serious. That didn't stop her from trying to lay claim to me in other ways, though. She'd already run one girl out of Briar Hall for daring to get too close to me. I didn't doubt that was precisely what she planned to do with this new one, too.

The mere thought of the new girl had my cock

hardening beneath my jeans. She was not what I expected, and I'd gotten good at knowing what to expect. How to play those expectations to my advantage.

Ava Jade was frustratingly, and refreshingly, divergent from all my expectations. I didn't know what to make of her.

Callous. Vulgar. Sly as a fox.

And smarter than she looked.

We shared AP calculus third period, and she finished her work for the day *before me.* I thought she'd handed it in unfinished, or riddled with errors, but I saw the look on Mr. William's face when he marked her answers. Looking at her like she was some fascinating puzzle he'd like to unravel.

I couldn't blame him.

Hers was not a conventional sort of beauty. Not the type best suited to be wrapped up in silk or adorned with flowers and jewels.

Ava Jade's was a brutal beauty. Forged of sharp edges and heavy contrasts. Lips bowed and turned down at the corners. Eyes dark despite their arctic color, hooded and calculating.

Rook elbowed me hard in the ribs, and I cleared my throat, readjusting my cock as Diesel stood from his seat to go to the bar.

The warehouse was a temporary meeting place since the new headquarters weren't finished being built. We'd grown out of the old lodge but still laundered money through it—and about eighteen other properties from here to Stockton.

Thirty or more shot glasses were lined up in two neat rows along the bar, filled to their brims with whiskey. Enough for nearly everyone here to have two if Rook didn't drink his usual five first. Whispered conversations from the other members quieted as Diesel lifted one.

His cut-glass eyes skimmed the faces of the members. Pausing briefly at the low table where the other guys and I lounged near the open doors and the barbeques pouring burger scented smoke into the night outside.

"To Randy," Diesel said, suspending time for an instant before knocking back the whiskey and upturning the glass on the bar.

His eyes glimmered with malice as he licked the shine of the drink from his lips. "His death will be avenged."

A few shouts of assent rang through the gathering.

Diesel moved aside for the next member to pay his respects to a drumbeat of fists pounded on cheap tables until someone flicked the radio back on.

"What's up with you?" Corvus asked, his jaw working as he picked at the label on his beer, eyes boring a hole into me. Looking like he knew exactly what I'd been thinking about and didn't fucking approve.

"Bri," I lied. "She's still in a fit about homeroom."

Corvus rolled his eyes but visibly relaxed, smirking. I

got the sense he was glad Bri decided she didn't like Ava. Less work for him if he wanted to get rid of her, which seemed like exactly what he wanted to do.

Stooping to helping *Bri*—a bitch he'd made no secret of disliking—set the girl up for theft? Since when did Corvus need help getting rid of a body? If he wanted her gone so damn bad, then why was she still here? I had a feeling there was more to it than I thought. He must've seen something in her, or knew something about her that we didn't. I wouldn't have been all that surprised if he'd already nicked her file from the office and used our contacts to dig into her past. He didn't like wild cards.

"What is it about the new chick that's got you all twisted?" I asked, regretting the question almost as soon as it left my lips. His cheekbones flared, and I was narrowly saved by Diesel coming to the table.

He slapped his hand down onto Corvus' shoulder and gave a squeeze. "I'm going to need you this weekend," our adoptive father said, slipping into the chair next to Corv, the mask he wore for the others slipping around the edges.

His exhaustion was apparent in the heaviness of his shoulders and the flare of red veins in his eyes.

Diesel rubbed the edge of his mouth, thinking, before wiping his palm down his short blond beard. Barely forty, but in this moment he could've passed for closer to fifty with all the hard lines creasing his forehead.

"Recon?" Corvus asked, running his tongue over his teeth as he turned his mind from the banality of Briar Hall back to business.

Diesel nodded.

"I don't think it was the Aces," Corvus said. "Doesn't sit right."

"We can't assume anything. Not until we have something concrete to base it on."

Corvus clearly disagreed, but said nothing else.

"Good?" Diesel asked, his gaze resting on each of us briefly before he stood again.

"Good," he said when none of us rebuked his order. We rarely did. "Now go pay your respects and get out of here. It's late. Grey, I'll get Cook to wrap you up a plate."

My stomach pinched at the mention of food even though I'd just eaten before we left home. "Thanks, Dies."

Corvus was the first to get up, abandoning his half-drank beer to head to the bar.

Rook stared on, his leg bouncing rapidly beneath the table as he twisted his lip ring around and around with his teeth between drags of his cigarette.

Corv was right. He had the itch. If we didn't get him some action soon, he'd go catatonic. "Hey, man," I said, nudging him. "Let's go get some whiskey, yeah?"

He rolled his shoulders and tipped back the rest of his beer before getting up, stomping out his smoke, and looking bored. A dangerous thing for Rook Clayton to be.

"Want to rally on the way home?" I offered and his lips twitched into a grin. We owned a good-sized patch of dirt just outside Thorn Valley with a few buildings on it. The Saints mostly used it for storing shit and taking apart stolen cars. We used it as a racecourse to destroy old junkers for kicks.

"No pussy shit," he said, framing it like a question even though he already knew what my answer would be.

"No pussy shit," I agreed. "We'll bust out that old Subaru SVX Corv found. I might even let you drive."

"You want to die?" Corvus said, reappearing like a fucking ghost out of thin air. "Because that's how you die. You want to rally at one in the morning, fine. But Grey drives."

"Suits me," Rook said as though he didn't care. We both knew he'd drown himself in whiskey before we left, anyway.

A familiar beat poured out from the speakers overhead and my throat went dry at the sound, all movement stilling as the first lyric dropped.

Corvus' face slackened as he registered what it was and calmly crossed the room to change the radio station.

Rook's black eyes scanned the room with unease before finding Corvus again, his analytic stare changing to a pained sort of pride.

I lowered my voice as Corv returned, still reeling but doing a good job of hiding it. "Man, was that just playing on The Edge—"

"Shut the fuck up," he hissed. "Not here."

I snapped my mouth shut.

"You coming with?" Rook asked him, the moment erased as though it never happened.

"No," Corvus said in a shaky breath. "I'm heading to the gym."

"*Man*," I started, but stopped myself when I saw the look he gave me.

Corvus barely slept, that was normal. He woke at the smallest sounds around the house and refused to wear earplugs or move out to the loft where it'd be quieter. But lately, it'd been worse. Like he wasn't bothering to try to sleep at all anymore.

For a guy who didn't let us have any secrets, he sure kept a lot of his own. He knew everything about Rook and me. Our pasts. The things we'd done, both before we wound up at Barrett's Home for Boys and during. I shuddered out of the memories trying to pull me under.

He never talked about his own past though. Not ever. I'd have been lying if I said I didn't wonder what kept him up most nights—what led him to Diesel and the Saints years before we were in the picture.

"Check in when you get back to the Crow's Nest," Corvus added as he stalked out the open door and into the night, not bothering to look back as he picked up his pace, starting a slow jog back toward town.

"Should've brought his Ducati if he was going to ditch," I mused aloud, my gut twisting as he vanished from view, swallowed up by the dark.

I shook my head. He'd be fine.

"I'd be shook, too," Rook said, clearing his throat. "Shit's on the radio now. There's no taking it back."

"Think Dies will recognize his voice?"

"Nah. I doubt it."

A muscle in his jaw twitched before his gaze trailed away from the cool night and back toward the bar. "Let's grab a drink and head out. I'm not in the mood for mourning."

"I'll let you have your fill first," I joked. "Let me know if there's any whiskey left when you're done."

He licked his lips and tossed me a wink before carving a path through the throng to the bar. I had to remind myself it wasn't drugs, that at least we'd gotten him off his weeklong coke benders. Booze and cigarettes we could deal with. When he was on blow, he was a fucking hurricane, and neither of us could do a damn thing to stop him.

Watching the other members, most almost twice his age, part like the fucking Red Sea made me smirk. People outside of the Saints always assumed Corvus was the psycho, but he was just the most lethal of us. Rook was the one they needed to be wary of. Where Corvus would plot your murder, taking into consideration every risk and possible outcome over a course of weeks before acting, Rook was liable to just snap at any moment.

And that moment was coming.

I'd have to call Julia tomorrow. See if she had anything new for us from the helpline.

My pocket buzzed, and I dug it out in a rush, thinking it must be Corv. That the Ace who carved that shit into Randy's chest was still around. But it was just Bri. *Again.*

Her message, the twentieth since lunchtime today, flashed over the screen.

Brianna: Meet you at your place around seven before school? I'll let you make it up to me...

My brows pinched, and I looked down at my traitorous cock. The thing wasn't even the least bit excited to get some action.

I readjusted myself.

Nothing.

Frowning, I thumbed out a quick reply. Annoyance washed through me, but I wasn't sure if it was directed at myself or her.

Grey: Busy.

Her reply was immediate.

Brianna: Are you serious?

Was I? I'd never turned her down before. The annoyance I'd felt before magnified as the new girl's face blew through my mind again. Bri didn't have any sort of claim on me. It was time I stopped letting her act like she did.

I started a reply that I would've regretted the next time my cock craved pussy but deleted it. The worst punishment for a girl like Bri would be not to answer her at all.

Ava Jade

EIGHT

Ms. Wood nodded as I left detention for the second time this week, her stubby fingers knuckle deep in the bag of Takis I brought her.

Becca was right. Ms. Wood was easily plied with a simple bribe of soda and snacks from the stash she kept in our shared apartment.

The only vending machine in the school was stocked with zero sugar protein bars, rice chips and some fruit things that looked like they belonged in the compost.

I didn't blame Ms. Wood for wanting a bit of junk food.

With her off-label clothes and unwaxed upper lip, she looked like she'd gotten the job at Briar Hall based more on her willingness to deal with the worst of the students than anything else. In fact, I think she might have worked at Lennox High for a while during my freshman year. As a janitor if I was remembering it right. I rarely forgot a face.

Becca was right about Bri, too. The bitch never showed yesterday. Looked like money and status really could buy you anything. Even a one-way ticket out of high school detention. I snorted to myself, hefting my books down the hall to the main atrium and the stairs leading up to the dorms.

Talk about a waste of power…

I fully expected another attack from her today in homeroom, but she didn't show up there either. Or anywhere else on campus for the rest of the day. Then again, neither did blondies 1, 2, or 3, so I had to assume they were all ditching together. Fixing their spray tans, I bet.

If I thought ahead, I might've been able to sabotage that…

Oh, well. There would always be next time. I'd have to learn where Bri liked to frequent just in case she was intent on continuing to try and make my life hell.

Two could play at that game.

I paused in the atrium, peering down the hall leading in the direction of the cafeteria. It was vacant save for the chatter of students eating dinner, just like it had been yesterday. And I had it on good authority—*thank you, Becca*—that the Crows didn't board here, which meant they'd already be gone for the day.

No one would know.

I backpedaled across the marble floor and used my elbow to jab the button on the elevator, bouncing on my heels as I waited for it to open. The thing was ancient, but at least it was better than lugging all these textbooks up three flights of stairs.

What kind of asshats *claimed* an elevator, anyway? Total bullshit if you asked me.

The doors pinged open, and I winced at the volume of the sound before stepping inside. Despite the masochistic part of me that almost *wanted* to get caught, I sighed in relief when the doors shut, boxing me in without being seen.

I made sure to jab the button for the main floor when I stepped back out on my floor, not wanting there to be any question as to whether it'd been used. And by whom.

No reason to poke the bears, especially when they hadn't taken a swipe at me today.

I'd almost been disappointed—the three of them seemed distracted as hell in homeroom. Barely paid me any attention except to stare. I could feel it, even if I didn't allow myself to turn around in my seat to check if my suspicions were on the money.

It would be better if they ignored me, but I got the feeling they were only biding their time for a better opportunity.

The sound of the shower and sweet smell of Becca's shampoo greeted me when I shoved through the door, making sure to lock it behind me. I sagged against the frame for a second, happy for a moment spent utterly alone.

Detention wasn't a group activity here. Not like it was at Lennox High, with a good mix of jocks and junkies. Loud jeering, tossed notes, and music playing so loudly through headphones that the cacophony of nine different songs echoed off the walls.

There were only two students with me in the borrowed science classroom used for detention at Briar Hall. So quiet, too. Like they were afraid to provoke Wood's wrath.

Worked in my favor, though. I couldn't imagine a more peaceful place to do all the work I was expected to catch up on. At this rate, I'd be ahead of the class by the end of the week.

Eager to set my books down, I kicked off my sneakers, stooping to draw the fifty I lifted from a buff dude that kept looking at my tits in math today. It was practically falling out of his back pocket anyway. At a place like this it was likely to be swept up and tossed out with the rest of the trash.

I'd make better use of it.

Hope the fucker enjoyed the show.

My phone chirped when I entered my room, and I

tossed the pile of books onto the bed before flopping down next to them, snatching it from the nightstand.

Shit.

Twelve texts waited for me to read them, and if the cracked screen wasn't lying to me, three missed calls, too.

Dom.

I flicked through the messages, finding a slew from her. Asking me where I went. If I was coming back. If I was alive. And then, the last two, sent within the last fifteen minutes, assumedly after she decided to go looking for answers herself.

Dom: Holy shit, babe. I'm so sorry. Why didn't you tell me what happened?

Dom: I'm here if you need anything. Text me when you can.

My chest panged at the reminder, and I grimaced, closing her conversation without replying. Not ready to have that phone call just yet.

Here, people didn't know. They wouldn't treat me with pity or with any added scorn. I liked it better that way. I wasn't ready to think about it too hard. Not yet.

Dom would understand. We were friends, but not the kind who really knew each other's business. I didn't know how to be that kind of friend, so Dom had to settle for a halfway friendship. The kind where we shared self-defense training and sometimes some fast food afterward. Where she poured her heart out to me, and I listened.

Giving next to nothing in return.

I flicked through the other notifications, bristling as I came across one from my Aunt.

Female Hitler: Detention on the first day, Ava Jade. Not off to a good start.

Female Hitler: Answer your phone.

Not wanting to ruin my chances of a big payout from dear ol' Auntie Humphrey, I thumbed a quick reply.

Ava Jade: Won't happen again.

Big allowance. Big apartment in the city. Freedom. Big allowance. Big apartment in the city. Freedom.

I repeated the mantra in my head, trying to picture myself in that life. Just a girl in college, with aspirations of being a…whatever the fuck college girls wanted to be. With a cushy savings account, a nice boyfriend, and a local eatery on speed-dial for late night study sessions.

Yeah. Nope. Couldn't picture it. I'd spent too long in the dirt, up to my elbows in bills and my mom's vomit. At least Mom was someone else's problem now if she weren't dead.

I wouldn't be like her, not if I escaped this place. I could be the college girl I pictured. Carefree. On the road to a good paying nine-to-five, taking vacations twice a year. It's what I should want.

I mean, it's what I *do* want.

I groaned at the next message. Sent from Kit.

My Ticket to Ride: You missed the last session. Dom's

worried about you. Want to come over for a bit?

My thighs squeezed at the offer. I'd been fucking Kit for almost as long as he'd been giving Dom and me self-defense lessons. She thought it was gross, since he was nearing thirty, but he was the only guy who'd ever been able to give me that big, glorious *O*. I wasn't about to give that up over something as trivial as an age gap.

Fuck. I could use the release right now, but he was an hour away and I had no way to get there. Maybe he could come...

No.

Sighing, I shut off my phone and rolled onto my back, setting it on my chest. It went off not two seconds after I shut my eyes, and I groaned inwardly, lifting it to my tired eyes.

I assumed it was another scolding message from my Aunt, or a worried one from Dom, but it wasn't either of them.

Unknown: Hello, Ava Jade.

I clicked through to see the number, but didn't recognize it. A grand total of six people had my cell number. Six. And none of them would be giving it out in a hurry.

I considered how to reply. Obviously, the person had the right number...

Two sharp raps on my door had me bolting upright, a sizzle of heat racing up my spine.

"*Whoa,*" Becca said, holding up her hands as she appeared in the doorway. "I come in peace." She grinned, crossing her arms over her chest and leaning against the door frame as I relaxed.

Her hair was still dripping wet from the shower, but she had it pulled back in a long ponytail. Dressed like she was going out.

"How was Wood? She miss me?"

"Yeah, she made a point of mentioning that detention just isn't the same without you," I drawled.

She put her hand to her heart, sighing dramatically before bursting into a laugh. "Thought you'd be down at dinner. You eat yet?"

I shrugged. "Not hungry, I guess."

"You sick or something? Or just finally full? I never met anyone who eats like you, except maybe Grey."

I swallowed, a prickle of unease making goosebumps rise on my skin as my screen flashed to life again.

Unknown: No run today?

"Did you give my number to anyone?" I asked, ignoring her other question. Other than my aunt, she was the only one in Thorn Valley that had it.

Her eyes narrowed, glancing between me and the phone clenched tightly in my palm. "No. Why?"

I shook my head, tossing the phone back onto the nightstand with a clatter. "It's nothing. Someone must've lifted it from the office."

Becca pursed her lips, but didn't disagree that it was a real possibility. Probably Bri. Trying to scare me away with ominous messages. How very boring.

"Well, *uh*, I have to go out for a bit. Help yourself to anything in the fridge if you're hungry. I had this eating *issue* a few years back. Now my dad has the fridge stocked with fresh groceries every week. It usually ends up in the trash so just help yourself."

I cocked my head at her, considering her thin frame in a different light.

"I don't have that problem anymore," she assured me, a muscle in her jaw ticking. Her body language shifted to discomfort. Shuffling on her feet. I looked away, clearing my throat.

"I didn't say anything."

"You didn't have to."

"You want company?" I offered as she pushed off the wall to leave, but her hesitation told me everything I needed to know.

"Actually, I forgot I have a history assignment I have to finish for tomorrow," I rushed to say, beating her to the punch. "I'll just go for a run if there's time after."

"You do that a lot. Run, I mean. Friendly tip? Stick to the main trail at the back of the field."

"Why?"

"There's an old service road that runs parallel to it. It goes up the cliffside to the Crow's Nest. You don't want to be anywhere near there."

"Crow's Nest?"

"It's where they live," she said offhandedly.

"There's a joint in the tin under the coffee table by the way," she offered with a wink. "History is better high."

I grinned, unable to disagree.

"Oh shit, I forgot. I got you something," she said, rushing out of my doorway and back across the apartment.

"You got me something?" I called after her, confused.

She reappeared a minute later with a crisp white shopping bag and tossed it to me. She had terrible aim, but I managed to catch it before it hit the floor by my feet.

"I guessed your size."

My stomach clenched.

"If you don't like it..." she started, trailing off. "I mean, I can always return it."

I peered inside, finding a swath of dark fabric. My fingers brushed the satiny dress and I grimaced, drawing it out of the fancy bag.

My first instinct was to bite her head off. I didn't need new clothes. Nothing was wrong with my clothes. I didn't need or want to look like the girls who went here.

"You don't like it," she said after a beat of tense silence, and I found her uneasily chewing her bottom lip.

I bit my tongue, seeing how clearly self-conscious she was about the whole thing. Maybe Becca was just as shit at having friends as I was.

Ease up, Ava Jade.

"It's actually amazing," I said.

And it was.

With a tight bodice and deep cut V in the front and a keyhole cutout in the back, it was a dream. The color was incredible, too. Black at first glance, but with a tint of dark navy and galaxy aqua when the light hit it just right.

The price tag almost gave me an aneurysm, though. It would eat up a quarter of the money I had stashed away if I were to have bought it myself. Plus, I didn't have the time or resources to case out a job in this town yet.

I hoped she didn't want me to pay her back.

"You shouldn't have bought me anything, though. I don't uh…"

"Have access to Old Lady Humphrey's bank accounts?" she finished for me.

I shook my head.

"I figured. I don't know much about her, but her tight purse strings are legendary in Thorn Valley. It's no biggie anyway, it went on Daddy's AMEX like everything else does."

Must be nice.

"Uh, well. Thanks."

"Welcome," she said, noticeably more chipper. "I thought you could wear it to the party tomorrow."

My mind immediately jumped to conclusions.

Wondering at her ulterior motives. She probably didn't want to be seen with me in my regular off-brand, thrift store clothes. Or maybe she was just wrapping me up as a gift to feed to the wolves to earn herself favor. Maybe…

Guilt gnawed at my stomach, and I shut down the part of my brain that always had to be suspicious of everything. Admitting there was a very good chance Becca just wanted to do something nice for her new roommate.

That thought was a harder one to swallow, and made my throat tight with emotion I didn't know what the fuck to do with.

"Yeah," I muttered. "Can't wait."

Corvus

NINE

"This it?"

Grey pulled the car we borrowed from underground parking in town up to a neat white house with blue shutters, a doubtful frown turning down the edge of his mouth. "Thought that asshole lived down on Freemont, near the trailer park. That's where we picked him up the last time."

Rook chewed his lip ring in the backseat, already hedging to the door, his hands twitching.

"Yeah, I'm fucking sure," I growled, cutting Grey a look. "What? Shitty people can't live in nice houses?"

He inclined his head, knowing that all too well himself.

I inhaled deeply to calm down, knowing I was ornery

as fuck. I'd have preferred to plan this little visit over at least a few days, if not a week, but we were running out of time.

Tomorrow was the monthly full moon party down at the docks and we needed to be there. The location, though it was perfect for parties, was right on the edge of our territory. The *one time* we didn't go, a group of junior Aces crashed and almost drowned a chick. We couldn't have that in our town.

If we didn't do this now—for Rook—then we'd have to leave him behind. I hated that idea almost as much as the idea of bringing him with us when he was like this.

"What are we waiting for? Let's fucking go," Rook gritted out, his tatted hand poised on the door handle in the backseat.

"Hold it. We need to scope it out. Julia said the kid usually leaves around this time to sleep out with a friend. We got to make sure he's gone."

A muscle in Grey's jaw twitched and Rook kicked the back of the seat, cursing.

I'd already gotten everything else into place, this was the one moving piece that I wasn't sure of, and it made my fucking skin itch.

"Stay here," I said, slipping out of the car and around the side of the house, skirting the hedges. It was a quiet rural street, and all the lights in the neighboring houses were out. Silent as the grave.

Except this house.

Around back there was a light on in the kitchen and the radio playing on low inside.

I crept to the sliding door and peered within, finding the whitewashed kitchen empty save for the row of empty brown bottles by the sink.

Soft footsteps drummed down the steps after two minutes of waiting and I lowered myself next to the door, crouching to be hidden by the deck's banister.

A boy, no more than eleven, rushed into the kitchen on quick, quiet feet, his runners in his hands. A fresh shiner bloated the flesh around his left eye and what looked like a fresh cigarette burn sat angry and red just below his jaw. I'd seen enough just like it on Rook, though his asshat of a step-uncle preferred cigars. His new tatts hid the scars well unless you knew where to look for them.

The boy's name was Thomas.

He'd called the number on our flier three times in the last six months after calling the cops did nothing to help him. Twice, we'd given his joke of a father very straight forward warnings about what would happen to him if he didn't stop. But apparently a broken arm and five cracked ribs weren't enough.

First warning, we scared them. Told them what would happen if they didn't comply.

Second warning got them at least five broken bones. A burned appendage. Maybe some missing fingernails.

Depended what kind of mood Rook was in.

But three strikes…

He's out.

The same rule didn't apply to child molesters though. They didn't get second chances.

Better no parents at all than ones like Thomas'.

We knew from the helpline that Thomas had an aunt he could live with, who'd been trying to get custody of him. But the ones who had no one else…we saw to it that they had the right connections in the system. That they weren't hurt anymore.

We weren't heroes.

We were just boogiemen who developed a taste for the flesh of villains. Someone had to sate that need. Who better than pieces of shit like Frank?

I vanished into the shadows beneath the deck as Thomas eased the patio door open and pushed through, his breaths coming quick. His shoulders up to his ears. Inside, a loud thud made him jump and gasp before he took off like a shot into the dark, sprinting through neighboring backyards until he disappeared over a low fence and was gone.

No better time than the present.

I walked back to the side of the house and nodded to my brothers in the old Camry before tugging the ski mask from my back pocket and pulling it over my face.

Rook's breath clouded in the cool night air as he came

around the back of the house, his chest wide and heaving.

I nodded.

"We take him," I ordered before setting him loose. "I don't want to clean up a crime scene here."

"Fine."

"No blood."

"*Fine.*"

Rook went into the house first, and Grey and I followed, double checking the yards and area for anyone who might see.

All clear.

Even if the name *Saint* was enough to ensure we wouldn't be bothered, at least on our own turf, I liked the added layer of security. The residents of Thorn Valley may not go to the cops, but a few had tried blackmail in the past. Didn't work out for them the way they hoped, but I'd rather not deal with that shit.

"*No!*" came a shout inside the house, and my jaw locked tight as I followed Grey inside and shut the door behind us, flicking off the lights.

"*Rook,*" I hissed, following the sounds of struggle through the kitchen. "*Too fucking loud.*"

A second cry was abruptly cut off with an *oof* of breath, and I heard Rook breathing in through his nose like he was snorting a line. He liked the smell, he said. The smell of a man's fear.

I had to admit, it was a favorite of mine as well.

Almost as nice as the smell of a woman's.

Rook dragged the guy into the kitchen before Grey and I could get any deeper into the house, his bulging biceps cutting off poor Frank's air supply.

He struggled, his bloodshot brown eyes going wide as he took in the sight of Grey and me standing in his kitchen. Recognizing our masked faces from the last two times. Knowing what it meant that we'd returned.

The fucker doubled down his efforts to escape, tucking his chin to bite into Rook's arm like a feral dog. He got free, rushing forward like he actually thought he could get through us. Stumbling on his drunk ass feet.

Rook's blood spurted onto the tile floor, and he bared his teeth, rushing forward after Frank.

What a goddamn mess.

I shoved Frank back as he ducked in an attempt to slide through Grey and me and the fucker ping ponged off of Rook and then the kitchen fridge, making it pop open.

Rook got a hold on him again, but the damage was done.

Grey stared at the bare refrigerator, his eyes glinting venomously in the blue tinted light as he took in the empty shelves. Two slices of processed cheese and six beers.

Nothing else.

"Grey…"

His fists clenched.

Rook licked his lips.

"There he is," Rook whispered with excitement, his tongue sliding over his teeth as he took in Grey and held Frank steady for him.

My youngest brother shook as he turned his fury on Frank, and I stood watch as Rook shoved the asshole forward, giving Grey his turn.

The *crack* of his fist against the bastard's cheekbone was sweeter than any music I could create.

Grey hit him again *and again,* mute, his face a mask of stoic calm with only the barest glint of rage. He didn't stop until Frank was unconscious and lying in a puddle of his own blood on the floor.

"How hard is it to buy a loaf of fucking bread, you piece of shit," he seethed, getting one more good kick in before he began to settle, his shoulders dropping as the rage went out of him. He wiped the sweat from his upper lip, panting, and Rook stared down at Frank with glee.

There was a difference between inflicting pain for business—on orders from Diesel—and doing it for pleasure. This?

This was *all fucking pleasure.* For all of us.

"You finished?" I asked Grey with a raised brow. If he'd killed him, we'd need to find another asshole for Rook to play with. Luckily, he was just knocked out. Fucker would have one mean ass headache when he woke up. But not for long...

"Yeah," Grey said on a breath, slamming the empty

fridge closed and rolling his shoulders back, a calmness stealing over his features.

"Good. Go find the bleach. You're cleaning that shit."

Ava Jade

TEN

My breath fogged in the air as I jogged down the trail, one earbud in and the other tucked away in my pocket. The road ahead was gravel, narrow, winding up a fairly steep incline.

I told myself I just wanted to see which road Becca was talking about—to know where to *avoid* going but…

It was past midnight, and I couldn't sleep. I kept thinking about Dom, and Kit, and where the hell Becca kept going at all hours of the early morning and night. And, if I were being honest with myself, I couldn't stop thinking about *them*, either. This burning urge to know more ate at me.

Know your enemies.

I'd feel better if I knew what I was dealing with.

Where they lived. If I knew how far it was from the school.

It didn't take much to convince myself before I was stepping off the gravel road and into the shadows of the trees running alongside it, speeding back up to a run over the leafy ground.

A cool wind stole over the ridge, flash cooling the sweat slicking my arms and back, making the small hairs there stand on end.

I clenched my teeth, tapping my earbud to switch off the husky whisper of Primal Ethos singing to me of savages and saints. Just in case.

Statistics would warn against it, but night runs were my favorite. Especially in the hours just after midnight or just before dawn. When the whole world seemed to hold its breath, steeling itself against the coming of a new day. Only the night creatures chirped and chattered in the dark. Creating their own sort of music.

The house came into view about two miles up, where the road began to level out onto a flat, treed lot.

I squatted in the shadows, putting my hands to the damp earth as I squinted through the branches, keeping low as I moved closer.

I could see how the place got its name.

The Crow's Nest was a modern structure, tall and narrow, built of grey wood with big square windows and a sharply slanted roof. Orange tinted light shone out around the heavy black curtains on the middle floor, but every other light within was out.

There was a garage, built similarly, next to the odd house, and a smaller structure down to the right, almost hidden in the trees. A shed?

It wasn't built to match the others, it looked old. Ancient, really. And I wondered if it was the original structure here before they built the monstrosity of a house.

A camera hid in the alcove above the big black front door, facing downward. I checked for others before mentally giving myself a smack.

It was habit. Casing the place for weak points to exploit.

I mean, it looked like the sort of place where I'd find a metric boatload of cash. Probably weapons. Jewelry. Watches?

With only one camera, it was doable—

No, Ava Jade.

Jesus fuck.

What happened to not poking the bears?

Worst. Idea. Ever.

I sighed, deciding to leave well enough alone, placated knowing that they were at least eight miles from the school in total. Not far enough, but at least they didn't live on the grounds.

The sound of car tires chewing gravel made me duck lower in the shadows and I narrowed my vision. An old model light blue Camry sped into view, peeling into the lot in front of the house and coming to a jarring stop.

I should leave.

I should really *leave.*

I settled in, biting my lower lip as the engine went dead, and I held my breath to keep from making a sound.

A bulky shadow spilled out of the passenger door and pulled a black ski mask from his face. As he lifted his face skyward, taking a long breath, I saw that it was Corvus. Odd sounds filtered to me on the breeze. Whispers, and was that…

Was that whimpering?

"Get him. Let's get this over with," Corvus said as Grey and Rook popped out of the small car, both of them heading for the back of it.

Grey opened the trunk, and what was unmistakably a man with his hands bound clambered out and fell onto the driveway with a thud and a groan, breathing heavily.

Fuck.

With a reach like the strike of curved talons, Rook grabbed a fistful of the man's hair, wrenching his head back.

"N-no," the man choked. "He's lying. I-I didn't do anything. If you let me go, I'll…I'll pretend I never saw your faces. I won't say shit. I-I can pay you. I can—"

"Shut the fuck up," Corvus growled, slamming his door shut to join the others around the back of the Camry. "We warned you, asshole. And you didn't listen. This is on *you*."

"Please…"

It was hard to tell this far away, but it looked like Rook was fucking grinning. And not just like a little grin, either. He was fucking *beaming* down at the guy. Like he wanted to lick the smears of dried blood off his face.

"Take him," Corvus nodded to Rook, and he licked his lips, hefting the guy to his feet by his hair alone. Like it was nothing.

The man spat at Corvus' feet as Rook began to drag him away.

Corvus just stared at him like he was the most insignificant thing on the planet. A speck of dust in the wind.

"Fuck you!" the man shouted at Corvus, spewing more saliva with his words as he turned his attention to the others. "Fuck *all* of you."

The smell of blood and urine reached me on the wind, and my nose wrinkled.

"Fucker pissed himself," Rook said, holding the guy out at arm's reach with a scowl as he roughly manhandled him across the lot, carving a path to the shed at the far right of the property.

Corvus followed and Grey rushed ahead to unlock it and flip a light on. From my angle, it was hard to see inside, and I leaned to get a better look, snapping a twig.

Corvus froze mid-stride, his back lifting.

I clenched my teeth, sinking as low as I could go without moving too much.

He turned, his face cast in moonlight looking so violent, all bones and shadows and contrast, that for a second, he looked like a skeleton come to life. Like a grim reaper searching for prey.

His hollow-eyed gaze swept over the lot and the trees before he continued, following his brothers into the small shed and shutting the door behind him.

It took about five seconds before the screaming started. Loud at first, and then muffled as though someone had stuck something in the man's mouth. They were torturing him.

My stomach lurched.

In Lennox, the Kings ruled the streets, but they didn't have the reach the Saints did. Or even the Aces. The Kings stayed in Lennox, keeping to their turf, never expanding.

I supposed I could see why.

If the junior members got their kicks torturing people, then how were the senior members?

Fucking gangs.

My upper lip twitched into a snarl.

Gangs stole my innocence. They ruined my mother. And now they'd taken my father, too.

Fuck the Crows.

They were just bad news wrapped up in pretty paper.

For a heartbeat, I considered setting the shed on fire

with them inside of it. It'd be easy. Older cars were simple as fuck to hotwire. I'd just back it up to the door, blocking their escape, pop open the gas tank and drop in a match.

I'd probably be doing the world a favor.

But I was short exactly one match.

And the energy required to run for the rest of my life from one of the largest gangs in the western USA.

Tearing my gaze away, I stood and turned from the Crow's Nest, right at the exact second the shed door banged back open and Grey strolled out, shutting it firmly behind him and rubbing a palm over his jaw.

My heart vaulted into my throat.

He started toward the front door of the house, and I allowed myself a small breath, backing slowly away from the house, never letting my gaze falter from his back.

Grey stopped before he reached the door, tilting his head to one side.

No.

He whirled around, and it was too late to react.

Our eyes met.

I was fucking *gone*.

Without bothering to see if he was giving chase, I bolted through the trees, skidding down a slope and barely clawing back to my feet as I pressed forward, heedless of the trees jutting out of the earth like long fingers trying to grab me. To stop me from getting away.

I weaved through the forest, my focus dialing in like

it always did when that blessed spike of adrenaline injected itself into my blood. My feet moved with more surety, keeping an unfathomably quick pace as I expertly avoided the worst of the branches, knowing exactly where to step on instinct.

As the drumbeat echo of my pulse quieted, my ears opening back up to the world around me, I heard him.

It was a second too late.

The inclined path worked in his favor as he tackled me from behind. My face and chest collided with the earth, skidding through sharp twigs and over gritty earth. The taste of blood and dirt coated my tongue as I worked to get him off, coughing, my hand reaching down to my ankle, to the blade strapped there.

His knee dug into my back, pressing me down as his hands wrapped like iron manacles around my forearms, effectively pinning me beneath him.

A little tremor of fear ricocheted up my spine when I couldn't wriggle free. When my mind immediately went back to another time. Another place.

Another man holding me down.

"Let me up you *motherfucker*," I spat, just managing to eat more dirt.

"*Ava Jade?*"

The knee in my back let up just enough for me to get my feet under me, prying his metal grip from my forearms. I sent a backward kick into his face but missed, hitting him in the shoulder instead.

He groaned, reeling back enough for me to get to my feet, drawing my blade as I rose.

I held it out in front of me, blinking the grit from my eyes. It was a shame I only had one or I'd throw it. I hadn't practiced in over a week, but I rarely strayed from a bullseye.

Not worth the risk of losing it if you miss…

Grey panted in the dappled moonlight, taking me in with narrowed eyes as though he couldn't believe what he was seeing. He held his hands out, his eyes jerking to the glint of the silver blade, back to me, and behind him.

Like he was waiting for something. Or someone.

Backup.

Had he tripped some sort of alarm? Did he somehow have time to fire off a text in the split second before he gave chase? Did he shout? I couldn't remember.

But I liked my chances against one a hell of a lot more than my chances against three.

I darted forward, taking a stab at him when he twisted for another look behind him. He only *just* managed to knock my hand away, going for a grab of my wrist, but missing. I slipped free and danced back two steps, ready to try again, my body electric with energy.

"Shit," he cursed. "What the fuck are you doing?"

He tipped his head to one side as though seeing me in a new light.

"Who are you with?" he asked suddenly, his bright eyes darkening, hooded by drawn brows. "Who the fuck sent you?"

He stepped forward and I gave a warning swipe. "Don't think I won't carve up that pretty face," I warned. "Just turn your ass around and *leave*."

"I can't do that."

A moment of brittle silence passed between us, and a scowl twisted his features. I hadn't noticed before, he usually wore long sleeves at school, but now, in nothing but a loose tank, I saw that he was covered in tattoos. Just like Rook. One entire arm. A half sleeve on the other. Except Rook's seemed to be done in shades of black and Grey's were all painted in vivid color.

"Who are you with?" he asked again, each word dripping venom as his fists clenched. "The Aces? Did they plant you—"

"I'm not with a gang, asshole," I spat, trying to judge whether or not I could get away if I tried a second time to run. I'd have to incapacitate him first. A good slice to the inner thigh would do it if I could get close enough. He might even survive if someone found him within a few minutes and got him to an emergency room.

But I didn't hear anyone else coming. Besides, then what would I do?

Run? Hide?

Grey's eyes carved a path up and down my body,

taking in my jogging pants and cropped tank. My running shoes.

"Little late for a run, isn't it?"

"I couldn't sleep," I muttered, not sure why I was continuing a conversation with a guy who was clearly part of a murder-in-progress not even half a mile up the hill.

Grey lifted his shirt, turning to show that he was unarmed. He stooped to lift the edge of his jeans, too, showing his ankles, keeping a steady eye on me the whole time. He had more tattoos on his calves and the outline of something started on his ribs.

"I'm not armed," he said. "You say you're not with a gang? I'm going to need you to prove that if I'm going to let you go."

Let me go?

"Yeah, right," I said under my breath. As if he was just going to let me go after what I'd just witnessed.

He arched a brow. "You see something you shouldn't have?" he asked dubiously.

"I didn't see anybody."

Shit.

"I mean, I didn't see *anything*."

"Well that *nobody* earned what he's getting tonight...if it makes you feel any better."

"I don't give a fuck. Not my business."

That seemed to surprise him, and he pursed his lips, eyes flitting to the blade and back to me again. "I'll ask you again, new girl; Did you see something you shouldn't have?"

"Depends," I countered, challenging him. Praying that he wouldn't tell the others I was here. "Did *you*?"

He grinned. "Maybe. Maybe not. *Depends.*"

"On?"

"Whether or not you have gang ink."

I frowned.

"I'll need to check," he said, his teeth dragging over the corner of his lip as he looked over me again. "Or you could just take it all off for me."

"*Hell* no."

"Then I'm afraid I can't help you," he said with a shrug and lifted two fingers to his lips, ready to whistle.

"Wait!"

His lips split into a mischievous grin again and he crossed his arms. "Shall I check, then? Or would you rather give me a show?"

There was no way I was stripping down naked in the fucking trees. I wouldn't be able to keep a steadfast hold on my blade.

"You can check," I decided, inhaling deeply.

"You going to put that away?" he asked, nodding to the blade.

"Nope."

His jaw flexed, and he hesitated before stepping toward me. I liked the uncertainty in his expression. That he didn't know whether or not I'd cut him.

Hell, neither did I.

I stood very still as he closed the gap and slowly lifted the edge of my cropped shirt, exposing my black bra and breasts to the chilly air, making my nipples harden beneath the worn-out fabric.

He tugged at the waistband of my joggers, and it took everything inside of me not to use the opportunity to put him down like a dog. But if he was serious, if he was going to let me go when he found no gang ink, then I'd rather avoid a war.

I'd rather pretend this never happened and stay the absolute fuck away from the Crows and their murder nest.

I was an idiot for coming up here. A damned fool.

Grey circled me, tugging my joggers a bit to check my ass.

"Like what you see?" I gritted out when he seemed to be staring a little too long.

He grunted, letting the elastic waistband snap back against my hips before bending to check my ankles and calves. His hands sliding up my legs to push away the fabric made my breath catch, and I had to snap my mouth shut to keep from making a sound.

He moved to my back next, lifting the shirt out of the way to inspect my shoulder blades. Nudging my messy ponytail to one side to check my neck and behind my ears, his warm breath fanning over my neck, the twin sensations of danger and desire making me…

"You finished?" I snapped, pulling away and whirling on him. "Satisfied?"

"Not even remotely," he replied, his voice a low rumble as he took me in with new appreciation.

I *really* didn't like the way he was looking at me.

But my greedy vajay sure as fuck did.

Why? Why were the bad ones always so fucking hot?

His brothers are up there murdering *someone,* I reminded myself. Or at least they were torturing him. I should *not* be turned on right now.

Bad vajay.

"Who are you?" Grey asked in a distant voice, as though the question was more for himself than for me to answer. Good, because I wasn't about to tell him anything more about me.

"Can I go now?"

He ran a hand through his blond hair, considering something.

"One last thing."

"What?"

He didn't reply at first, but the bulge in his pants told me everything I needed to know. "I'm not fucking you," I bit out. "And I'm not sucking you off either, so forget it."

He barked a laugh that sent tremors racing up my spine, making my nostrils flare in worry that someone might've heard. How long did we even have before one of the others realized Grey was gone? Before they came looking?

I needed to get clear of here. *Fast.*

And hope to fucking god that he didn't tell them.

"You think I'm the kind of guy that needs to blackmail blowjobs, babe? No, when I fuck you, you're going to beg for it. You're going to scream my name until your throat is as raw as your pussy."

"You're a pig," I snarled, tough words coming from a girl who might be kind of, sort of, a little bit wet.

He smirked. "Just a kiss."

"You're kidding. A kiss? What are we, twelve?"

He shook his head. "A fair trade, I think. A kiss in exchange for *not* telling my brothers you were spying."

"I wasn't—"

"*Uh, uh,*" he warned. "Don't lie to me."

I pressed my lips into a tight line.

"What do you say? It'll be like this never happened. Like you were never here."

"Or I could just gut you and run."

"You could, but something tells me you won't."

"Won't your girlfriend be jealous?"

He snorted. "She isn't my girlfriend."

"But you knew exactly who I was talking about, didn't you?"

He licked his lips, ignoring me, even though I saw a knot form between his brows. He didn't like the idea of people thinking he belonged to her. I didn't think he liked the idea of people thinking he belonged to anyone.

"We doing this or are you gutting me? I haven't got all night."

My knuckles turned white as I lowered the blade. "This is fucking juvenile."

"Then it should be easy."

I stiffened as he came to me without warning, his hand coming up to grip the back of my neck as his mouth came down on mine. Heedless of the blade I was still holding at my side. Testing my will to use it against him. Daring me to.

Motherfucker.

His rough fingers pressed hard on either side of my neck, locking my lips to his, tipping my head up as he pushed inside with his tongue and stole all the breath from my lungs. Breathing me in like he could reach inside and snatch my soul clean off my bones.

He tasted like salt and caramel.

Felt like hot coals.

His hand skated down my side, gripping my hip to pull me hard against him. His hard cock pressed into me, and it was that touch that woke me to reality. Sending a burning fury licking down my spine to pool in my stomach like acid.

I shoved him back, breathless, lips swollen.

I didn't even realize I'd cut him until he inhaled

violently through his teeth.

Grey gripped his biceps. Dark fluid dripped down to his forearm, rising to the surface even as he worked to stop the bleeding.

Oopsie.

It would need stitches, but he'd be fine. Not my fucking problem.

"We're square," I said, the words hollow as I strode past him.

He caught me by the arm, and I jerked to a stop, giving him a look that I hope conveyed how fucking glad I would be if he gave me another reason to cut him.

"Don't come back," he hissed. "Next time, I won't save your ass."

I tore my arm from his grip, a snort of derisive laughter steaming in the air between us. "Next time I won't hold back."

Rook

ELEVEN

Frank came apart beautifully.

His seams loosened bit by bit until his eyes grew wide and distant with hysteria. Until his sounds were nothing but whispers falling from quivering lips. Until his insides became his outsides.

With every piece of him that fell away, a piece of myself was returned. Until I was whole. And he lay broken at my feet.

His dirty soul in exchange for a moment of peace for mine.

Corvus coughed, and I remembered he was still there, standing at my back, like he always was.

I turned off the blow torch, stepping back to properly admire my masterpiece, tilting my head to get a better angle.

Bits of incinerated Frank floated in the sweltering heat of the old woodshed, sticking to my sweat slicked arms and bare chest. "I think it's my best work," I muttered with a smirk, looking to Corvus for confirmation.

He had his mouth covered with his ski mask, brows pinched from the smell. Corvus didn't like the smell of cooked asshole, but I'd grown accustomed to it.

Corv cleared his throat and dropped the mask. "You think the Met might be interested? We're low on cash. Could use the payout."

I snorted. "Dip him in epoxy and...*maybe*."

Corvus shook his head. "Nah, the fucker doesn't deserve to be admired."

"To the lake, then?"

"I was thinking the woodchipper, then bury the rest."

"Even better."

Corvus pushed out the door, and I hollered after him, not quite finished in here. "Can you pick me up another acetylene tank? I'm almost out."

I tossed the near empty one to the side and let myself fall onto the short stool in the corner of the shed, where I could watch the little Frank flakes dance in the moonlight on their way out into the dark. I fished out a cigarette and lit it lazily, twisted the pre-rolled mix between my blood and ash coated fingers before taking a drag.

Fuck.

I tipped my head back to rest against the rough wood wall and inhaled deeply through my nose, relishing the feel of *nothingness.* The stillness of my body. The quiet in my head.

Fucking *peace*.

Just like the first time.

Grey followed me that night, when I snuck out of Barrett's Home for Boys. I knew he was there, tailing me in the shadows, but I didn't tell him to go back. I think part of me wanted him to watch. So he'd be scared away. As he fucking should've been.

But he didn't come out. Not when I stole an empty jug from the back of a department store. Or when I siphoned gasoline out of a car.

Not even when I snuck into my aunt's house while she was out at Bingo, like she always was on Wednesday nights. Or when I doused my uncle's bedroom in gasoline and set it on fire.

Grey didn't come out until the windows were bright with orange flame and inside, we could hear my uncle screaming until he didn't scream anymore.

He sat with me, slung his arm over my shoulder, and didn't say a fucking word until the firetrucks and police and ambulances showed up. With all the chaos, they didn't even notice we were there, tucked away in the dark entry of the abandoned house across the street. It wasn't until they had the fire almost completely subdued that he stood up and extended his hand.

"Best barbecue I've ever been to," he said. "But I think we should get back before anyone notices we left."

That was when I knew: he was more than a kid I met at some lame excuse for a group home. He was my brother.

I could still taste the phantom flavor of gasoline on my tongue. Acrid and tangy. I licked my lips.

"Well, Frank," I said, stretching out my kinks as I stood again, snubbing out my cigarette on the top of his charred skull. "It's been a pleasure."

Grey cursed when I stepped into the doorway to leave and almost ran him over. He grimaced, and I wasn't sure whether it was me or Frank that offended him. Probably both. I was almost as covered in gore as our buddy inside.

It took me a second to register why he was standing awkwardly, his hand clutching his upper arm.

"The hell happened to you?" I asked, my veins flooding with heat. My hand jerking back in case I needed to draw my gun. I peered over his shoulder, looking. Listening.

Grey pushed past me, using one hand to dig around the various tools of my trade. "I thought I heard something," he said. "Ran into the trees to check it out and sliced myself good."

"On what?" I asked, scrutinizing the amount of blood

soaking his arm. Still trying to squeeze past his fingers. "Are trees growing fucking razorblades?"

"Do you still have that stitch kit in here or not?" he hissed, shooting me a glare. I didn't miss how his eyes kept darting outside.

Either he was expecting company, or he didn't want Corvus to see this.

"*Rook?*" he pressed. "A little fucking help, bro?"

I gave my head a shake, deciding I didn't exactly care what happened, as long as the idiot didn't let it happen again. Hopefully, he learned his lesson.

I knocked a still smoking Frank from his chair and brushed off his ashes. "Sit down. I'll get the kit."

Ava Jade

TWELVE

"You think Bri will be there?" I asked Becca as we got in her Audi, the all-black interior swallowing us up before she started the ignition and the dash came to life, painting her in shades of blue.

Becca pulled out of the school lot, giving me a curious look. "Why? You miss her?"

Turned out she went on a shopping trip to LA. Or at least, that's what Becca thought. Bri went every year around this time for some big annual sale a designer put on in the fall. It would be just my luck if she got back in time for the party.

"So much it hurts," I replied, my voice dripping sarcasm.

It was a relief not having to deal with Bri the last

few days, but I'd still had to weather the Crows this morning. I'd have been lying if I said I wasn't just a little bit on edge walking into homeroom, not knowing whether or not Grey would hold to his word to keep last night's unfortunate rendezvous between us.

It seemed he had, though. Corvus was his usual quiet, menacing self. Rook looked almost...*serene.* And Grey? Grey just kept on fucking staring at me. Not even bothering to try to hide it, either. Earned himself a solid jab to the ribs by Corvus at one point, too. Though I didn't know why.

Best not to question it.

Not to even think about it at all.

Banishing all thoughts of the Crows from my mind, I sank back in the seat, letting the supple leather conform to my curves. "Hey, nice car by the way."

"Thanks."

I took note of how the passenger side seat was slid all the way back and lowered, as though someone tall frequently sat in it. I wanted to ask, but it wasn't any of my business. I wondered if he was handsome. Older, I was betting. Maybe a teacher?

Becca had the air of someone much older than she was. I could totally see her banging a teacher. I just hoped it wasn't that Harry Potter wannabe from homeroom. *Ugh.* Or Mr. Williams from AP math. That guy gave me the creeps.

"What?" Becca asked after a few minutes of quiet driving. "Do I have something on my face?"

I laughed. "No. You're good."

"You clean up pretty nice, yourself," she said, giving me a smirk as she jabbed some buttons on the center console, connecting it to her phone, and Halsey came on. I should have known we'd have similar music tastes.

"It's amazing what a bit of mascara and a new dress can do, am I right?" she asked.

Well, she wasn't wrong. Even though I was loath to admit it.

The dress fit unlike any second hand one ever could. Hugging my body like it was made for me. The deep 'v' showed off just enough tit to be sexy, but not enough to be straight up slutty. The length was perfect, too, not so short that I would have to keep tugging it down, but not too long that it bordered on prudish.

The short heels Becca lent me to go with it, and the small miracle she worked on my unruly hair, really brought the whole thing together. I looked fucking *amazing* and I knew it. All thanks to Becca.

"So, anything I should know before we get there? It's at the docks, you said?"

Becca turned the music down a click as we veered off a main road and onto a side one without any streetlights. Though it was harder to see in the dark, she didn't slow. She clearly knew the road well, even though it wound and curved down the hillside.

"It's an old pier. Been abandoned for a few years now. It's basically just an old warehouse building on stilts over the lake."

"Sounds super safe."

"Not really," Becca said, checking her lipstick in the rearview, signaling to me that we were almost there. "But only one person ever actually drowned. Lots of close calls, though."

Noted.

"Just stay away from the balcony on the far side," she continued. "The boards are rotten. Bri got her heel stuck in one once, almost broke her ankle."

"I'd have paid good money to see that."

Becca lifted her shoulders and sighed like she got a case of the warm and fuzzies. "It was glorious."

I laughed, reaching to turn up the music as my current fave came on.

"You like Primal Ethos?" Becca asked as I hummed along. "Not many people have heard of them."

"I've been listening since his really old stuff."

"I heard he's on the radio now. Oh! And there's a show in Lodi next month. You *have* to come with me. It's going to be epic."

"I didn't think he was doing any more shows?"

She shrugged. "Guess he changed his mind. People are dying to figure out who he is. There's this whole online forum dedicated to sleuthing his true identity."

I wasn't surprised. I had to admit I didn't really care as long as he kept making music, but even *I* was a bit curious. When the video went up of his first live show, his face was done up in *killer* skeleton makeup, black hair slicked back. Eyes covered in whiteout contacts.

He was a mystery.

Honestly, I was no expert, but it seemed like nothing more than a great marketing ploy.

"No shit. Who do they think he is?"

She snorted. "*A prince.*"

"A prince?"

"Yeah, like of some European country. Hiding his identity and coming to Cali so he can do what he loves without the royal family breathing down his neck."

"I would've pegged him as an ex-con or something. I mean, have you paid attention to his lyrics?"

I turned up *Gravedigger* so the next lyric could play loud and clear, proving my point.

"Maybe he's just a twisted prince? Like that one from Game of Thrones, *oh fuck,* what was his name?"

"Joffrey?"

"Yeah! That fucker."

She had a point. "Maybe. Power does go to your head."

As we wound around another sharp curve in the road, the docks came into view and the thumping bass of music in the distance warred with Becca's playlist in the car. She turned it down as we drove down and into a parking lot running along the water's edge.

The pier was alive with a crush of people in the parking lot smoking and chatting. Others walked down the narrow planks out onto the water where the building perched on stilts loomed at the end.

It didn't look as beat up as I thought it would. But I should have expected that. If it was too atrocious the students from Briar Hall wouldn't dare go near it. As it was, the 'docks' seemed like they would be something of a novelty to them. Like rich folk who spent their weekdays in condos and their weekends 'roughing it' in cottages on the lake.

"Pretty cool, huh?" Becca said as she turned off the radio and parked.

I nodded. "Not bad."

The rough plank exterior of the building was done up in swirls of graffiti. I thought I caught the signature fleur-de-lis tag of the Saints amidst the blocky letters and vulgar art. Discernible from the religious symbol by the elongated bottom, formed to look like a blade. There was an *A*, too. The gang tag used by the Aces. Though it'd been badly covered over in artwork.

Clearly this was disputed turf. Noted.

The whole roof was strung with hundreds of little lights on strings—the only light illuminating the area for

118

miles save for the moon and flashlight beams on camera phones.

The music grew louder as we stepped out, the sound of it echoing off the lake making the bass reverberate in my breastbone. I only recognized a few faces from the school, the rest looked a bit older. Anywhere from late teens to late twenties seemed to be in attendance.

Thorn Valley didn't seem a particularly large city though, and I was willing to bet there was very little *this* exciting happening here on any given Friday night.

Becca looped her arm through mine, taking my cell phone from my hand to pop it into her purse since I didn't own one of my own. "I don't see Bri's car," she said excitedly as we made our way to the dock leading out to the pier. "That's a good sign."

I hadn't seen the Crows yet either.

Could it be that I might actually have *fun* tonight? A smile pricked at my lips as we waded into the sea of bodies walking the plank.

The floor shook under our feet as we crossed into the large building and I instinctively put my arms out to stabilize myself.

Becca laughed at the expression on my face. "Trust me, it won't fall," she shouted over the music. "There'll be twice this many people here within the hour. Then the floor *really* shakes."

Jesus.

I let Becca drag me to an area to the right, weaving through dancing and chatting groups of people, many already piss drunk. The colorful strobing lights made their movements seem jerky and robotic with each flickering color change.

Despite the cool night air outside, it was fucking hot in here, and I was glad I'd accepted the dress from Becca instead of wearing the jeans and long sleeve I'd planned to.

She swiped a red cup off a stack from a table, and I snatched it from her, eyeing the punch bowl with horror. I could smell it from here. Artificial sweetener and way too much booze and likely a whole lot more than that.

It was wide open, ripe for drugging.

"You're not seriously going to drink that, are you?"

She cocked her head at me, smirking as she drew a mickey of gin out of her bag. "I'm not drinking at all," she said, pushing the gin and cup into my hand as she drew a joint out from between her tits. "And if I were, do you really think I'm stupid enough to drink *that*?"

No, I thought, a bit guiltily. I really didn't think she was that stupid. I gave her an apologetic grimace, and she bumped my shoulder with a smile, lighting up her joint to take a long drag.

"Don't worry about it. The punch is probably safe, anyway. This is Crow territory. No one would dare roofie the punch unless they wanted their eyeballs used as ice cubes in Rook's bourbon. But still," she shrugged. "Better safe than sorry."

I grimaced, able to vividly imagine Rook poking out eyeballs with a skewer after hearing the screams from their shed last night. *Ugh.*

Biting my lower lip, I considered the gin and cup before handing them back to her. If the Crows were here after all, then I should tread lightly.

"Maybe in a bit," I told her, stealing the joint for a quick puff instead. She shrugged and put it back in her purse, discarding the cup.

Me and alcohol had a rocky relationship at best.

Let's just say my particular flavor of darkness liked to bathe in whiskey. I'd once blacked out a whole evening only to find out the next day that I'd apparently ripped a chunk of Bethany Vargus' hair out and shaved off her brother Kenny's eyebrows after he passed out drunk. Their crime? Not caring that their family dog went missing during their party.

I was only fifteen.

And I really liked dogs. I also thought I was letting them off easy.

It happened again last year, but that time someone wound up being taken away by ambulance. No one knew who hurt the guy, but I did. Even if I couldn't remember. Those cuts could have only been inflicted by someone who knew their way around a blade. And mine were stained red when I woke up the next day.

Probably best not to see how gin affected me.

"Come on," Becca called over the music, taking back her joint. "Let's dance."

She skipped through the party goers, finding a place in the middle of the floor, already rolling her shoulders with the beat.

All around us, warm, half naked bodies grinded against one another in time with the thud of the music. Lips met in sloppy kisses. Hips rolled and greedy fingers grasped and groped. These spoiled rich kids might've thought they were better than all the rest, but they were just as down and dirty as any you'd find in Lennox. Hell, maybe even more so.

I was pretty sure that girl over there was straight up getting finger fucked on the dancefloor, but by the way her head was tipped back against the guy's shoulder in ecstasy, I didn't think she minded the audience. Probably enjoyed it.

A group of scantily dressed girls next to us shouted *cheers!* and tapped their little white pills together as though they were champagne flutes, before swallowing them down with shrieks of elation.

A guy with a black backpack counted cash one of the girls stuffed into his hand and nodded toward the back of the building.

That was when I saw them.

The Crows roosted atop a raised platform at the back of the warehouse-like structure. With the majority of the overhead lights pointed at the dance floor, they were mostly concealed by shadow, little flickers of their faces visible with the brightest of the colors.

Behind them stood a pair of double doors, their square windows showing low lighting within. A guy, barely visible on the other side, pressed down on a pretty blonde head and then tipped his back in ecstasy. Uncaring that everyone outside could clearly see his slack jawed expression as the chick sucked him off.

"They call it the Red Room," Becca explained, her voice rising over the din of music and conversation. "You know? Like Fifty Shades?"

So they had an orgy room…

Classy. I rolled my eyes before unintentionally letting my gaze fall back to them.

The Crows sat on a long black sectional, looking like kings overseeing their kingdom.

Rook, with his feet kicked up on a low table, took a swallow from a silver flask before passing it to Grey. I spotted a bit of white gauze poking out from beneath the sleeve of his t-shirt and felt all warm inside. Knowing that marking was mine, and that it would likely scar, forcing him to remember me every time he looked at it.

Corvus leaned forward over his knees, his eyes laser focused as they dragged over the bodies crowding the pier. Until they found me, and stopped.

"Show me what you got!" Becca shouted, spinning in a circle as she shook her hips to a top forty song, oblivious to the eyes watching us. Now three sets instead of just one.

A muscle in my temple jumped as I clenched my jaw, willing them to look away. Nothing to see here. Move. *The Fuck.* Along.

Instinctively, my gaze slid to Grey, and I found him smirking, leaning back to settle in, crossing his arms over his chest in a move that told me he wasn't planning on looking anywhere else anytime soon.

Fine. They wanted a show? I'd give them a show.

I came here to have a good time. Something I hadn't had in too long to remember. And they weren't going to ruin it for me.

I began to dance, feeling the music, letting it pull and twist and curl my body, closing my eyes to welcome it in and block them out.

"Damn, girl!" Becca said as she dropped the last of her joint on the wooden floor and stomped it out with the toe of her boot. "You can move!"

"Got my mom's stripper hips," I hollered back, regretting the admission as soon as it slipped out. I danced around Becca so my back was to the dais, and the Crows, but I could still feel them watching my every move.

Becca's eyes narrowed for an instant, lines of confusion between her brows before she seemed to decide she didn't care, or that it wasn't her business.

I wondered what dive of a strip club my mom was undressing at these days. Or if, maybe, she was finally dead.

After what she did, she was lucky Dad didn't kill her. Hell, she was lucky *I* didn't. But that was before I became *this*.

This broken thing filled with hate, running on instinct and reflex like some kind of animal. Something less than human.

I didn't know what to do when she hurt me. Or how to react. I hadn't seen it coming. At least, not from her. She was always a druggie and a bad parent all around, but she hadn't ever done *that*. Not until she got the dirty drugs, cut with who the fuck knew what, and decided I was the devil incarnate.

Explaining the bruises to Dad the next day when he came back after losing all our money at the racetrack was the hardest conversation I'd ever had. For a second, I thought about lying. Covering for her. But...I just couldn't. I was done. Done covering for her. Done being the grown up at barely thirteen.

Dad made her leave that same day.

She never came back.

"Need a break?" Becca asked as I began to slow, sagging beneath the weight of the memory. Why did I have to bring her up?

I panted, my mouth parched from the heat and exertion. "I think I'll take that drink now."

She lifted a brow questioningly, but handed me the gin. I twisted the cap and drank straight from the bottle. Not too much, just enough to feel the burn of it slithering down my throat, pooling warmly in my belly. Fixing the ache there.

I recoiled from the taste, shaking my head to get rid of the lingering tang of juniper.

"Better?" she asked as I took one more swig for good measure and passed it back.

"Much."

The air was clogged with the smell of smoke, both tobacco and pot. Thick with a muggy dampness that clung to my skin.

"Hey," a deep voice rumbled into my ear and I spun, my pulse picking up speed, but it wasn't a Crow who'd slipped into our tight twosome. It was a guy I recognized from my second period math class. "It's Ava Jade, isn't it?"

"Josh?" I tried, though I was good with faces, I wasn't always as good with names.

His alcohol glazed eyes widened in appreciation at my memory before narrowing coyly, snaking down the line of my body. "Yeah," he said, moving his hips in time with the beat, inching closer. "Want to get some air? I could show you my truck."

Annoyance flared through me before I could fully

stifle it. "Well, *Josh*, I'm dancing with my friend. Or did you not notice?"

Becca laughed, putting her hands on my hips seductively from behind, beginning to pull me away. "Sorry, Josh, this little birdy is all mine."

"Catch you in class, then?" he called as Becca attempted to save me from being preyed upon. Little did she know it was a hell of a lot more likely she was saving *his* ass.

I almost slipped on a puddle of spilled beer trying to turn around amid a cluster of hot, dancing bodies. I caught myself on Becca with a yelp, who giggled as she spun me away from the mess to drier ground. And right into a bubblegum pink catastrophe.

"*Lennox*?" Bri sneered, her upper lip curled in disgust as she dissected my outfit with her eyes, casting an accusing stare in Becca's direction. Because clearly it couldn't have been me who put an outfit like this together. Ha! There was a difference between *having* style and *having the money* to fund that style.

"Barbie?" I countered, making my eyes wide with false surprise. "Thought you'd be taller."

Her glossed lips pressed together as her little group of minions stopped what they were doing to stand behind her, their stares just as skeptical as their master's when they recognized me.

"What? Never seen real tits before?" I asked the one

on the right and her head snapped up, moving her line of sight where it ought to have been from the start. I mean, I was flattered but…

"You trailer trash *hoe*," Bri said on a laugh, smug as fuck with her hands on her hips. And *god* that outfit was awful. So pink it hurt to look at. Paired with sky high stilettos that proved she hadn't learned from the first time she almost broke an ankle here.

I grimaced. Damn, the hem of her dress was about two inches from showing the entire party her lady bits.

She wanted to call *me* trash? While she was wearing that?

"Whatever you say, Malibu Barbie. If you'll excuse us—"

I moved to brush past her with Becca on my heels but she stepped once to her right, blocking our path and forcing me to stop or plow her over.

She was lucky I was trying so very hard to be good, even though I could already feel the rush of that unnamable *thing* inside of me rearing its ugly head. Uncoiling like a snake.

Rising like steam until my cheeks flushed red and my scalp dampened with sweat.

"I don't think so, Lennox—"

"It's *Ava Jade*," I bit out, interrupting her.

"You don't need to be here, hon. Don't make this difficult. Just go back to where you came from, 'kay?

Nobody wants you."

I opened my mouth to form a reply, but Becca beat me to it.

"Oh, fuck off, Brianna. *I* happen to like Ava. She's much better company than you ever were."

"You little fucking bitch—"

Bri made a grab for Becca and that was it. When her manicured claws curled into Becca's hair, I saw *red*.

Letting go was always easy, even when I wished it weren't, but this time it was a motherfucking pleasure. I bristled with ecstasy in the split second before I launched my closed fist at her ugly ass face.

She released Becca the instant my knuckles cracked into her nose, a stunned look making her eyes round and distant as she staggered back, blinking to keep from passing out.

I didn't even realize I'd hit her again until I tasted blood on my tongue and realized I was splattered with it.

Someone screamed and hearing the sound of approach, I whirled, ready to take on whoever else wanted a fucking piece. I didn't even want to use my blades right now. I would if I had to, but the sting in my knuckles was *giving me life*.

The blonde who'd raced forward to try to attack me backed off when she saw the look on my face. Everyone backed off. Even Becca. The music continued to thud even with a floor devoid of dancers.

In the blink of an eye I'd transformed them from carefree partiers to stunned onlookers.

One of my best tricks.

Let them watch, my darkness whispered. I wasn't finished. Not quite yet.

I went back to Bri, who had fallen and was trying to get up on shaking legs, slipping on the smear of her blood. I gripped her by her hair like she'd gripped Becca's and ripped her head back.

She screeched, clawing at my hands, but I couldn't even feel it. The darkness was flowing freely now, blocking out the pain. Blocking out anything and everything I didn't care to feel. Anything I couldn't *use*.

"You'll pay for this, Lennox," she cried. "I'm going to fucking *end* you."

I put my mouth level with her ear, twisting her wrist back behind her when she made a swipe for my face. "1323 Rochester Lane. Big white house. Blue shutters," I whispered in her ear and reveled in the way her breath caught in her throat. The way her body stiffened.

It was easy to find her address, and one of the first things I did that very first day after the cow set her sights on me. A bit of social media sleuthing and reverse google image searching and *voila*. I had it. Just in case.

"Go ahead and come after me. See what happens."

I threw her head down and let her clamber to catch herself on the floor, inhaling deeply as the rush began to wear off, lingering only in my twitching fingers and the heat licking up my spine.

Three sets of eyes found mine when I lifted my gaze.

The Crows watched from their makeshift throne, expressions of shock and hostility reigniting my embers to flames. Did they want a turn?

"Come on," Becca said, and I flinched when she grabbed my bloodied hand. "We should get out of here, like *now*."

I let her pull me out, drunk off the rush, and grinning ear to ear.

Corvus

THIRTEEN

The music pulsed as I leaned forward on the couch to watch as Ava Jade collided with Bri's backside, and the bitch turned feral. I had to admit, I was curious how she would react to the self-proclaimed queen of Briar Hall.

"Hey man," a kid no more than sixteen stepped up onto the dais, blocking my view. "You think I could talk to—"

"No," I growled. "Now get out of the fucking way."

"But Grey said that maybe—"

"*Move.*"

The kid opened his mouth a third time, but one look from me silenced him and he bolted for the exit. Practically shaking.

"Dude, that was Jesse's kid. He wants in," Grey

hollered. "He wants to take the trial."

I shook my head, searching for the new girl again in the crowd. "He isn't ready," I retorted. "The kid was about to shit himself."

I wasn't wrong. And Grey didn't argue. I wasn't about to stick my neck out for some pipsqueak with Diesel when I knew full well he wouldn't last a *second* in the trials. Besides, Dies didn't take on kids. You had to be a legal adult to be initiated into the ranks.

Bri sneered something at Ava Jade, and I took in how her body shifted, the miniscule movements seeming second nature, putting her in a fighting stance whether she was aware of it or not.

Her file had been missing from the office when I went to have a look through it the other night after Randy's send off, but that didn't stop me. It took me a couple of days, but I now knew all there was to know about Ava Jade Mason.

She lived in a trailer park with her dad before he was killed. His very brief police report alluded to gang involvement, but it didn't look like they were doing anything about it. I doubted they ever would.

Her mom was a mystery. It was noted in her files at Lennox High that she was no longer a point of contact, so I assumed she split.

Ava Jade wasn't pictured in any of the yearbooks aside from the obligatory class photo each year which led me to believe she was a loner.

A loner who seemed to know how to handle herself, and who carried a blade. I wondered if she knew how to use it. Why she felt the need to carry it in class?

Bri turned her venom on Becca, but it was Ava I couldn't peel my eyes away from. I'd already noticed her curves, despite the fact she liked to hide them beneath baggy sweaters and ripped jeans, but tonight...

Tonight she wasn't hiding. In that dress, with everything she had on display, she was fucking taunting giants. She knew it, too. I saw the way her face changed when she noticed us watching. Flustered at first, but then rife with defiance as she began to dance.

My brow furrowed as she stiffened now, her body going rigid as she watched over her new roommate. When Bri launched herself at Becca, Ava Jade was primed and ready.

When her fist flew, sending Bri staggering back, my cock throbbed in my jeans.

Grey moved to stand, but I signaled him to stay put. I wanted to see how this played out. She had an audience now, even Rook was sitting up and taking notice, a gleam of appreciation in his dark stare. His cigarette forgotten, left to burn out between his fingers.

There would be no taking this back. Ava Jade was royally *fucked*.

Bye-bye, little sparrow.

In a move not even I could've anticipated, she fucking hit her *again.* As if once wasn't enough to seal her fate. You didn't mess up Gregory Moore's daughter's face and get away with it.

Bri's nose shattered under Ava Jade's fist on the second hit, spraying blood in an arc over her face. Somehow, the red warpaint suited her, and I ground my teeth to keep my body in check at her savage beauty.

"Jesus *fuck,*" Rook groaned, and I caught him pawing at the front of his jeans, practically salivating, his shoulders shaking with a shiver of rabid desire.

A hollow chasm gaped open in my stomach. That wasn't good.

Ava Jade wasn't what I thought, and I didn't know if I should be as turned on as Rook, or even more wary of her than I already was. I hadn't wanted something, *someone,* in a long time. Dolls broke too easily under pressure and the ones here were made of porcelain.

Ava Jade was made of something much stronger. Maybe not even a doll at all.

Would she break under my fingers? Would she shatter?

I'd been worried about what a girl like her could do to us, from that very first moment my brothers and I saw her. Their interest had me on guard, eager to get rid of her as soon as possible. My primal nature viewed her as a threat and my job had always been to eliminate those. To eliminate any possibility of distraction, but...

Bri fell to her knees, choking and spluttering. Ava Jade was on top of her in a second, ripping her head back to whisper something in her ear, and *the fear* on Bri's face. If that wasn't the most beautiful fucking thing I'd seen today...

What did she say to her?

For a second, I had to wonder if she'd use her blade. I knew she carried. I clocked it the very first day. Not because I saw it, or even its outline through her jeans. It was the way her fingers twitched low, toward her means of protection. The way her ankle hitched up when I stood to use the bathroom, just to get a better look at her. If she drew, I'd have no choice but to stop her.

My own hand inched to my gun, jaw tightening. Maybe we should stop this before it got any worse.

Bri's tear-stained gaze lifted to us, pleading without the need for words. Hurt and anger brightening her dull brown eyes.

A sneer curled my upper lip, and she let her head hang, defeated.

"Should we do something?" Grey asked, hollering over the music.

I shook my head. "I'll do it. You stay here, keep an eye."

Becca pulled Ava away, and the pair weaved their way out. I let out a breath as they shouldered past awed onlookers as Bri did her best to look *not* like the bag of shit she clearly was. Batting away helping hands left and right with a scowl.

"Corvus," Grey warned before I could leave. "Let me do it?"

I didn't like the look on his face. The way his eyes darted to her and away, or how his brows were drawn, jaw clamped tight. He was...*worried*...about what I was going to do. To *her*.

The beast inside me stiffened, making my blood sizzle in my veins, but I didn't let that show. Instead, I fixed Grey with an impassive stare.

Not for the first time, I questioned the truth of his excuse for vanishing last night. And for the too-perfect slice in his arm. He was keeping something from me. I had a feeling I knew exactly *who* it was.

"Nah," I replied easily, searching his eyes for any betrayal of emotion. "Why don't you shovel Bri off the floor? Looks like she might need a hand."

It was easy enough to find them. The partygoers scattered like roaches from an exterminator as I passed, letting me catch up to them without needing to hurry a single step.

When I stepped onto the dock, any lingering people outside fled too, except for the two girls who hadn't yet noticed I was trailing behind them.

Ava Jade tipped her head back and howled a laugh at

the moon halfway down the dock while Becca continued trying to tug her along.

"Fuck," I heard her curse, her body shuddering on a long sigh. "That felt *good*."

Becca stopped short, yanked to a stop with Ava Jade. "Look, crazypants, that shit might fly in Lennox for keeping the wolves at bay, but it won't here. You just started a war."

Ava Jade leveled her stare on Becca and smirked, giving a one-shoulder shrug. "Worth it," she said, and Becca shared in her next laugh.

"We'll see how *worth it* you think it is on Monday. Come on, let's get back."

"Rebecca," I growled and her back stiffened. "A word with your new friend, if you don't mind."

Her throat bobbed as she glanced at Ava Jade, whose full attention was squarely on me. Where it should be.

"*Uh…*" Becca started, her discomfort evident in the tension between her eyes. In her stilted movements.

"No thanks," she answered, her icy stare narrowing to slits that would cut a lesser man down to the quick.

My lips twitched. "I wasn't asking."

"Corvus," Becca started, "Bri was—"

"I don't give two shits about Bri."

Ava Jade looped her arm back through Becca's, lifting her chin with a false smile. "We have somewhere to be."

I shook my head. "You're making a mistake."

"Am I?"

Becca tugged her close and whispered something in her ear, prompting her to roll her eyes before pulling her arm back from her friend.

"*Fine*," she gritted out through clenched teeth. "But I'm not going anywhere with you while you're armed."

Smart girl.

I stared at her, trying to read the truth in her pinched expression, but for once, came up empty handed. She was a wild card, this Ava Jade. I didn't like that. Not one fucking bit.

"I'm not—"

"Don't fucking patronize me," she said, *interrupting me.* Heat licked up my neck, making my shoulders strain with the sudden urge to hit something. An urge I never let get the better of me, no matter how hard it tried to.

I closed the gap between us, sensing more than seeing the group gathering at the entrance to the pier at my back. She didn't balk at my approach, even though I stood almost a full head taller than her in heels, and she wasn't even that short to begin with. Maybe five-six.

I drew my gun from the back of my waistband and watched as her keen stare alighted on it, while her fingers jerked toward the hem of her dress.

Becca flinched when I passed the gun to her. "Go on," I told her. "Take it. If there's even a single scratch on it when you give it back…"

I left the punishment up to her imagination, keeping back a laugh as she grabbed it out of my grasp with two fingers, holding it as though it might explode if she weren't careful. "Safety's on, sweetheart," I told her. "Maybe best to keep it out of sight, yeah?"

She swallowed hard before carefully setting it into her purse and stepping out of my way. She mouthed *sorry* to Ava Jade, and I swept an arm out for her to take the lead.

"You first," she insisted, not budging an inch until I took the first step, guiding us down the dock and through the parked cars along the water's edge. She kept up, only a few steps behind me. I could feel her tension like a rubber band stretched as far as it could go, waiting for its opening to snap.

We rounded the last car and stepped off the gravel and onto the dirt where a sheer rock face jutted up out of the earth, curving like a hand cupped around the edge of the lake. You could climb it from just down the trail. Jump in from the forty-foot height if you were brave enough.

It wasn't exactly a thrill I was seeking tonight though as much as the silence and privacy the dark shadow of the cliffside would provide.

"Well, you got me out here, all alone. Congratulations. Now what the hell do you want?"

I cocked my head at her, not used to being spoken to that way by anyone, never mind a girl. I didn't know whether I wanted to sew her lips shut for the offense or lick away the blood still staining a corner of her frowning mouth.

"Do you have any idea what you just did in there?"

"Thought you didn't care?"

"I don't."

"You have a funny way of showing it."

"Where were you last night?" I asked, changing tactics. Needing to clear my head.

A flicker of recognition danced over her eyes before they settled back to a glare.

"What?"

"Don't patronize me," I said, using her own words against her, but she didn't squirm under the pressure of my accusation. "You wouldn't happen to know what happened to Grey, would you? Seems he had a run-in with a particularly feisty tree branch."

She crossed her arms, making her tits swell above the cut of her dress. They, too, were freckled with crimson, and I locked my jaw, grinding my teeth at the sight.

"I don't know what to tell you. Maybe he needs glasses if he's running into trees."

A laugh got stuck in my throat, held back by the dam of my lips.

"Bri's right, you know," I uttered, side stepping her, forcing her to mirror my movements to keep the distance she was so set on maintaining between us. "You don't belong at Briar Hall."

"I don't think you do either," she muttered, seeming to regret the words once they'd vacated her lips.

I lifted a brow, my body hardening as I began to cage her in, making her back up toward the rough rockface. Not knowing if I wanted to see how those lips tasted or toss her over the bank and into the lake. Would she cut me, too, if I tried?

I might like that.

I couldn't remember the last time I wasn't able to make a decision. The uncertainty was foreign. Yet another thing I was quickly growing to hate.

Once I had her boxed against the cliff side, I decided. I'd see exactly what I was dealing with here. Either she'd fight, or she'd crumple.

Which would it be?

Ava gauged my move a moment before I made it, her hand reaching for the blade she had concealed beneath the hem of her dress as I rushed in. My fist closed around her wrist, trapping it to her thigh while I blocked a hit from the other, pinning it to the stone at her back.

She panted through a snarling mouth, trying to get her hand free. I squeezed, forcing her to drop the blade with a little grunt. I kicked it away and it ricocheted off the rock before sailing like a glimmering arrow over the edge of the bank and into the lake.

If I thought she was pissed before, she was furious now. She tried harder to get free of my grip. Her relentless

struggle made me have to use my hips to pin her. My thickening cock pressing against the
cool bite of metal zipper.

"You're a monster," she spat, her harsh tone and curled upper lip disguising the truth her body couldn't hide from me. She was fighting the same indecision I was. Unsure if she wanted to fuck me or bite my head off.

She shivered as I leaned in, putting my mouth at her ear.

"You're damn right I am."

A bitter grin pulled at my lips. *Fuck.* I couldn't remember the last time I'd smiled.

"You should run, little sparrow. While you still can," I warned, unsure I'd even give her the chance to if she tried.

"And if I don't?"

"Then I'll swallow you whole."

Her resistance waned and for the briefest second, her blistering cold stare settled on my mouth—before she heaved her hips forward, knocking me off balance.

I staggered back a step, licking my lips at the ache in my hip bone.

"If I can't find it," she hissed. "You owe me a new blade."

She stalked past me like a panther, dark hair wild and blowing in a sudden gust of wind. She stopped for a second to tear the heels from her feet, tossing them to the side. Completely unbothered that her back was now to me. That if I wanted to, I could get my hands around that pretty neck and…

"Oh, and Corvus," she added as she unfurled back to her full height. "I'm not going anywhere."

She tossed me a wink over her shoulder before she dove, dress and all, into the lazy waves below, pushing herself deep into the black water to hunt for what she'd lost.

Rook

FOURTEEN

I took another swallow of my whiskey, rolling my neck as the warm burn of it forced my muscles to relax even with the thud of the music rattling my bones. I was still a bit hard from the new girl's spectacle. She was fucking brilliant.

A goddess.

I'd admit it, I was intrigued by her coarse nature from the start, but now...

Fuck.

My cock twitched in my jeans, re-hardening at the mental image of her covered in blood. The pattern of it splattered over her sharp cheeks. How she didn't even fucking flinch as it sprayed over her. The way her eyes went hyper focused, and also blank as she hit Brianna for the second time. Like she didn't even realize she'd done it until it was too late for her to stop herself.

I shivered, my fist clenching and unclenching until I curled it around the arm of the weathered sofa to stop the habit, my teeth twisting my lip ring instead.

I wanted her.

My jaw twitched, resisting the admission.

Another swig of whiskey and the flask was empty. *Damn.*

Grey knocked his knuckles on my shin, and I followed his line of sight to the door, where Corvus was making his way back inside.

That was quick.

Corvus' brows were pulled tightly together, shadowing his deep-set eyes as he stormed through the crowd. He cast a curious stare at Brianna as her friends tried to help her clean the blood from her face near the punch bowl, before he jumped up onto the dais.

He gave Grey a look before running his tongue over his teeth, clearly still inside his own head. I knew that look. It was the one he got when he was trying to plan out a particularly difficult job. His mechanical mind going over every option. Every possibility. Finding ways to control the situation in our favor.

Exhausting.

I'd rather have one of them shoot me in the head than have my every move planned out to within an inch of error. That wasn't living. Where was the thrill in that? Where was the fire?

But Corvus needed that control. It was why Grey and I didn't often challenge the fucker. If he didn't have his control, he got so goddamned nasty that neither of us could stand to be around him.

So he made plans. And we mostly followed them. Sometimes ruined them. It was a tossup on any given day.

"You scare her away?" I called to him over the music, not really giving a shit if he had, but curious all the same. She'd only just sunk her fangs in, gotten my interest. I didn't really want her gone, I realized. She was too interesting.

A spec of vivid color on the otherwise dull canvas of my life.

"Not fucking likely," Grey replied, securing himself another scowl from Corv.

Corvus said something I didn't catch over the music, and I gestured that it was too loud. "Can't hear you, Brother," I hollered, lifting a hand to signal the pledge standing down at the end of the dais to get me more whiskey.

He rushed over, catching the flask when I tossed it to him. "Fill it," I ordered and he vanished, lost in the crowd on his way to the tiny, locked office where we kept some personals.

"She's going to be fucking trouble," Corvus said, and

I was left piecing together his grumbled words through the music.

A vein in his temple throbbed, and he tightened his jaw as he turned away from us, signaling the two chaps by the door to keep an eye out. They were seniors at Briar Hall. Two in a small group of five that wanted an in with Diesel.

They knew the best way to do that was through Corvus. They did what we wanted, when we wanted, on a fucking prayer that we'd give them the *in* they so desperately wanted.

One of them might even be worthy of the opportunity. The others were not.

Corvus jerked his head toward the Red Room for us to follow.

My buzz intensified as I stood from the sofa and I reveled in the staticky numbness, following my brothers through the double doors.

Red tinted light played over naked bodies as people fucked on every available surface. The sounds of their ecstasy and pain blotted out the music as the doors shut behind us, mingling with the wet slap of bodies on bodies and lips wrapped around cocks and
tongues toying with clits.

My feet unconsciously drew me toward the girl three guys had strapped to the spinning table. One of them pounded mercilessly between her legs while the other choked her with his cock at the opposite end. Her throat visibly swelling with each of his thrusts.

A third guy leaned over her tits, snorting a line of blow from the tops of each mound. I bristled, my eye twitching at the sight.

I was stopped short when Grey pulled at the back of my shirt. "Focus," he said.

"*Out,*" Corvus thundered, his hulking frame seeming to grow in the red lights like a shadow come to life.

I drew out a cigarette, lighting it and inhaling deeply as the fucking stopped all at once and heads swiveled to the door.

Fun ruined.

"I said get the fuck out!" Corvus bellowed and the nude statues frozen mid-fuck burst into action, gathering up clothes and shoes, rushing to remove strap-on dicks and unstrap people from the various devices stationed down the hall-like room.

I watched the cocaine slip from the woman's tits as she was unstrapped and ground my teeth as the phantom taste of it burned at the back of my throat. I finished my cigarette in the second inhale, dragging it all the way down to the butt before dropping it to stomp on its carcass. The need mellowed, at least for the moment.

The few red lights affixed to the low ceiling made the naked bodies look like cattle being prodded through a narrow corridor as we stepped out of the way for them to leave like they were told.

My fingers found a pretty throat, locking around it before the girl who'd been strapped to the table could escape. She gasped, her baby blue eyes going wide as she took me in, her body going rigid.

"Rook," Corvus warned as I leaned in, inhaling the sweet aroma of fear and arousal on her still mostly naked body. I bent, dragging my tongue over the remains of the blow on her tits with a groan.

"Wait outside," I told her, licking my lips. "This won't take long."

Someone needed to take care of the ache in my jeans.

She managed a nod and tried to swallow past the dam of my palm pressing against her windpipe. A taste of what she was in for. She gasped as I released her, and she scrambled out the door, uncaring that she dropped her panties.

The doors sealed out enough of the loud music and raucous shouts from the crowd outside that we could speak without shouting or being heard in here. I sighed, leaning against the black-painted wall to cross my arms.

"What's up, Brother?" I asked him, my attention briefly pulled out the window, checking to see if that little rat was back with my whiskey yet.

"That girl is going to be a problem," he repeated, huffing as he tipped his head up to the ceiling. The red lights deepened the shadows beneath his eyes, exposing the exhaustion he was trying hard to hide.

Even half drunk, it was easy to tell. He was my brother. I didn't have to cut him open to know what I'd find inside. We were made of the same stuff, just different flavors.

Grey's gaze roved over our brother, a knot forming between his brows. "Man, I think you just need to get some sleep. You know how you get when—"

"I don't need fucking sleep," he snapped, stepping up to Grey in a way that would've made him reel back a year ago. "*I'm fine.*"

Corvus began to pace, his eyes shifting over the floor at his feet like it might hold an answer he was looking for. "She's got to be part of a gang," he muttered. "Maybe the Aces? Kings maybe since she's from Lennox? Planted here to keep an eye on us? I've looked into her and there's no evidence to support the theory but she's...it would just make the most sense."

Not surprising that he'd already dug into her past. I should've guessed he would.

I considered what he was saying, casting her in a rival's role in my head, but the image wouldn't stick. It wasn't impossible for her to be a member of a gang. Rare for a woman, definitely, especially one so young, but not impossible.

Diesel's wife had been a full member of the Saints. And apparently, she was the most brutal of them all.

Quietly deadly. A snake in the grass. How I wished I could've met her.

There was a woman in the Lodi chapter, too, but she was nearing thirty and had earned her *in* when she put herself between a bullet and Damien St. Vincent. One of the original three Saints.

"She isn't part of a gang," Grey said, making Corvus stop pacing to glare up at him.

"How would you know that?" he demanded.

Grey shrugged. "I just do."

He was growing some balls. *Fuck.* Didn't think he had it in him.

"And she won't be a problem," Grey continued. "Not if we can get her on our side."

"You're fucking serious?" Corvus scoffed, scrubbing a palm over his chin. When Grey didn't budge, staring down our brother with a *give-me-one-reason-why-not* look, Corvus ground his teeth. "Even if we wanted that, her dad was killed by the Kings. She's not interested in having anything to do with us. Or any other gang."

Hmmm.

Maybe Grey was onto something.

We didn't need to bring her in, and judging by the look on Corvus' face that wasn't an option, but maybe...

"Leverage then," I said, kicking off the wall to join Corvus and Grey at the middle of the floor. Thinking through the problem as best I could with my brain swimming in whiskey. If we could control her then whatever threat Corvus insisted she posed would be neutralized. We could go back to business as usual. And maybe get a little something extra in the deal.

"We don't need to bring her in, we just need some leverage."

Corvus' brows furrowed.

"Control," I added, speaking his language. "Give the dog a bone."

Grey's lips pressed into a tight line, but Corvus was intrigued.

"What the fuck are you saying Rook?"

"I'm saying we help her out. She just made a huge mistake with Brianna Moore. What if we cleaned it up for her? And in exchange, we get her docile obedience. You get to keep your reign of terror at Bitch Hall, and we get a new pet."

I let my proposition sink in, picturing Ava Jade's face contorted with pain and pleasure as I tore her sweet cunt to shreds, as I made her scream...

I swallowed, leveling my stare on Corvus. "I might even share her," I joked, smirking now. I liked this idea.

"If there's anything left when you're done with her," Grey muttered, seeming wholly uninterested in this plan. I thought he'd be all for it. He was clearly into her. He spent the entire hour of homeroom staring at her back like he could will her to want him as much as he so obviously craved her.

I may not have been as attentive as Corvus, but people were easy to read. And Grey had always been an open book.

Corvus brooded silently as he considered my idea, shifting from foot to foot.

They wouldn't blackmail her for sex, which really was a shame, but then again any of us could get that whenever and wherever we wanted. We hadn't had a drudge in a while, though, and I was willing to bet the idea of controlling the uncontrollable was *right* up my brother's alley.

"Awe come on, Brother," I pushed. "You can't tell me you aren't at all interested. I see the way you've been watching her. I bet you'd like to have her play fetch for you."

Corvus was more difficult to read than Grey, but his obsession was clear from the start, and it'd only gotten worse in the week that she'd been here.

His jaw tightened.

It seemed I'd misread him, too.

"Or maybe I've read you wrong," I baited him. "If you aren't interested at all then at least don't spoil the fun for the rest of us."

"She won't go for it," Grey warned, and I knew he was probably right. I had to admit, I'd be disappointed if she did.

I shrugged. "Didn't know we were planning on giving her a choice."

After another few seconds of thought, Corvus lifted his chin, fixing Grey with one of his rare expressions of support. "You good with this?" he asked. "Bri will shit a fucking brick."

I grinned darkly to myself, knowing damn well she would. But she wouldn't deny us if we told her not to breathe a word of what Ava did here tonight. If we told her to lie about what happened. Keep it hush. Grey would bear the burden of this call, though.

No more heiress pussy.

And he would be the one who had to deal with her hysterical ass when she realized that we'd chosen to protect this new girl over her. No matter the reason. Unlikely that he'd give her one anyway.

Grey nodded solemnly. "Bri was just a decent lay who happened to have connections we needed last summer. It should've ended a long time ago."

He wasn't fucking wrong there.

Corv and I had been telling him as much for *months*.

I bristled with anticipation, waiting for Corvus to give the word.

His gaze slid back to me, calculating, trying to read my intent.

I gave him nothing.

"We'll try it your way," he decided, and I let a fresh

smile slither over my lips. It was the closest thing to an admission we would get from Corv that he wanted the girl, too. At his beck and call. Submitting to his every whim. That's how he liked them.

"Don't look so smug," he growled at me before turning to face Grey again. "Go find Bri before she calls the fucking cops."

Ava Jade

Unknown: I'll admit I had my doubts you were the same girl I saw near the railway tracks years ago, but tonight those doubts were erased. You are perfect.

I read the message for what must've been the twentieth time since I woke up Saturday morning to see it staining my phone screen. And now, Monday morning, the feeling of dread still lingered.

Four years ago near the train tracks in Lennox, I went full dark.

It consumed me, and I let it.

Those repressed, terrifying, *powerful* feelings took the wheel...and I killed a man.

This wasn't Bri. It couldn't be.

She couldn't know that.

No one knew about that. No one was there.

It had to be a coincidence. I could remember walking along the tracks a handful of times back from downtown, anyone could've seen me. This didn't mean anything. Right?

But then who was it? Why the anonymity?

The number that sent this message late Friday night wasn't the same one that sent the others on Thursday, but the feel of them was the same. If they were sent by the same person, then why use two different numbers?

I could reply. Ask who it was. But my gut told me that would only be inviting even more messages from someone who was giving off major stalker vibes.

Ignore it and whoever it is will get bored and stop.

"Are you waiting for it to sprout legs and run away?" Becca asked, sweeping out of her bedroom fully dressed for the school day. The smell of her earthy body spray filling the room with her.

I blinked, glancing up from my phone and realizing how tightly I'd been holding it. Any tighter and I might've cracked the screen even more than it already was. "Oh," I swallowed. "No. It's just...I got this weird message on Friday."

She cocked her head at me, and I lost my nerve, not wanting to give whoever this creep was the attention he or she so clearly wanted. Not wanting to give Becca even the tiniest clue as to the potential meaning of the message still trespassing on my phone's drive. What would she think if she found out what I'd done?

"Never mind," I shook my head, stuffing my phone down deep into the pocket of my jeans.

Her eyes narrowed for an instant before she seemed to decide not to press. "So," she said, dropping onto the soft leather beside me on the couch with a snicker. "How excited are you for homeroom?"

I groaned, letting my head fall against the backrest with a roll of my eyes.

All weekend I'd been waiting for the *Bri* hammer to drop. Becca warned me that there would be retaliation, if not actual police involvement. Apparently Mr. Moore, the poor fucker who sired the queen bitch, didn't take kindly to people touching his precious girl. Being more of a strait-laced sort of fellow, his retribution would likely come in the form of a lawsuit or some other legal bullshittery that I did *not* want to deal with.

Frankly, I'd rather he send a hired gun. I had a much better idea what to expect and how to handle that than I did a lawyer.

If he dragged police and shit into this there would be no way to keep it from getting back to Aunt Humphrey. *Good-bye ticket to freedom.*

"That excited, hey?"

"Why hasn't she done anything yet?" I moaned.

Becca barked a laugh. "She must be cooking up

something *really* special for you."

I'd spent the weekend catching up on assignments for the most part, but I also spent a solid three hours doing recon on Bri. I now knew where she went to get her nails and hair done. Where she liked to shop and grab coffee. What type of car she drove *and* her license plate number — what kind of dumbass doesn't at least blur that out for a social media photo?

I felt pretty confident that if she retaliated in any way not legally driven that I'd be ready to beat her right back, even if just the idea of wasting that kind of time on her was exhausting.

"Bri can be a cantankerous bitch, there's no doubt about that," Becca added as she got back up to pillage a handful of peanut M&M's from the kitchen counter for her breakfast. "But if I were you, I'd be more worried about the Crows."

The mere mention of them made me sneer. I hadn't been able to find the blade Corvus lost in the lake. I searched for a solid fifteen minutes in the chilly lake water, digging through seaweed and litter, but it was gone. I had three more from the set, but that wasn't the point. They were a gift from my dad. The last thing he ever bought me.

I now kept *two* on me at all times. If I'd learned anything from my run-ins with both Grey and Corvus last week, it was that one just wasn't enough. At least, not for them.

"That asshole owes me a blade," I grumbled, crossing my arms over my chest.

Becca snorted. "Yeah, good luck with that. I can't see Corvus James replacing your precious metals, babe."

Oh, he'd replace it. Even if it wouldn't be the same.

"Is that his last name?" I asked. "James? Why didn't Diesel give him his last name when he adopted him?"

Becca shrugged. "None of them are St. Crows. They all kept their last names. People say it's because Diesel only adopted them for his wife after she died. Because she always talked about wanting to give a few kids a better life."

"What do you think?"

"I don't think it's that. I've only seen him with them a couple times, but he definitely considers them his sons. I'm sure there's some other reason."

"Like?"

"Like maybe a *don't forget where you came from* kind of thing? Or maybe he wanted them to have a choice about joining the gang. If they took the St. Crow name, they'd have big ass red targets painted on their backs. Using their given surnames adds a layer of anonymity."

I lifted a brow. This girl was smarter than I gave her credit for. *Damn.*

Becca hopped up with a sigh. "I'm going to grab a water, want one?"

I shook my head, mulling over everything I knew

thus far. At least one thing was for certain: Monday morning felt like a point of no return.

Bri told me she didn't want me here. Corvus told me I should run.

If I wasn't a stubborn ass with an ax to grind, I'd already be long gone. But their threats only made me dead set on staying. Nothing was going to ruin my chance at a ticket out of here. A ticket to a completely new life. One without gangs or worrying about casing the next job before I ran out of funds. Speaking of…

After a little jaunt into town with Becca to buy some new bedding and a couple incidentals, I was running dangerously low. I could ask Auntie dearest for an allowance, but honestly, I'd rather suck a goat.

I'd take the apartment in the city and college tuition when the time came, but for now, I'd do what I'd always done: take care of my damn self.

"Shit, we should head down," Becca said, rushing to toss her phone back into her bedroom. "The bell's going to ring any second."

Sighing, I saw that she was right. At least I'd get to see the look on both Bri and Corvus' faces when I deigned to show myself in homeroom this morning. It would be worth whatever came after.

I tossed my phone onto my bed and hurried to follow Becca out the door, making sure she locked it.

She split off from me as we reached the bottom of the

stairs just in time for the bell. "See you at lunch!" she hollered, rushing to make it to her homeroom class before the tardy bell rang in three minutes.

I rushed across the atrium, knowing Mr. Harry Potter Glasses wouldn't let me in if I was even a second late. And I was *not* missing my chance to rub it in their faces that I wasn't going anywhere.

"Oh! Ava Jade, could you come here for a moment?"

My brows furrowed as I caught sight of a woman with a tight blonde bun sticking her head out of the office. She gestured for me to come to her, and I forced a face that wasn't the death glare I wanted to give her.

"Sure," I chimed as I hurried over, gauging how much time I had left to make it to class on time.

The woman held the door open, and I stepped into the quiet office, my nose wrinkling at a terrible vanilla musk scent that reminded me of something, but I couldn't place it.

A secretary typed away on a computer behind the main desk, and a few staff members chatted lazily in the corridor beyond that.

"I'm so sorry for your loss," she said, catching me off guard.

"What?"

"Your, *um*, your father, was it? He recently passed?"

My jaw clenched. "What is this about?"

"I'm so sorry, I'm the Vice-Principal, Mrs. June. It

seems our secretary misplaced your file—"

"I told you, Caroline, I didn't misplace it. I wouldn't—" The secretary paused mid-typing to huff.

"Yes, yes." Mrs. June interrupted the secretary, waving off her words and earning herself an ugly face from the woman behind the desk. "Anyway, I seem to recall there being a request for you to see the counselor. I just wanted to let you know that she's been away on vacation this week but that she should be back by next week to see you, all right? If you need anything in the meantime, my door is open, just ask Janice here, and she can buzz you back."

Well fuck me. I really hoped this wasn't some hidden stipulation of Aunt Humphry's because that was a *hell fucking no* from me, thank you very much.

"You must be mistaken," I said with my best apologetic smile. "I see a private counselor online."

The lie rolled off my tongue like butter and the VP lapped it up, looking relieved to be off the hook. "Oh, that's great. Well, if you find you need any more support, just let us know and we can try to set something up."

I nodded. "Sure thing. I should probably…"

"Oh, yes. Go on. Don't want to be late."

"Fucking counseling?" I muttered to myself as the door shut behind me, and I rushed down the vacant hallway, shaking my head.

The last time a school forced me to see a counselor I

lasted a full five minutes before vowing to never subject myself to that again. I mean, Dom went to therapy and she said it helped her and that was great and all, but when people asked me prying questions, my first instincts were to either stab or run.

The counselor at Lennox high was lucky I'd decided on the latter.

The bell rang just as my hand closed around the handle of the door, and I stepped through before it finished ringing.

"Cutting it a bit close, Miss Mason?" the teacher drawled, peering at me from the corner of his eye while he sat atop his desk, hands folded over a knee.

"Sorry, sir," I bit out. "I was—"

"Don't care," he said with a strained smile, and I braced myself, my blood flooding with enough adrenaline to make me shiver as I turned my attention to the class, making my way slowly to my seat.

What was this?

I caught the briefest glimpse of Corvus' smirk before he dropped it in favor of his trademark scowl. He was fucking *pleased* to see me. The bastard. He knew I wouldn't run. His shoulders flexed beneath the leather of his jacket, making an audible creak.

Rook stared openly from beside his adoptive brother, leaning over his desk like he might launch an attack at any given second. His dark hair shadowing his even darker eyes. His knuckles popped as he cracked them into his palm one by one, the tattooed letters spelling his name moving like a wave.

Grey slouched back in his chair, running a thumb over his lower lip as his eyes scraped down the length of me inch by inch. He had his tattoos on display today in a short sleeve V-neck that showed off a lot of muscle I hadn't paid proper attention to before. Not to mention, the bandage still in place over the cut that was no doubt crusting over into a good scar by now.

Their interest wasn't missed, not by anyone in the class, but least of all by motherfucking Brianna Moore.

I took a good long look at her, *sitting at the other end of the classroom*, before I slid into the one vacant seat, directly in front of Corvus. Like he planned it that way. For all I knew, he did.

I smiled to myself as I set down my books and settled in to listen to the drone of the teacher prattle on about some shit that he prefaced by saying wouldn't be on a test—which basically meant I didn't care at all what he was saying. Good, because I was too busy replaying the epic visual of Bri in my head and biting my lip to keep from laughing.

No amount of makeup could hide the two black eyes, and *man* did she look absolutely ridiculous in that nose splint. I was surprised she came at all, though I had to assume it was to host her very own pity party.

But to sit all the way on the other side of the classroom? To not even give me a good *glare* when I came in?

Had I scared her that much?

Huh.

If a little threat was all it took, then I'd have done that to start with. Avoided this whole mess of bullshit drama.

"Find what you lost?" Corvus asked in a rumbling whisper behind me, and I wriggled in my seat, not liking what the sound of his voice was doing to me.

I really needed to get laid…

"You mean, what *you* lost, jackass?"

An intake of breath from someone nearby made me smile to myself.

"You owe me a new blade," I reminded him when he didn't reply, and got a pointed look from the teacher that I studiously ignored. I got what I came for, he could kick me out now for all I cared.

I missed the peace of detention with Ms. Wood.

Though, I really didn't relish the thought of having to explain myself to my aunt again. Yeah, *fuck that.*

"Is that so?" came Corvus' delayed reply, and I stiffened, feeling his fingers brush against my back and curl into my hair. For a heart stopping moment, I thought he might jerk my head back right there in the classroom, punish me for daring to speak like that to him. Right in front of everyone.

He might've even gotten away with it.

But he didn't, and I let out a breath as his fingers retreated, shivering. Telling myself I'd have had his hand nailed to the table with six inches of sharpened steel if he tried it.

"Yeah," I said, wetting my suddenly dry lips. "And it better be a nice one. The one you so rudely stripped me of was a gift."

He grunted as though amused, and I sensed more than heard him sitting back in his chair, leaving the conversation only half finished. If he thought I was kidding, though, he was dead wrong.

Not wanting to incur the wrath of the teacher and earn myself another week of detention, I decided *not* to poke the bears any more than I already had. At least for today. Surprisingly, they seemed keen to just lounge in their chairs and stare at the back of my head.

I had to admit, it had me feeling a little...*special?*

No, maybe that wasn't the right word.

Powerful.

Yeah, that was the one.

I'd hardly done anything to warrant it, but apparently speaking your mind and not letting bullies push you around was enough to make the notorious Crows sit up and take notice.

It'd be easier for me if they *didn't* take notice. I knew that, but taunting them was kind of...dare I admit it?...fun.

I hadn't felt this alive since what happened to Dad. Maybe longer than that if I were being honest. Maybe all the way back to that night at the train tracks.

Run, the rational part of my brain demanded, at war with the dominant part that whispered to push them to their edges and see what they did when they fell.

Like a cat pawing a glass of water, nudging it to the edge of a countertop. Unable to help myself. Wanting to crouch down and peer over the edge to see the broken pieces after it fell. Tail flicking with satisfaction.

Stupid? Definitely.

Tempting as fuck? Hell yes.

I gathered my books and left before the teacher was through speaking at the end of class, not wanting to linger there with them barely a step behind me. Not trusting myself enough to not say anything more than I already had.

Be good, I reminded myself, mentally fighting those dominant urges. Just one fucking school year of this bullshit and I would be free, but only if I followed Female Hitler's rules.

I got to the front atrium, almost to the stairs when I was jolted to a full and complete stop by his voice alone.

"Hey, Sparrow," he said, his voice booming in the cavernous atrium, drawing a lot more attention than just mine.

I gritted my teeth as I turned to find him standing in

the elevator, Rook and Grey behind him. Students scurried past the gaping metal doors as he thrust an arm out to hold them open.

They cast me worried and curious stares as they went.

"Join us," Corvus said. Not a question. Not a command. But somehow both at the same time.

"I'm good," I replied, sending him a beaming smile I hoped screamed *fuck off* as loudly as I was screaming it in my own head. "But you boys have fun in your little box of privilege. Wouldn't want to spoil your VIP sausage fest with a street taco."

Corvus lifted a brow as a dark grin pulled at his mouth. "It was good enough for you on Friday," he said, and my lips parted but no sound came out as I choked on another sarcastic reply.

How had he found out? Who the fuck told him?

Reflexively, my gaze swept the atrium, hunting for the telltale red glow of surveillance camera lights. But I found none.

This was so fucking stupid.

Corvus stepped out of the elevator and Rook held the door as his brother crossed the floor to me. All six-foot five of him radiating the kind of smugness that only came from an overabundance of power.

The VP, Mrs. June, stepped out of the office for a moment but turned around the instant Corvus locked his eyes on her. He hadn't even needed to say a word and she was *gone.* Closing the door behind her and averting her stare.

Maybe I'd underestimated these three just a smidge.

"Get in the elevator, Ava Jade."

I clutched my books tighter to my chest, wondering how hard I'd need to swing them at his head to knock him off balance long enough to get away. If it would be worth the fallout afterward.

"Or what?"

Fuck!

I scolded myself as the air left my lungs, forced out by the pressure of his shoulder as he easily tossed me over it, scattering my books on the floor. *I could've stopped him*, I told myself, face heating.

"Put me *the fuck* down," I snarled, pounding on his back, helplessly unable to reach the two blades strapped to both of my ankles in this position.

"Stop squirming," he growled, locking me in place with his biceps and holding my legs down with his other arm. "Grab her books," he said, and footsteps sounded on the parquet floor. I got an upside-down view of Grey collecting my books from the floor before he followed Corvus back to the elevator.

He all but threw me down as the elevator door shut, leaving me to wobble unsteadily for a second before I was able to find my footing, my face burning from all the blood rushing to my head.

Corvus jammed the emergency stop button, and I dove for my blades.

"*Whoa*," Rook said from behind me, and I spun in the enclosed space, blade drawn. "No need for that. We just want to talk."

The bell rang, signaling that I was now late for class. *Great.*

I pressed my back to the elevator wall, holding my blade out in case any of them dared come closer. "Don't think I won't use it," I warned. "I can have the three of you on your asses and be halfway to Canada by morning."

Rook pointed at me, giving Corvus a *told you so* look that made me think I was missing out on some private joke between them.

"I know you could use it," Corvus replied, sliding his gaze stealthily to Grey and the arm I'd sliced open just a few days ago. "But I don't think you will."

Cocky fucker.

"What do you want?"

He lifted his brows as though affronted by my question. "It's not what we want, Sparrow. It's what we can give you."

My face must have pinched up because his smugness intensified.

"Brianna Moore," Grey explained. "You wonder why you weren't hauled off by police Friday night? Why she hasn't retaliated?"

I had to admit, I was wondering that, but the idea that they had anything to do with it just infuriated me even more.

"It's because we paid her a visit before she returned home to daddy dearest," Rook whispered huskily, his eyes gleaming with malice. "Saw to it that she wouldn't speak a word about her little *accident* at the docks."

"And why would you do that?"

It dawned on me as soon as the question left my lips: to bring me under their control.

They were offering me a life vest, a ticket out of the mess I made Friday night, but in exchange for what? I had to admit having queen bitch off my back permanently would make finishing out this year and getting my sweet, sweet freedom so much easier, but at what cost?

Corvus shrugged. "Call it a gesture of goodwill."

"Everything has a price."

He licked his lips. "Well, now that you mention it, there is one thing we all agreed would be a fair trade for our services."

"And what's that?" I spat.

Corvus' icy blue eyes flicked to both of his brothers before settling back on me with his reply. "Your obedience. You fall in line. Do as you're told. We say jump, you ask how high."

Unable to help myself, I barked a laugh, so caught off guard that my hold loosened on the blade for just a second.

Hot tears stung my eyes and I flicked one away before it could fall, sniffling at the absurdity of it all. "Oh my god," I said once I settled down, seeing that none of them looked even the least bit joking. "You're serious? You want me to be your little bitch girl, is that it? At your beck and call?"

Corvus' brows drew together, his stare turning deadly instead of just spiteful, but he didn't deny that was exactly what they were after. They hated that they didn't control me. Couldn't fucking stand it.

"That's not exactly it," Rook deadpanned, and I turned my blade on him, but that only perked him up. "But I'll accept your *full* surrender if you're offering. I've never tried Lennox pussy."

He licked his lips, stepping forward until the tip of my blade was at his throat, just above the edge of a tattoo peeking out from beneath his black t-shirt. He pushed harder, until the freshly honed edge drew a droplet of crimson from his flesh.

My breath rushed out through parted lips, and my traitorous cunt throbbed beneath my jeans as Rook devoured me with a single look.

"We'll keep the bitch at bay," Corvus explained, placing his hand against the flat side of my blade to push it away from Rook's throat before he could impale himself on it. "But in exchange, you will belong to us. You will do as you're told."

"I'm not a fucking possession. You can't *own* me," I

scoffed.

"I can, and I will. Whether you agree to it or not. This way's easier, Sparrow. Don't fight it."

He reached out a hand like he might try to smooth out the sour pucker tightening my lips, but I knocked it aside with a scowl.

"Hard pass," I hissed. "I can handle my own shit. I don't need your help."

His smug look faltered and pure satisfaction raced through my veins, bringing a smile to my lips.

"Fine," he seethed through a false smile. "Have it your way."

Corvus jammed the emergency stop button again and the elevator completed its trip to the second floor. The doors *pinged* open as he stepped out of my path, but he stopped me before I could leave. His hand curled around my upper arm.

I let him have his moment of control, even though if I'd wanted to, I could've sliced his fingers clean off his palm.

"Don't forget your books," he said, and Grey passed them to Corvus, who held them out to me, releasing my arm. "Last chance, pretty bird. All you have to say is yes and you can be living on easy streets for the rest of senior year…"

I snatched my books, burying my blade between the pages as a student ducked her head and scooted past the open elevator door. "I'd rather die."

Corvus nodded, pursing his lips as he pressed another button inside the elevator and the doors began to close before Grey slipped out.

"Walk you to class?" he offered with an entertained gleam in his eyes as the elevator whisked the other two away.

I groaned, frustrated heat licking up my back as I stormed away.

The sound of his muted laughter followed me to class.

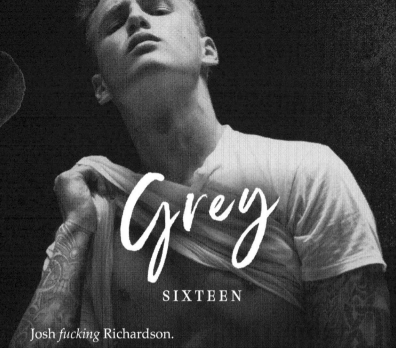

Grey

SIXTEEN

Josh *fucking* Richardson.

You have got to be kidding me.

I knew something was up the minute he slid into the seat next to hers in math today. He always sat in the bottom left corner of the classroom. Where he could play games on his phone in the shadow of his desk without being noticed. Josh Richardson was the kind of guy that escaped notice most days anyway.

Flying below the radar of popularity even though his family was among the wealthier ones at Briar Hall. He treated school like a holding cell. Like it was just a thing he had to sit through to make it to whatever came next. I didn't think I'd ever seen him hand in an assignment, and yet he was still here. Still just below the top of the class. At Briar Hall, your money didn't just buy you nice clothes and a straight-toothed smile. It could also buy you halfway decent grades. I wondered if his parents would continue paying for A's when he went to college.

I didn't give a flying fuck about Josh *fucking* Richardson. Until today.

He leaned into Ava Jade's side, whispering something I couldn't hear from four desks back.

I should've sat next to her.

Why hadn't I sat next to her?

Oh, right, because I didn't want to push my luck and get fucking stabbed again. She'd do it. I had no doubt. But I also wanted to give her a little space. A little time to think over Corvus' offer without me right there, hovering. Show her that not all of us were as hard as Corvus or as bloodthirsty as Rook.

Being the nice guy got you absofuckinglutely *nowhere*. Corv was right about that. It turned out he was right about a lot of things.

When Ava Jade laughed at something Josh said, my jaw clenched tight. No matter how hard I tried to relax it, to not let this *thing* inside of me swell too big, it didn't work.

Was she trying to goad me? Was that it? Was she doing this on purpose?

She couldn't be serious, right? This had to be a joke.

This guy?

I caught the way her arctic eyes flitted over him. In an

analytical way. Like she was taking a measure of him. Of his ability to please her. Like she might eat him alive if he couldn't perform. She twisted her ankles together beneath the table, and I wondered if she was imagining his cock inside of her. Pressing her thighs together against the ache forming between her legs.

My pencil snapped in my hand and a few eyes turned to me before they fled back to their work. But not her. Ava Jade didn't turn. She didn't look.

I dropped the pencil remnants to my desk and ran my teeth over my lower lip, leaning forward slightly. Trying to hear.

Was he handsome?

I critically evaluated the fucker from head to toe. He was tall. My height maybe. Not as tall as Corvus. A decent face, young and bright, like the darkness of life hadn't tainted him yet. Hadn't seeped into the hollows beneath his eyes or carved premature lines in his forehead.

His hair was dark, a chestnut brown that shone in the classroom lights like it was covered in a thin film of oil. I grimaced. Did she prefer men with darker hair, then? Men who looked like they would take you for a late breakfast at IHop after fucking you gently and texting another side bitch in the bathroom when you weren't looking?

Fucking *Christ.* I was jealous.

I was *jealous* of Josh *fucking* Richardson.

I couldn't remember ever being jealous with Brianna.

Not for even a fucking second. I wasn't even sure if that *was* the emotion I was feeling. Couldn't remember ever experiencing it before. But I knew one thing for sure, the idea of jumping to my feet and smashing Josh's smug ass face into his desk sounded really good right now. Magical, even.

I wondered if she'd smile at him then? When his nose was broken and his face covered in blood.

No. She might like that.

...*fuck*

This is madness.

The bell couldn't ring fast enough. I gathered up my unfinished work, stuffing it into the crook of my arm as Ava Jade put her hand on Josh's arm.

"Thanks," she said, and he grinned at her like a starved kitten who'd just been given a bowl of milk.

Thanks? Thanks for what?

He nodded vigorously. "No probs," he said, the epitome of douche.

As she went to hand her work in to Mr. Williams, I rushed Josh, not even fully aware of where I was going until my shoulder collided hard with his, almost knocking him on his ass.

"Sorry," he muttered, gripping his shoulder as he steadied himself on a desk. "Didn't mean to get in your way."

"Watch it," I sneered at him and caught Ava Jade

smirking at me from the head of the class, where Mr. Williams was casually trying to get a peek down her shirt while she was distracted.

"Yeah, man, my bad," Josh mumbled, stooping to lift his scattered blank pages and binder from the floor.

I tore my gaze away from her and stalked from the class, my body flooding with unspent adrenaline, making my muscles shudder and twitch.

Maybe Corvus was right. That girl was trouble with a capital T. Bolded. Underlined.

But I didn't want her gone. I wanted her all to my fucking self.

I wanted all her smiles. Her laughter. I wanted her thighs to squeeze at the image of *me* inside of her.

They would, I decided, picking up speed as I thundered down the corridor and jabbed the elevator button.

Yes, I thought, the rage that'd been making my stomach clench loosening by the second now. *I will have her.*

I relaxed, rolling my taut shoulders back and cracking my neck. Grinning to myself in the solitude of four metal walls.

No girl had ever refused me, and I'd never backed down from a challenge. I wasn't going to force Ava Jade into Corvus' agreement. I would have her eating out of my palm without the need for forced coercion. It would just take some time, and time I had, since she'd made it very clear she wasn't going anywhere.

My phone buzzed in my pocket and I dug it out, seeing a message there from Corv.

Corvus: Cafeteria.

I snorted. Knowing now that she had her talons in him just as deeply as she had them in me. We rarely ate in the cafeteria, preferring to take the Rover out to the Crow's Nest or get takeout instead. Since Ava Jade showed her pretty face on the streets of Thorn Valley, we'd only missed a single school-provided meal. Not the coincidence I originally thought it was.

I wasn't sure how to feel about that. Or the fact that Rook clearly wanted to take a literal bite out of her, too.

I didn't feel the same *thing* toward my brothers, as I did Josh, but Corvus... He'd always been possessive. If he decided she belonged to him, there would be no room for negotiation. Unless...unless...

Oh. *Oh.* This would be good.

I found my brothers in our usual spot, set near the back of the cafeteria, in the only spot that afforded us an unobstructed view of the entire room. I nodded to them before going for the food. I snatched a tray from between two queuing students and skipped ahead of the line to grab what I wanted, not really paying attention to the *what* as much as making sure I had enough to fill the unfillable void that was my stomach.

Rook tipped the contents of a flask into his glass of OJ, securing himself a scowl from Mrs. June, who seemed to be on cafeteria duty for the day. She didn't say anything, though, and she wouldn't. He'd been working her since our first day at BH. If Diesel St. Crow wasn't enough for the majority of the teachers and staff to turn a blind eye to us, Rook had the VP herself by her married little cunt.

A word from him could ruin her career and her marriage now. He had tapes of them. Several. They liked to fuck in the mornings in the rarely used chapel. He had one of Jesus' eyes carved out and replaced with a micro camera. It had to be some sort of blasphemy, but if there was a hell, we were all headed there anyway.

I fell into my seat opposite Corv and dug into my food, considering how best to broach the topic.

Rook rubbed a coin between his thumb and index finger, rolling it through his knuckles and flicking it to spin atop the round table. He was oddly pensive as he sipped his boozy afternoon drink.

I followed his line of sight to where she sat with Rebecca Hart. Honestly, she was about the only other girl at this school who wasn't a vapid, self-absorbed debutante. I'd be glad they were friends, if it weren't for the fact that Rebecca Hart would *definitely* be smart enough to warn Ava Jade away from us instead of goading her toward us, like the majority of the others bitches here would.

Ava Jade *inhaled* her lunch. Putting Becca's small bowl of low-sodium soup to shame with a tower of finger sandwiches and a bowl of fruit that I wonder if she knew was meant to be scooped from, not taken in its entirety to her table.

Was she left alone as a child?

Had she gone hungry?

Was she forced to fend for herself?

My stomach audibly rumbled, prodding me to pick up the next in a row of sandwiches on my own plate and take a large bite.

There was a time when a sandwich the size of the one in my hand right now would have looked like a feast to my 8-year-old eyes. When all there was were crumbs to be found beneath kitchen cabinets and mom had been gone for two weeks.

She came back sometimes. But the guilt of seeing me, rail-thin, gaunt, and starving always drove her away again.

I didn't only starve for food. I starved for her. For human connection. To not be left alone in the house out in the country with only my dead stepfather's library for company.

If a teacher from my school hadn't come by the house to check up on me after the phone was disconnected, I wouldn't be sitting here. I was almost gone. At the point of organ failure.

Literally starved to death.

My stomach turned now, remembering that pain. The *ache*. The eventual nothingness that followed.

Stop it.

I gave my head a shake, coming back to the present. Deciding there was no better way to do this than to just give it a shot. I set down the sub sandwich dripping tomato juice down my wrist and swallowed the tasteless lump in my throat before speaking.

"I have a proposition."

Rook's glass halted an inch from his lips. He raised a brow, setting the glass back down.

Corvus cocked his head at me, trying to read the words I hadn't yet spoken in my stare.

"A game," I explained. "Winner takes all. Winner takes Ava Jade."

Rook perked up, leaning forward over the table with a gleam in his eyes. I had his attention.

"You want her," I said, telling Corvus what he wouldn't admit. "So does Rook."

I sat back, sighing. "So do I."

Corvus crossed his arms over his chest, his jaw working behind the wall of his lips. "What are you suggesting?"

"You were right," I admitted. "She was never going to go for our deal."

"Thought we weren't going to give her a choice?"

Corvus asked, eyeing Rook before turning his attention back to me.

"She'll fight us tooth and nail," I said, shaking my head. We didn't know her. Not really. But that much I thought we could all agree on.

No one denied it, so I went on. "What if we didn't use...the usual tactics? What if we tried to reel her in instead? The only way she's going to be controlled—unless you want to get rid of her..."

I let that thought hang in the air, banking on them not wanting to vote for that option. Their eyes widened before they settled back into mute scowls, trying to play it off like they didn't give a shit. Liars.

"...is if it's on her terms. Like, if she were with one of us. We make it a contest, first one to fuck her wins. First one to fuck her gets to keep her."

Rook liked this idea, I could tell by the way he twisted his lip ring with his teeth, his breathing heavy.

Corvus' face pinched. He stared at me like that, unmoving, for so long I almost began to squirm in my seat. But letting on that he was getting to me would only boost his already massive ego.

"You want to *date* the new girl?" he hissed, studying my face for a reaction.

My stomach twisted, but I kept my cool.

Did I?

Was that what I was suggesting here?

188

Shit.

"Never mind," I muttered, snatching up my water bottle for a long pull. This was a stupid fucking idea. What was I even hoping to accomplish? All I'd done was show my cards. Admitted I was a pussy. Right to their faces. Proved to them how weak they already thought I was.

Probably made Corvus even more certain that he needed to make her disappear. Proved to him that she was the threat he thought she was from the start. A thing that could come between us. Distract us. Infiltrate our ranks and destroy us from the inside out.

But I'd win, the thought whispered through my head. *And they know it.*

It was at that moment Josh Richardson entered the cafeteria, carving a path through the tables toward the one Ava Jade and Becca shared across the room.

"Get your head straight," Corvus uttered, stealing a thin chicken strip from my plate and tossing it into his mouth. I lifted a brow at him, not over what he said, but over the fact that he had just eaten a fucking strip of breaded, deep-fried chicken.

"What?" he grunted, but dropped it when Josh stopped at Ava Jade and Becca's table.

Josh flashed Ava Jade a smile, leaning down onto his elbow to put himself closer to her eye-level as they chatted. Becca glanced between them, her interest clearly piqued by the whole encounter. Ava Jade hadn't told her friend about her little conversation with Josh Richardson in math class today. Was that because she didn't think it was important?

Because it didn't matter?

"The fuck is Richardson doing?" Corvus demanded, swiping the back of his hand over his grease-stained lips.

I wondered if it looked the same to my brothers as it did to me: like a fucking golden retriever propositioning a lioness.

Fucking *cringe*.

"He was all over her in math today," I told my brother. "I think they exchanged numbers."

Corv couldn't whip his head to me fast enough, his accusing stare fixed on me. "And you let that happen?"

My mouth popped open. "Should I not have?"

"We gave her an out this morning," he said. "Made a deal. She is *ours*."

"She didn't agree," Rook corrected him. "In fact, I'm pretty sure she said she'd rather die."

"And we're just going to let her get away with refusing us?" Corvus demanded, his slanted eyes cutting between Rook and me. "Have you gone soft there, Rookie?"

Rook frowned, back to looking like his usual bored self. Exhausted with Corvus' antics.

He wouldn't rise to the bait. He rarely did.

When I made no reply, Corvus fell back in his chair

and pressed his lips into a tight line, his disappointment clear as he let his eyes track back to Ava Jade. She was still locked in conversation with the senior prick, smiling in a sultry way that told me she knew exactly what she was doing to him.

When Josh rose to say his goodbye's, he remained slightly hunched, angling his body away from Ava Jade. Hiding the chub in his pants.

Becca immediately descended upon Ava Jade, leaning far over the table with wide, glimmering eyes, demanding details.

Corvus' chair screeched against the linoleum floor as he shoved back and stood, following Josh Richardson from the cafeteria, without another word.

Ava Jade

SEVENTEEN

I let the murdery lyrics of Primal Ethos' *Fuckface* drive me onward, using the unfiltered rage searing through my veins as fuel for the cruel pace I was forcing my body to endure. My sneakers pounded the blacktop and the chill of the evening licked at the warm sweat on my arms and chest. Stoking the fire inside.

Downtown Thorn Valley wasn't much to look at. Especially not at ten on a Monday night. All the shops running along either side of the historic city center were shuttered for the night. Their wide windows dark, *come back tomorrow* signs hanging in doorways. The only lights still on that I could see were from a small cafe at the end of the block, and the low lights from the Valley-Mart I'd already passed four blocks before.

The hill from town to Briar Hall was the only chunk of this route not alive with at least some public activity, and I was delaying the return trip.

Fucking asshole.

Whoever sent that text was ruining my only escape. I'd been running down the hill and through town since Saturday. Only using a short arm of the trail behind Briar Hall in emergencies of frustration to blow off some steam between classes before my lid could pop.

It wasn't that I was afraid, at least, not really. It just creeped me out. Whoever was sending these messages was clearly watching me. They knew I liked to go for runs. They were at the docks during the party Friday night. For all I knew they'd *been* watching me all this time, though something told me that wasn't the case. That coming here somehow triggered this. This person was from Thorn Valley, but had seen me in Lennox years before. I was on their turf now.

Running alone in the dark through the trees, where no one except maybe the Crows might hear me scream just didn't have the appeal it did a few days ago. It irked me that someone could be out there, where I couldn't see them, fucking jerking off behind a tree or some shit.

Gross.

I vacillated between wanting to avoid it at all costs and going on a fucking hunting trip to find the bastard and carve his eyeballs out. I might still go on that hunting trip, but maybe best to let everything else die down first.

I held no illusions that my refusal of Corvus' idiotic offer meant that my 'protection' from Brianna Moore and her wealthy father had been terminated. It was only a matter of time now before she launched her attack.

Corvus.

Fucking Corvus.

And the rest of them.

Smug bastards. As if they thought I would actually agree to...*to be their plaything*. To kneel like a peasant at their gilded feet and open wide for them to use my mouth like a fucking cum dumpster. I'm sure they would love that. They were probably getting off on just the *idea* of breaking me. Corvus for sure.

The worst part was that for the briefest second, I actually considered it.

My little *problem* with Brianna would evaporate. No legal problems. No cops. No retaliation. No more issues with teachers. No more detentions. Not while I was under their protection. Fuck, I'd even get laid.

I bet they were good, too. I bet...

Don't go there, Ava Jade. You are not for sale.

Besides, Josh would do.

He was tall, stalky. Big feet. Long thumbs. All the telltale signs that he should be at least somewhat well-endowed downstairs. Whether he knew how to use it or not was a mystery, but one I'd solve soon enough. He didn't strike me as the type of guy who dated, which suited me just fine. I wanted a fuck buddy.

Like Kit.

Speaking of, I really should message him back. And Dom, too. And okay, *fine,* Aunt Humphrey as well.

I slowed, hunching over with my palms braced on my knees to catch my breath for a minute, my throat burning. Sweat dripped down my temples and between my breasts. I could taste the salt of it on my lips.

I'd been out here too long. I needed to get back. Get some water. Some food. Sleep might also be a good idea. Hadn't had much of that in the last few days.

A long shadow stretched down the sidewalk from up ahead, bouncing lightly as the person approached. I moved to the side, resting my back against the shop next to the illuminated cafe so the late-night walker could pass.

But he stopped, instead. "Ava Jade Mason?" he asked, and a sliver of adrenaline spiked into my bloodstream, making me vividly aware of the stranger's nearness. Of his height and build. Of my hand's proximity to the blades at my ankles.

"Who's asking?" I panted, tipping my head up to get a look at his face while remaining hunched, overacting my tiredness to emphasize that I was weak. No threat to him. So that he wouldn't be expecting it when I proved to be the opposite. Keeping my hands on my knees because that's where they were closest to my blades.

The man wore a dark windbreaker over black slacks. His shoes were polished leather, scuffed lightly on the sides. His hair was cropped short. His face square, clean-shaven, light eyes searching.

He had a certain look to him that made warning bells ring loudly in my ears, but I couldn't place what it was about his demeanor that was throwing me off.

Was this my stalker?

No.

This guy didn't look like a stalker psycho, he looked...

The man reached into his windbreaker and I drew my blade, ready to disarm him, but he came out with something I hadn't been expecting instead, rushing back two steps with wide eyes as he took in my weapon. My fighting stance.

Oops.

He held his other hand up. The one not holding the police badge.

Slowly, I lowered my blade and tucked it back into the sheath at my ankle, covering it over with the edge of my sweats. "Sorry," I muttered, hands raised slightly to show that I was no danger to him while trying to assess whether or not he was carrying.

The officer narrowed his gaze on me before tucking the badge back into his windbreaker and clearing his throat. "Name's Vick," he said, still studying me warily.

"Was I running too fast or something," I sniped,

panting lightly from the run and the burst of adrenaline still thrumming through my swollen muscles, making me feel lead-limbed and tired. I didn't want to deal with this right now. Whatever *this* was.

Officer Vick let out a breathy laugh at my smart-ass response. "Nah. Nothing like that. Could we talk? In private?"

He gestured to an alleyway carving a dark path down the side of the cafe and scanned the street up and down. What was he looking for?

"*Uh*," I hesitated, feeling a creep of unease set in like phantom fingers tripping up my spine. "What for?"

If the cops in Thorn Valley were anything like the ones in Lennox, going down that alleyway with him could be just as dangerous as going down it with any random dude off the streets. Maybe more so.

"Just a talk."

The officer lifted his jacket, doing a slow spin, showing me that he was unarmed.

"Can I see that badge again?"

The man balked, but when I didn't move a muscle, he wrinkled his nose and retrieved the badge, holding it out to me again.

Victor Stoll. Thorn Valley PD.

Okay, looks legit. That doesn't mean he isn't here on an errand from Mr. Moore, though. A hired gun sent to intimidate the girl who dared raise a hand to his daughter.

I gave him another once over and decided I could take him if I had to. I didn't need to add a cop to my list of enemies in Thorn Valley unless I had no other choice.

"All right," I agreed, and followed him into the alley, going no further than just into its shadowed mouth.

When he saw that I would go no more he stopped, sighed, and leaned casually against the brick wall, kicking a bit of trash out of his way. He folded his arms and fixed me with an investigative stare.

I should have had him pegged as a cop from the moment I saw him. It was written all over him. The shoes. The haircut. His posture. The fucking navy windbreaker. Standard issue.

Christ, I needed to get out of my own goddamned head and pay closer attention.

"I hear you've made some *friends* at Briar Hall," he said, the words a verbal nudge. A prompt he wanted me to finish.

I didn't.

His jaw ticked. "All right. No beating around the bush." He lifted himself to his full height, all traces of *good cop* gone. This was business now. "It's been brought to my attention that you've drawn the interest of a particular three students. You might know them as the Crows: Corvus James, Rook Clayton, and Grey Winters."

This was *not* where I thought this was headed.

"I'll take your silence as a yes," he continued, not

even bothering to give me more than a few seconds to formulate a response. "Now, I've done some digging. I know that your father, a Mr. John Mason, was recently killed in a gang-related incident."

My skin prickled with heat, fists curling.

"That's not how the cops in Lennox see it," I bit out.

He pursed his lips. "No. But you seem like a smart girl. I'm sure you know that these things aren't always dealt with as they should be."

He and I could agree there, but he wasn't painting himself in the best light. What made him any better than those useless badge-toting rednecks in Lennox?

"I want your help," he said, surprising me for the second time. "The Saints are squeaky clean. My department can't seem to make anything stick to those slippery bastards. And my boss...let's just say his allegiance is and always has been *questionable* at best."

That was a serious accusation. One he was making to an eighteen-year-old girl in a dark alleyway at nearly 11pm.

He wants my trust, I realized. He was trying to put himself on my level. Make it seem like we were in on some private secret.

I don't trust it.

"Why don't you just ask for a cut and turn the other cheek like all the other asshole cops do?"

A knot formed between his bushy brows.

"It's...personal," he offered, giving no more than that.

I nodded silently, imagining a million possible scenarios without his needing to utter a single word.

"Okay. So what do you want?"

"I think you'd like to see those boys and their entire empire fall just as much as I would."

The screams of the man in the shed returned to me in sharp clarity.

Corvus' rough fingers around my wrists.

Rook's malice.

Grey's attentive stare.

"I want your help," he repeated again. "I need an informant. One Diesel and his psycho sons won't see coming."

"I don't—"

"Wait," he interrupted, rushing forward a step like he might try to cover my mouth. Stuff my refusal back in. "Don't answer now. Think about it. If you've seen anything—if you *see* anything—just..."

He dug into the pocket of his slacks and opened his wallet, digging out a crinkled white business card. He thrust it out to me. "Just call me. The Crows don't mess around, Miss Mason. I can help you. We can help each other."

Victor Stoll left me standing there in the alley with his card in my hand as the only evidence that this encounter happened at all. Heels clacked on the sidewalk not far away, and I slipped the crumpled paper into my bra as a woman appeared in the entrance to the alley. A black apron covering her long-sleeve gray dress. A trash bag held at arm's length.

"Uh, you can't be back there, hon," she said, pointing up. "Read the sign."

Corvus

EIGHTEEN

"What do you think he wants?" Grey asked as we made our way into Sanctum.

"He has a job for us," I muttered, holding the heavy door open for my brothers, allowing classic rock music to spill out onto the midnight street. I didn't know for certain, but that was usually the reason Diesel asked to meet us here. He had something for us that he didn't want to take to the table. Something unofficial. Usually.

The bar at the edge of town was one owned by the Saints. Complete with an illegal boxing ring in the basement and a fully functional escort service running out of the two upper levels. Top tier. Two-dollar hookers weren't welcome in our city. Only the finest for Thorn Valley's privileged upper-class.

The boxing ring had been Rook's idea.

The escort service had been mine.

And with Grey helping run the books, the money was cleaner than it'd ever been.

Sanctum brought in a good chunk of the gang's income and helped tide us over when things got tight. Like they were right now.

Sasha winked at me from the bar as we entered, leaning over the ledge to show her new tits off to a drunk guy who looked like he was about halfway into a midlife crisis. He'd already removed his wedding band, the white slice of untanned flesh on his ring finger probably brighter than any silver or gold.

She could be his for the night if he could afford the ride.

"My sons," Diesel called to us from the back of the bar where he was setting up a shot at one of the pool tables. Playing himself and winning.

"Want some real competition, old man?" I asked him as we approached, shrugging off my jacket to toss it over a chair back. This late on a Monday night, there was little happening at Sanctum, and the echo of Diesel's 8-ball sinking shot rang through the mostly empty hall.

Diesel snubbed out his cigar and removed the ashtray from the table side, his silver rings glinting in the vintage table light above. "Always. Here, rack it up, and then we'll talk, yeah?"

He tossed me the rack, and I caught it, emptying the ball return to set up the game while Rook signaled Sasha for a drink, and Grey slumped into the nearest booth, frowning at his phone. Probably still dealing with an onslaught of messages from his former fuckbuddy. He still hadn't given Bri the green light to hit back at Ava Jade, even though I'd told him to the moment she refused us. He thought I didn't know, but it was obvious. Bri would've had Ava Jade carved like a Thanksgiving turkey by now if she thought she could get away with it. Or, she'd have at least tried to.

I'd let him think he was in control, at least for now, until the right moment.

Diesel polished off his beer and sighed. Not a great sign. He rarely drank. That, coupled with the deep lines in his forehead and the darkness beneath his eyes told me he was more stressed than he was letting on.

The more vocal members of the Saints were calling for blood after what happened with Randy. They wanted retaliation, and he promised it would come, but only once we had solid intel. The A carved in Randy's chest could just as easily have been an A for Arty. A member of the Kings who Diesel gunned down last year for stepping where he shouldn't. Or it could've been a member who acted alone.

There was that one time a year back when they tried to retake the docks. We lit them up like Christmas morning. Bells and all. Two Aces fell that day. It was only because their leader wasn't aware of the attack that the Aces still existed at all.

Or the whole thing could've been a set-up.

Dies wouldn't act until he knew what he was dealing with, no matter how vocal they got. But it was him who needed to deal with them all in the meantime.

"All right, son," Diesel said, giving a tight jerk of his head for me to have a seat before we started our game. "Let's talk."

I nodded and followed Dies to Grey's booth, nudging my brother to move further in so I could sit across from our leader. Grey obliged and Diesel slid in opposite me.

Rook joined a second later, whiskey in hand. Diesel clapped him on the back, giving his shoulder a tight squeeze. "You look good," he told Rook. "Up for a fight in a couple weeks? Some upcoming MMA aspirant wants to take a stab."

A sly grin played over Rook's lips.

"Has he ever done an underground cage match before?" I asked, needing more details before Rook could agree to it.

Diesel pursed his lips. He hadn't.

I shook my head. "Rook will kill him, Dies. Bad for business."

"I'll make sure he knows what he's signing up for," Diesel agreed. "We could use the cash."

That was the end of that then. Diesel had already decided. And Rook looked like a pig in shit. Swirling the golden liquid in his glass with a shiver of delight.

"Anyway, that's not what this is about."

"What's up Dies?" Grey asked, slipping away his phone to give our old man his full attention.

"I'm going to need you boys over the next couple of weeks. I know you have your own shit going on, but that's all going to have to be put on hold. I'll need your focus. All of it."

My skin bristled and without warning, a mental image of Ava Jade surfaced in my head. Put her on hold? I wasn't sure if I could do that. But for Diesel, if he needed it, I'd try.

"What do you need?"

"I've set up a gun deal with the Reapers MC. They have a shipment for us, coming in next week. We need some more firepower and I have a buyer for half the order down south."

Damn. I thought it was the last time *last time* we made a sale to the Mexican cartel. I didn't like being involved with them. But neither did Diesel. He wouldn't be setting this up unless we really needed it.

"I need you boys to case the trade point and find out where they got the guns. The Reapers don't usually run guns. Drugs are their MO. I don't want fucking blowback after the deal is made. Make sure their source is legit and report back to me."

"You got it."

This was something I could do. Something I was good at. Planning. Recon.

The things Diesel used to do himself before I came along. His need for control *nearly* rivaled my own. Trust no one but family, that was his adage. And I had no doubt it was the only reason he was still alive at almost fifty.

"I don't want you missing too much school," he added before I could start asking more questions to flesh out the situation. My jaw clenched.

We all knew how Diesel felt about our education. It was a stipulation for us to join the ranks of the Saints. He didn't give two fucks about college but wanted us to do what he didn't in his teens and finish high school. Graduate. The whole idiotic shebang. He made a very generous contribution to Briar Hall to get us in. So generous in fact that they even took his suggestion of a motto change and ditching the antiquated uniforms.

They didn't know they were letting a pack of wolves in to have their way with the sheep. Or maybe they did but didn't care. The antiquated academy was on the verge of going under. It *ran* on hush money and bribes from wealthy parents now.

"We'll swap out," I offered. "Two of us on the job, one in class to pick up assignments. Good?"

"Good."

He leaned back, blowing out a breath. There was more.

We waited.

"That's not all," he admitted. "I've set a meet with the Aces."

"What?" I growled, fists clenching beneath the table. "When?"

"Two weeks. Right after the gun deal."

"Is that smart?" Rook asked and his trepidation lent weight to the question. If he of all people questioned the sanity of the decision, then I felt fucking justified in my rebuke.

Diesel's jaw set and he lifted his chin. The minuscule movement undetectable to most spelled the words *no fucking reproach allowed* clear as day to me. He'd already decided this. It was too late to change his mind.

"I want you three there. I can't trust the others to keep level heads. Randy was...he meant a lot to them. Like a surrogate son to some."

He didn't have to elaborate. Though we did larger jobs with the other members from time to time, we were a unit unto ourselves. Joined and yet somehow also separate from the rest. We didn't form attachments. Not beyond this.

Not beyond family.

"We need to know if they were involved... If that mark carved in Randy's chest was theirs, then they'll own it. Why else make it so obvious? And if it was them, we deserve to know why. If the bastard who did it acted alone or on behalf of Lenny Ace. We'll have to retaliate. I need to keep my men under control. This needs handling."

"Bloodshed?" Rook asked, his brows lowering, but not enough to shadow the gleam in his dark eyes. "Or a trade?"

"If the person acted alone, a trade. The killer's life for Randy's. If Lenny doesn't agree to that then, yes. There will be blood."

"And if it was them? If Lenny sanctioned the kill?" I asked.

His dark look said it all. If it was sanctioned by their leader then we wouldn't be the ones to initiate the bloodshed. They already had.

"Where is the meet point?"

I wanted to case that out, too. Make sure there was an escape route. No way for them to come at us with uneven numbers without us knowing well in advance.

Diesel signaled Sasha for another beer, also signaling that this conversation was coming to an end. "Haven't decided yet. We'll give it to them same day. Like usual."

No time for them to set anything up, but plenty of time for us. It would be up to them if they wanted to take the risk and honor the meet. If they didn't, it would mean they had something to hide and we'd find them and kill them anyway.

If it wasn't them, all they had to do was say so and Dies would walk away. He would find out the truth eventually, he always did. And if they were smart, they'd know that lying to Diesel St. Crow bought you nothing but a bullet with your name on it.

"Let me do it," I offered. "I'll find a good meet point. Somewhere in no man's land. I'll scope it. Rig it. Make sure there's an easy escape if needed."

"You've got enough to do over the next couple of weeks, son. I can handle it."

I nodded, a muscle ticking in my temple, making my eye twitch. I'd rather do it myself, but Dies was the one person I trusted implicitly. He'd get it done.

"Everyone good with this?" he asked as Sasha dropped him off a fresh beer and slid Rook a fresh whiskey.

"Can I get anything for anyone else?" she asked, and Grey shook his head. She didn't wait to hear from me before leaving with a little extra pop in her hips. She'd been trying to get Diesel between the sheets since she started here. She wouldn't have any luck.

"Alright." Diesel clapped his hands together, effectively ending the conversation. His cunning stare slid to the pool table and returned to me with a renewed spark of life. "Ready to get your ass kicked, son?"

The king of pool at Sanctum, Diesel hadn't ever been beaten. Not by anyone. But maybe tonight would finally be the night that the apprentice overtook the master.

I scoffed, flipping my internal switch. There were enough hours between now and dawn that I'd have plenty of time to start the recon Diesel asked for after we left.

Business later.

For now, I had a Saint to dethrone.

Ava Jade

NINETEEN

Nasty.

I wiped drool from the corner of my mouth with a frown, my nose wrinkling at a cloying smell tainting the air of my bedroom. _Ugh._ What was that? I lifted an arm to make sure the gross limey odor wasn't coming from me.

"_Ew_," I mumbled, rolling out of bed to wash the drool off my hand and rinse out my mouth. I never drooled. Couldn't sleep deep enough for that. At least, not usually. I swished the cool water from the tap in my mouth and spat, opting to just take a shower in case I did actually smell like a fucking stale ass gin mojito.

At least the deep sleep brought with it some clarity and as the scalding water prodded my dead muscles back to life, a plan formed.

To be fair, it started forming the minute the

fucking Crows decided to try to cut me a very one-sided deal. The little visit from Officer Vick just cemented it.

The way they saw it, I had two options.

Option one: take the deal and become their little plaything. Kneel.

Option two: be forced to take the deal by whatever devious bullshittery they came up with to try to force me into it.

Officer Vick had provided me an option number three, but honestly? I didn't fucking like cops. Sixty percent were corrupt. At least thirty percent were power-tripping dickwads. The last ten percent were just fucking useless. Or stupid.

Biased? Maybe. But you haven't been a starving kid living in a trailer with a crackhead mother and a father with a gambling addiction. Or maybe you have. And then you know.

I was going for option number four. It was time to take these Crows down a peg. If I'd been smart, I'd have taken photos of the stolen car that night with the guy in the shed. I'd have filmed Rook dragging him to the shed. Captured his screams on camera.

Two could play the blackmail game. I'd been focusing my attention on the wrong threat. Bri was a blimp on the greater scale. The Crows were the real enemy. They were the ones who deserved my attention. I'd find out every little thing I could about them. Their dirty secrets. Their plans. And then I would use that knowledge to buy my freedom.

It would take time, and I'd have to do it right, but it could be done. I just had to make sure I didn't break along the way.

"You trying a new perfume?" Becca asked as I made my way into the living room, making a spectacle of plugging her nose. "Babe, that is so *not* your scent."

My shoulders slumped. "You smell it too?" I asked, relieved. I was starting to think I was going crazy when it didn't go away after the shower. It was somehow soaked into my blankets. In my pillows. Whatever I ate yesterday, I was never eating it again. *Barf.*

She poured herself a coffee from the elaborate chrome machine in the kitchen and pointed to a second cup. "Want one?"

I moaned, chasing the aroma of fresh coffee to the kitchen. "Careful," I warned. "I could get used to this."

She snorted, but set another cup under the weird coffee drippy thing and started frothing some milk. "Here," she said, nudging the already made cup with her elbow. "Take that one."

I took a sip, and it didn't even matter that it nearly scalded my tongue. It was fucking *divine.* Like, call me religious because I might have just been converted to a devoted member of the church of Becca Hart Lattes.

"*God.*" I groaned, clutching the mug under my nose

to inhale. "I'm going to steal you away from whoever you go see in the mornings and make you my coffee bitch."

Becca barked a laugh but didn't reply, instead eyeing my outfit. The usual knock-off jeans, softened by too many owners, paired with a long sleeve black t-shirt today. "No run this morning?" she asked as she finished pouring off the frothed milk into the espresso basted cup.

I shook my head. "Nah, I had to wash that stink off. Two showers in one morning goes against years of two-minute shower conditioning. Just can't do it."

"Speaking of," Becca said, leaning against the counter to sip her latte. "Maybe close the oven after you're done baking. When I got home last night it was hot as balls in here."

I winced. I'd always been taught to leave it open, especially when it was chilly outside. It was a waste of heat to keep it closed. But I supposed that wasn't a worry here, where the air temp was controlled to within an inch of its life by the crazy touchscreen panel by the fireplace. I probably only managed to make the AC work harder. I snorted. "Sorry. Habits."

She smirked, getting that look she sometimes got that told me she didn't really understand but was trying to.

"No worries. You saved me a cookie, so I guess I'll let you off this once."

"So kind."

Becca swirled the coffee in her mug. She looked

amazing in whatever the thing was she was wearing. A one-piece black romper with a long gold necklace and cage heels. But then, she always looked like a supermodel next to me. It was a wonder the Crows didn't take an interest in her instead. She wasn't like the other girls here, either.

Then again, maybe they had. What did I know?

"So," Becca started, a mischievous gleam in her brown eyes. "Has Josh texted you yet?"

I shook my head. "Nope."

She bit her lower lip. That wasn't what she wanted to ask. I could tell she was holding something else back.

"What?" I hedged. "Just spit it out. Is the guy a creep or something?"

Becca pursed her lips. "No, it's not Josh. It's just...people are saying they saw you in the elevator yesterday. With the Crows."

The flash of betrayal in her eyes cut me to the quick. "Oh."

"Oh?" she pressed.

"Look, I didn't say anything because I didn't want you to freak out."

Her brows lowered, worry creasing the spin between them.

"See?" I said. "You're already freaking out."

She smoothed out her expression and gingerly sipped her latte. "Well, what did they want? Someone said they saw Corvus *literally* fireman carry you into the elevator."

I gritted my teeth.

Becca set her mug down with a clatter and crossed her arms over her chest. "They're dangerous, babe."

"They wanted me," I admitted before she could say anything else. "They said they'd make what I did to Bri Friday night go away if I agreed to fucking bow down to their reign, be a good little girl and keep my pretty mouth shut unless they asked me to open it."

Becca's face screwed up into a scowl. "And you didn't take the deal, did you?"

"You think I should've?"

"*Hell yes*, you should've. I'd take *sit down and shut up* over possible jail time any day of the week and twice on Sundays. Never mind that your refusal means that you get to keep them as your enemies, too."

Heat licked up my neck, making my body shudder. "I'm not like that. I can't just..."

"Fuck. You're right." Becca huffed, pinching the bridge of her nose. "You're right. It's not my call to make. I just don't want to see you run out of here or worse, you know?"

I didn't know, but I was trying really hard to accept the fact that someone, a friend, did actually want me here. A smile beat back the frustrated heat still trying to find a toehold in my veins.

"I know. Don't worry, Becks. I'll handle it."

I always handle it.

"Taurus," she said suddenly, her eyes widening before a sour look took hold. "No, wait, that's not it, either."

"My birthday's in—"

"No," she interrupted, her mug clattering back down onto the counter as she reached over and slapped a palm over my lips before I could finish. "Don't tell me. I got this."

I laughed against her hand, and she pulled back, chewing her bottom lip as she considered me.

"Good luck with that," I muttered, finishing off my coffee. "While you stew over it, can I have another latte?"

I went into homeroom expecting to have to deal with the Crows, knowing it was likely they would try to corner me after class was through again, but...that didn't happen.

As I walked in, a full two minutes before the second bell, I found only a lone Crow there waiting for me. Grey met my gaze as I entered the room, tipping his head in greeting.

"Morning, AJ," he whispered as I slid into my seat and I turned to give him a warning scowl before settling in for the day's lecture. He said nothing else to me through the entirety of first period.

And then the following day, it was only Rook. He didn't speak a word to me, though I could feel his hard gaze on the back of my neck. Could hear the *chink* of metal as he spun his lip ring with his teeth.

Thursday it was only Corvus, and I realized they were all switching out through the week. One in class, to collect assignments, maybe to keep an eye on me, and the other two off doing god knew what.

That was what I needed to figure out. I got the sense something big was going down. They would be here to terrorize me every chance they got if there wasn't something monumentally more pressing that needed to be handled.

I had to up my game.

Corvus all but ignored me Thursday. He seemed so distracted. His face a pinched mask of focus.

As if that weren't strange enough, I was still waiting for Bri to hit back. She hadn't made a single move even though I'd turned down the Crows.

And I hadn't received a single text from the unknown number in days. I wasn't foolish enough to think it was a coincidence that I stopped getting the creepy messages at the same time as the Crows being too busy to continue trying to make my life hell.

It would be too much a coincidence, right?

It had to be one of them.

By Friday, if I were being honest with myself, I was fucking bored as shit. Frustrated that I still didn't have anything worth mentioning on the Crows. I'd been returning to the Crow's Nest at night for days. Watching like a shadow from the darkness of the trees. But there was nothing happening.

No one there.

At least not between the hours of ten and two a.m.

My other endeavors were coming up empty, too. Usually, a bit of cash was all it took to get information, but not with these guys. I'd gotten nowhere trying to get their records from before their adoption to Diesel St. Crow.

All I knew was that Grey and Rook had been together in Barrett's Home for Boys when Diesel snatched them up as a pair.

I knew that Corvus James was adopted three years prior to that, at the age of nine.

But I had a few little gems of info now that I didn't before.

For instance, I now knew that Corvus was adopted from fucking *Lennox*.

That's right. *My* hometown.

I wasn't the only one from the wrong side of the tracks.

I also knew that Grey was short for Greyson. Greyson Winters.

And that Rook was a nickname. His real name was Sawyer. Sawyer Clayton.

I wondered why none of them took Diesel's surname when they were legally adopted. If that was their choice or

Diesel's?

It wasn't enough though, none of it was really useful. None of it told me *who* they really were. What they'd done. What they'd been through. What made them tick.

I needed more. I needed something that I could use. Preferably before they were finished dealing with whatever it was they were dealing with and had the free time to harass me again.

After so many nights spent casing the Crow's Nest from a safe distance, I'd found a path. I had it all mapped out in my head. Exactly which direction I would need to approach from, where I would need to step, and pause, to be able to get inside without the camera seeing me. If I could get my hands on a decent bug, I could plant it. I doubted they were very careful with what they said while at home.

After all, no one was foolish enough to fuck with them in Thorn Valley.

I was so absorbed with my own thoughts, trying to figure out where would be my best bet to find what I was looking for in this foreign town *without* the Crows finding out, that I almost didn't see him.

"Josh?"

His back stiffened, hand stilling on the door handle to the office.

I only had about a minute before my last class for the day started. "Hey," I added when he didn't turn around straight away. I carved through the other students in the atrium rushing to class. "You haven't been in class."

He hadn't answered either of my texts this week, either, but I didn't really care about that.

My thirsty punani did, but she could deal.

"Where have you—"

He spun around and whatever I'd been about to say ghosted my lips.

The way he was looking at me, and also not looking at me, spoke volumes. So did the angry purple bruise swelling his left eye almost completely shut.

I could see the anger in the tension around his still usable eye. The embarrassment in the pink of his cheeks. The discomfort in the shifty way his gaze moved over the atrium. And I knew.

"What did they say to you?" I demanded, all desire to fuck this cowardly jackass gone in the blink of an eye.

Josh shook his head, his jaw tightening. "Look, I'm just here to grab my shit. I'm transferring to LA."

"*Josh*," I hissed, leveling the full weight of my stare on him. "What. Did. They. Say?"

He recoiled from me slightly, surprise flitting over his eyes as he took me in in this new light.

The bell rang, signaling that I was now late, but I didn't give a fuck. My muscles twitched, constricted beneath tight skin. So tight it made me itch. Made me sick.

"Fucking spit it out."

223

"It was Corvus, all right," he said, lowering his voice even though we were the only students still lingering in the atrium. "He...he warned me away from you. Told me I should leave."

"And you just packed up and went like a good little sheepy?"

His brows lowered, lips pressing tightly together.

"If you knew what was good for you, Ava Jade, you'd leave, too."

I laughed, shaking my head at the ludicrousness of this whole idiotic situation.

"What did he say, then, hmm? That I was his or some other bullshit?"

Without missing a beat, Josh replied. "Yes. And he didn't just warn me away. As of this morning, no guy in this entire school is allowed to go near you. They've...they've claimed you."

The way he said it, with pity, made my teeth grind. I got the sense they hadn't ever done anything like this before. Never claimed someone for themselves.

Fuck if I was going to let the bastard get away with it.

I wouldn't let them back me into a corner. Into a cage.

I said *no* to their deal, and I would stand my motherfucking ground.

A growl tore from my throat as I chucked my books to the floor and spun on my heel, storming toward the stairs, and leaving Josh in my dust. I shivered, my edges coming unglued, fingers of heat inching up the back of my neck.

My vision narrowed, tinted crimson.

My thoughts were a mess of disjointed things rattling in my head.

Those entitled motherfuckers.

Friday. Today was Friday.

Grey.

Grey was here.

Last period.

He would be in room 910. Biochem.

I was there so fast that I could barely recall from which direction I came, how I'd managed to climb two flights of stairs and jump down three different hallways. It felt like barely a second had passed since Josh poured gasoline on my fire.

The door flew open, battering loudly on the opposite wall as I stepped inside. Heads swiveled. Startled eyes took me in. But I was looking for a specific pair.

"*Excuse me,*" the teacher all but shouted, rising from behind her desk with a pointed stare in my direction. I didn't even have to look at her to know that she was five foot nothing, rounded through her middle, and absolutely no threat whatsoever.

"You," I growled, latching onto Greyson Winters at the back of the classroom with my eyes alone. "We need to talk."

"I said, *excuse me*," the teacher repeated. "We're in the middle of—"

Grey lifted a hand, silencing the teacher with a lazy *shhhh*, without taking his eyes off me.

My heart beat in my temples, thudding so strongly that the room seemed to expand in shades of red with each pulse. I inhaled deeply through my nose, regaining control as the initial burst of adrenaline leveled out into a steady rush, sharpening my focus. Centering.

If I'd found Grey one minute earlier, I might've bit his head off.

"Excuse us, Mrs. Waters," Grey said as he rose from his desk, inclining his head to the ruffled teacher. He left his books and pencil behind as he waded through the whispering students toward the door.

"AJ," he said with a nod as he approached, the tiny tick of enjoyment squirming at the edge of his lips was enough to set my blood boiling anew. I snatched his arm and dragged him through the door, slamming it behind us.

I didn't stop there.

"Where are we going?"

I growled to myself, curses falling from my lips as I towed Grey along with me until I found what I was looking for. I shouldered the door to the ladies washroom open and shoved him through it.

"*Um*, hello?" a small voice called from one of the stalls

inside.

"*Get out.*" I snarled.

The girl was spurred into action, rushing from the stall with a furtive and fearful glance between Grey and me before she rushed out the door. I checked the other stalls, punching the doors open one by one until I was certain we were alone.

I locked the door and swallowed back the acid in my throat. Crossing my arms over my chest, I faced Grey, unable to trust I wouldn't just haul off and deck him right in his stupid mouth.

"I thought I made myself clear," I started, surprised at the level tone of my voice, now only edged with a sharp bite. "I am not something you fuckheads can own."

Realization registered on his face and his self-righteous smirk morphed into a taut line.

"Watch your mouth," he said, his upper lip curling. Though it wasn't hostility I found when I met his heavy gaze. It was something else entirely.

Grey's fists clenched and unclenched at his sides as he took me in, his broad chest heaving beneath the crisp white t-shirt he wore. His tatted biceps flexed, stretching the inked images.

"Or what?" I challenged. "Going to put me down like you did that guy last Thursday night? If you are, just get it over with. But I'm warning you now, I won't go down without a damn good fight."

A muscle jumped in his temple, and his fists uncurled. "There are a lot of things I want to do to you, Ava Jade," he said, his voice dropping an octave, the sound of it making me squirm. "Killing you isn't one of them."

My breath caught in my throat.

Grey stepped forward, closing the gap between us, and I felt my own wetness like warm silk in my panties.

I didn't move so much as an inch as he approached; to back away or go for a blade would be giving him too much credit. He wasn't armed, at least not with a gun. I'd given him a thorough once over when I spotted him at the back of the classroom. I'd cased each step as he approached. He wasn't packing. At least not anything but the hard angled shape in his back left pocket.

His cell phone.

His cell phone.

I suppressed a grin, biting my lower lip.

Grey stopped before me, standing nearly a full head taller. Inches of space between us. His dirty blond hair burned with strands of gold in the bright vanity lights over the bank of sinks at my back.

I jerked, twitching toward my blades as Grey took my jaw into his hand, his callused fingers rough against my skin. He studied my face as though he could read something hidden there. A secret code. A riddle to be solved.

"Who are you?" he asked on his next breath, his gaze narrowing as if he looked hard enough he might find the answer he was looking for. He'd asked me the same question that night in the woods. This time, I'd answer him.

"Someone you shouldn't fuck with." I'd meant it to sound threatening, but it came out differently. My breath stuttering.

"Is that so?"

I swung my arm up to knock his hand away, my anger flaring again at his arrogance, but he caught my wrist instead, holding it there with a cruel smirk.

"Fuck you," I spat, tugging the arm he had hostage, but his grip only tightened, drawing me into him. His scent engulfed me. So familiar. Like the forest just before dawn. When the air is thick with the smells of settling dew and damp earth. The stronger smell of engine oil was at war with it, giving the heady, soft aroma a bit of unusual bite.

A small sound escaped my lips, and my traitorous pussy throbbed beneath my jeans, aching at his nearness.

I could feel more than see his smile as he dropped his lips to my ear. "I dare you."

Motherfucker.

I shoved him back and his hand snapped off my wrist. He stumbled back a step, surprise in his wide stare.

Grey grinned, recovering quickly and coming at me

with renewed spite pinching the skin between his brows. He shoved me back, and I let him, catching myself on the bank of sinks, lips parting.

I didn't even have time to catch my breath before he claimed my mouth, stealing whatever dregs of air remained in my lungs. His fingers twisted into my hair, securing me to him as he shoved me against the cool stainless steel. It bit into my lower back, and I clutched it until my fingers strained from the pressure, trying desperately to ward off the flutter taking over deep in my belly.

I don't want this.

Lie.

I don't want him.

Lie.

"Stop fucking fighting it," he demanded between kisses, pressing in between my hips, making me moan into his mouth as his erection nudged my belly.

Fuck it.

I released the countertop, letting him lift me with ease until I was seated atop it, able to wrap my legs around his middle. To yank his shirt off.

"*This means nothing*," I panted as it fell to the floor, my voice a breathy growl.

"Absolutely nothing," he agreed with a smirk.

I stopped his advance with a palm pressed flat to his warm chest, making him look at me. Forcing him to understand. He was still my enemy. I was not going to hold back. As long as they fucked with me, I would fuck with them. Mercy wasn't something I was ever given. I wouldn't be offering it up. Not to them. Not to anyone.

Understanding made Grey still, made his smirk fade.

"Now fuck me," I demanded, loosening my grip on him with my thighs to allow him closer. Regret slammed into me even before he unbuttoned his jeans and let them fall, showing off one of the most beautiful cocks I'd ever seen.

No amount of premature remorse was going to stop me from having him.

Grey undid my jeans next, looping his fingers through the belt loops to wiggle them and my panties off. He paused at the sight of the scars marring six inches of flesh on each of my thighs, and I jerked him closer, forcing him to look at me. Not at them.

"What—"

"None of your fucking business," I hissed as I kicked my jeans the rest of the way off and spread myself to him.

But the sight of them had distracted him, and his thumb bumped over the perfect white raised lines, making me shudder.

He dropped to his knees, and I convulsed as his warm breath skated over my inner thigh. A gasp turning into a cry as his warm mouth pressed against my scars, kissing my inner thighs higher and higher until…

Fuck.

Yes.

His mouth closed over my clit, making my back arch violently. I thrust against his face as he began a slow, tortuous pace with his tongue. The fast-building orgasm was a testament to how badly I'd needed this fucking release.

Grey ate my pussy like a man starved. Like this was a heist he'd been planning forever, and I was the prize. I bucked and writhed against the counter, making Grey have to lock his hands around my thighs to hold me down.

"Just like that," I moaned, feeling the build deep within. "Fuck, don't stop."

He slowed just a fraction, and I about lost my shit, digging my fingers into his golden hair to make him keep going. He obliged, quickening the pace with his tongue and adding his fingers to the mix, pushing them inside of me at the perfect moment to increase the pleasure past the breaking point.

I clenched around his fingers, writhing against his mouth as I shattered, my head smashing back against the mirror so hard I heard the glass crack.

I hardly noticed as he slipped his fingers out and flipped me. My feet hit the floor and my belly met the hard countertop as he thrust into me from behind, making my thighs slap against the metal and a gasping moan press out through my lips.

He groaned, his length filling me exquisitely.

I gasped into the counter, face down as he splayed his hands over my back until they were curled around my hips. I braced, my breath hitching as he drove into me again, using his grip on my hips to push in deep and hard, grinding his hilt against me.

My hands grasped for something to hold on to, finding faucets. My back arched with his next thrust, and I found us in the broken mirror.

A hundred fractured pieces of pleasure and pain. Of reserved fury and sated desire.

Grey was a myriad of ink and flesh. Of control and chaos.

The build of another orgasm began again, and I bent to the sensations ricocheting through my body like fucking buck shot, crying out as he pumped his cock into me. He set a blistering pace I was sure would leave me fucking bruised, but I didn't care. All we had was this, here and now, and I was *starving* for it.

Grey grabbed my ass, squeezing hard as the fractured reflection of his face hardened in the mirror and his body began to tense.

"*Fuck,*" he cursed through gritted teeth.

I slipped my hand down between myself and the counter's edge, my fingers finding my slippery clit. They brushed against his length as he fucked me, and he shuddered at the dual sensation as I rubbed myself.

233

"*Christ*, AJ," he grunted, and I splintered, then broke, coming on his cock as he bent over my back, gasping. His hand slid over my mouth, muffling my scream as we came. His hot release filled me as his hips jerked their last.

I let the satiated delirium take me, but only for a few seconds. Only long enough for me to catch my breath, then I slid out from under him and stooped to snatch my jeans and panties from the floor. Easily plucking the cell phone from the back pocket of his jeans to tuck it into the lump of mine in my arms.

I strode to the door and unlocked it. "Thanks for the ride," I muttered, unable to meet his stare. Unwelcome guilt swirling in my stomach. "Now get the fuck out."

Grey

TWENTY

I could still taste Ava Jade on my lips when I left Briar Hall for the day, deciding to swing by Sanctum for a long workout before heading home.

We had a decent home gym at the Crow's Nest, but I didn't want to run on the treadmill or bench today. The heavy bag was what I was after, and I didn't stop until my knuckles bled.

I couldn't figure her out.

She wanted me, that much I was certain of, but she was so hot and cold. One second, she was fucking my mouth, grinding her round ass against my cock, crying out, fucking *screaming*, and the next...

I hit the bag again, gritting my teeth at the sting.

What did she want?

Where did she come from?

For the first time in forever, I had an itch I couldn't scratch. I wanted to know more about her. I needed to know what made her tick. In my head, I considered every place Corvus might've put the files he'd gotten on AJ. I couldn't ask him for them. Didn't want to see the smug look on his face when he passed them over.

If I wanted to read them, to know what he knew, then I'd have to find them myself.

Breathless, I stopped my assault of the heavy bag and rolled my aching shoulders back, walking off the frustration still clinging to my bones.

At least there was satisfaction in knowing that if the guys *had* gone for my little contest idea, I would've won.

My phone buzzed on the stool near the back of the private warm-up area in the basement of Sanctum. Sweat dripped down my temples as I shucked off my gloves and tossed them in the bin, snatching up my phone with a grimace.

I'd fucking dropped it in the girl's bathroom this afternoon. I hadn't even noticed for almost an hour after AJ kicked me out. At least when I went back to look for it, it was still there. Face down against the wall beneath the bank of sinks.

The screen was cracked now, a single long slice running from one corner to the other, making the message from Corv look like it'd been cut down the middle.

Corvus: Where are you?

I thumbed a quick reply, sighing.

Grey: Sanctum. Heading home now.

His reply came a few seconds later.

Corvus: Good. We have work to do.

I swiped his message away and tapped on Chrome, my thumb hesitating over the search bar. Habit.

My gut twisted as I pressed the search bar, and her name came up as a recent search. Siobhan Winters.

Fuck.

Changing my mind, I deleted the search history and dropped it back onto the stool.

I didn't care where she was. I didn't care if she was dead or alive. I didn't care why she never came back.

I wiped a palm over my face and shucked off my gym shorts in favor of the clothes I'd been wearing earlier, purging her from my thoughts.

I'd wait to shower until I got home. If I didn't leave now, I'd get another message from Corv in fifteen minutes asking why the fuck I wasn't back yet.

At least I knew that if some shit ever did go south, Corv would be the first one to figure out what went wrong and drag my ass out of trouble. We had about a thirty-minute window for answering our big bro before he came looking. And if you took more than thirty minutes to reply, you better hope your ass was dead because you'd never hear the end of it.

I may not have known what it was like most of my life to have family. To know that multiple people had my back no matter what. But at least I did now.

I took the back roads home, sticking to the routes I knew AJ sometimes liked to run, hoping to catch a glimpse of her. No luck.

One of Diesel's cars, the nondescript navy-blue Impala was parked up near the front door, and I drove around it, parking along the side of the Crow's Nest. They'd been doing some recon work, then. Otherwise Corv would've taken the Camaro.

The smell of roasting chicken greeted me when I entered, and I inhaled deeply, scenting lemon and garlic.

Corvus was cooking, that was a good sign. He hadn't cooked anything all week, forcing Rook and me to live off takeout and leftovers. If he was cooking, it meant they had a successful day.

Rook was just wandering to the kitchen from the living room as I entered, leaving the video game he'd been playing running on the load screen. It almost felt like a regular Friday as I snatched a bottle of water from the fridge and fell onto one of the stools at the kitchen counter.

"Hungry?" Corvus didn't bother turning as he stirred sauce in a small pan atop the stove, pausing every few seconds to toss a pan of green beans.

"Fucking starved. How'd it go?"

"Good," Corvus replied as Rook settled into the stool

opposite me, pouring himself a fifth of whiskey from the bottle on the counter. He eyed me suspiciously as he swirled the liquid in the glass, his dark eyes narrowing.

"The MC's source is legit. We're good to go for the swap."

I snorted, impressed. That didn't take long. Now it would just be a matter of casing the meet point and then we'd be solid. More firepower. A solid payday. At least things were starting to look up, with that one thing at least.

"Any word from Dies? How's the meet looking with the Aces?"

Corv gave a shrug. "He's deep in it right now. Not sure what's up. He'll let us know."

He played it off like it wasn't a big deal, but I could feel the tension radiating off him from here.

"Shit, I forgot the bread in the car," he said suddenly, flipping off the burners and tossing the dish towel on the counter as he stalked from the kitchen.

Rook leaned conspiratorially over the counter, and I lifted a brow at him. "What?"

He inhaled deeply and let out a sigh, his lips curving into a sultry grin. "What happened at school today? Anything exciting?"

I couldn't school my face fast enough, the memory of AJ's tight pussy wrapped around my cock came stampeding back to the forefront of my mind. I swallowed. "Not much."

"*Liar*," Rook said, calling me on my shit with a knowing look. "Leave you alone for one fucking day…" He shook his head, tossing back his whiskey. "How was she?"

Fucking Christ.

It was my turn to shake my head at him. No one gave the fucker enough credit. They saw him as the crazy one. All fists and fury, no brains. But my brother was the full package. He saw things other people didn't. Saw them easily. Without even trying to. He'd always been that way.

I licked my lips, leaning back in my chair with a slow shaking inhale, conveying to him without the need for words just how goddamned good it was. Lips twitching into a suggestive grin.

He blew a breath out, shoulders twitching as a shudder rolled down his spine.

Corvus returned a second later, and I winced, hoping Rook would keep this between us, at least for now.

He tossed me a wink and poured another whiskey, sipping it this time, a distant look in his eyes.

"So," I said, clearing my throat. "Work tonight; are we doing the job Julia texted about earlier?"

Julia sent a group text to the three of us like she always did. She got a call this morning at the helpline from a pair of little girls. We'd already visited their abusive father once. So this would be strike two for Billy Parker.

We had the address of a butcher shop he owned and

intel that he often worked late Friday nights to prepare for the weekend rush. That he often worked *alone,* drinking in his locked up shop before driving home drunk to take out his rage on his five and nine year old daughters and their mother.

We knew Mrs. Parker tried to leave him once before, and that he almost killed her for it. She dropped her petition for sole custody less than twenty-four hours after she made it.

But...Diesel specifically said to hang up everything we were doing. He didn't know about our little humanitarian project, or at least, he pretended not to. Either way, he wouldn't like us going off to do our own thing with everything else going on right now.

It was why we all agreed to let AJ simmer on the backburner for the time being. Until we had more time to devote to her eventual surrender.

"Yeah," Rook answered before Corvus could. "It'll be quick."

There was no room for discussion, then.

Rook rarely took an assertive role, but when he did, it wasn't worth arguing. He'd go off and do it alone if we didn't follow him.

Corvus grunted his agreement, carving up and plating the chicken and beans, pouring the sauce over it.

He set our plates down on the kitchen island, drying his hands on the towel slung over his shoulder. "Eat," he ordered, turning his attention to me and wrinkling his nose.

I stiffened, thinking he could smell AJ on me as easily as Rook could, but then his gaze tracked to my sweat-greased hair. "And get washed up. We'll leave after dark."

Ava Jade

TWENTY–ONE

2248 Fletcher Street, unit 4.

I double checked the slip of paper I'd written the address on so I wouldn't forget it. This was definitely the place. The small L-shaped shopping plaza near the northern ridge of Thorn Valley had already emptied for the night. Only a single car remained in the lot, an older model Ford truck with rust around the wheel wells and a cracked side-mirror.

The large square windows of the shops were all dark, caged over with metal to prevent break ins. Except for unit 4. The window of Parker and Sons Butcher Shop still glowed with a dim light from somewhere deeper inside the narrow space.

I really had no idea what I would find here, but

this was the break I'd been waiting for.

After Grey left the ladies room, I locked the door behind him and *prayed* his phone wasn't solely fingerprint enabled or I would need a lot more time, and a computer, to bypass it.

I almost had a panic attack when it came up with the print scanner, but swiping across the screen brought up an alternative option. Not a code, but the option to draw a password shape.

I couldn't make out the finger smudges, so that was out. I had three tries before it locked me out and he'd know it was messed with. It'd been a hot minute since my pickpocketing days, but I still remembered the three most common shapes.

Grey didn't strike me as a basic bitch, so I threw out the first two options and went straight for the third. A simple enough swipe path, but not so common that just anyone would be able to get in. I got in on the first motherfucking try.

I wondered if Rook's or Corvus' phones would be equally simple to break into, but once I was inside of Grey's, I realized the reason it wasn't as protected as I assumed it would've been.

It wasn't a burner. Not exactly. But it was clear they did change phones semi-regularly. There were only three numbers stored in the device. Corvus. Rook. Diesel.

Every other call came in as an unknown number.

And aside from a few useless messages between Grey and Corvus (it was obvious he wiped the phone clean daily) there was absolutely nothing save for a single text message from an unknown number that was sent to all three of them.

Unknown: Billy Parker. Strike Two. 2248 Fletcher Street, Unit 4. He works late. Doesn't get home until after midnight on Fridays. Accept?

The only reply was a single word from Rook in the group chat.

Rook: Accept.

That was it.

I had a date and an address. A place where they were going to be tonight. I wasn't sure who Billy Parker was, but I was glad I wasn't him.

Strike two?

I had to assume it was something to do with a debt owed to the Saints. That they were going to collect or take payment in blood. If I could get something on camera, then maybe it would be enough to buy my freedom. Or at least, it would be a good start. I had no illusions that they wouldn't just as easily kill me if I tried to blackmail them, but if they took me down I'd make sure whatever footage I had of them went absolutely viral.

Dom once explained to me how to do that, because this one time the Kings did it to her dad. They blackmailed him with footage of Dom getting double teamed by two college guys at a frat party she'd snuck into. They told him *exactly* what they were going to do with the little movie they bought from the two dickwads at Theta Kappa Nu. Down to the minute details.

Dom never forgot because dear 'ol dad never let her live it down.

Her father saw to it that they got off on all charges like they asked, even though the mess they'd gotten themselves into should have wiped them off the face of the planet.

Fucking gangs.

I'd offered to castrate the little fucklets for their crimes, but Dom made me promise not to, something about not wanting me involved.

I crept around the back of the building, careful not to be seen. A single security camera watched over the parking lot from the southern corner of the plaza. Easy to stay out of view. Around back, in the wide alley between the plaza and a closed down pharmacy were the back entrances to each shop.

Big green dumpsters lined the alley opposite the back doors. There were no windows back here. None at all. No cameras, either. *Fuck.*

How the hell was I supposed to see what was going on inside without straight up peeping into the front window?

I settled next to one of the dumpsters, wrinkling my

nose at the smell, but at least I was out of direct sight here, tucked away in the shadows.

The text message from the unknown number insinuated that Billy Parker would be here until midnight. It was just past eleven now. No sign of the Crows.

My phone buzzed in my pocket and I quickly drew it out and tapped the side button to silence the sound. The screen flashed with two messages.

Becca: Hey, you asleep? Want to watch bad horror movies and get high?

Kit: Are you ever going to call me back?

Stage four clinger alert.

I swiped ignore on Kit's message for the moment, re-upping my promise to myself to get back to both him and Dom ASAP. Knowing that might not happen for a while. I really was complete and utter shit at being a friend.

Ava Jade: Out for a run, sorry. Raincheck?

I didn't wait for a reply, toggling my phone to silent and slipping it back in my pocket. I didn't run twelve fucking miles out to this sketchy ass plaza all the way on the other end of town for nothing. I was getting in there. One way or another.

Resolving to check the front again for a good vantage point, I stood only to drop back to a crouch as the door at the back of Parker and Sons burst open.

I tucked myself into the shadows, the cool nip of the metal trash bin biting even through my long sleeve black shirt and joggers.

"I can't tonight," a man said, speaking over a garbled voice on the other end of a call. He chucked a bottle into the bin I was hidden beside and it shattered. The smell of stale beer wafted to me on the cool breeze.

"All right, all right. Look man, borrow the truck, I'll leave the keys under the visor, but if you score, I want a cut."

A pause.

"Be back by midnight. You walking over?"

Another pause.

"All right. Yeah, yeah, I'm going."

Keys jangled, and Billy Parker cursed as he dropped his phone and fumbled to pick it up, angrily striding around the back of the other shops toward the parking lot at the front. The instant he was out of sight I sprinted across the alley to the door he exited and stepped through into the dimly lit shop.

The space was narrow. At the front, a long bank of refrigerated displays poured their blue-tinted light toward the front window. That must have been the ambient light I was seeing from outside. Nearer to the back, to the right of where I stood, was a large structure built into the wall. I crept to the front of it and found the door slightly ajar, leaking icy air out into the main shop.

A side of beef hung from a hook in the ceiling, all vivid red meat and yellowed fat and bone. Several stainless-steel shelves held long slices of aging beef along the back wall. More hooks dangled from the metal sliders in the ceiling, waiting to hold more mangled cow bits for Billy Parker to cut down to size.

Okay, think Ava...

Kicking myself into gear, I rushed for the front counter, digging in a low shelf between two display cases until I found what I was looking for. I began folding down a paper bag, my fingers working deftly until I was left with a good size chunk of paper. Peering over the display cases, I could see Billy Parker slamming his truck door shut to make his way back inside.

I let out a breath of relief when he veered left across the lot, going around the back of the plaza to the rear entrance.

Once he was out of sight, I hopped the counter and unlocked the front door, stuffing the wad of paper into the lock slot. There were no bells or anything else I'd have to worry about. If I needed to make a quick getaway, I should be able to slip out undetected through the front.

I padded to the right of the display case and sank into a crouch in the nook between the edge of the case and the wall just as the back door banged back open and Billy re-entered the shop. The exhaust fan from the display case pumped warm air around my ankles, but at least the soft noise of it would mute any sound from my shuffling feet as I maneuvered myself into place.

From where I crouched, facing the back of the shop, I could see the rear entrance door and the door to the massive walk-in cooler. If the Crows tried to come in through the front, I might be seen, but if they went around back I would be safely hidden from view by the metal cart piled with stickers and pre-cut butcher paper in front of me.

I was banking a lot on them taking the back entrance.

And this was only going to work if they attacked Billy Parker here in his shop. If they waited for him to leave to snatch him then this whole thing was just a total waste of my fucking time.

But it was the first bit of useful information I'd gotten. It would have been idiotic of me not to at least *try*. The Crows poked the wrong fucking bear and they would see what happened when the bear hit back no matter how long it took me.

A taste of their own medicine wouldn't kill them.

They tried to blackmail me first, after all.

The wait was longer than I hoped. Twice, Billy wandered too close to the front of the shop, taking breaks from sawing apart the massive cut of beef hanging in his cooler. Twice, I'd had to disappear into a tiny ball of black fabric and dark hair to avoid being seen. If he wasn't at least six beers deep, there was a good chance he'd have spotted me by now.

The guy liked to talk to himself, I'd learned. Though

maybe *mutter* was a more accurate word since I couldn't really tell what he was saying beyond a word here and there. Something about *little bitches* and *that hoe.*

He was an asshole. It was easy to tell. Something in the drunken swagger. In the way he carried himself. In his snarling upper lip and the way he tossed back violent swigs of his beer, seeming to grow more enraged with each one he finished.

His buddy came and took the truck, honking twice before he pulled out of the lot.

Billy Parker had a lot to mutter about that guy. Apparently he was a no-good piece of shit, but Billy was really hoping he'd score for them both. I wasn't able to get the best look at his face, but Billy was a tall, lanky guy. With lean muscle and a pin-up girl neck tatt. His skinny legs swimming in the bootcut jeans he wore. He ditched his Mötley Crüe t-shirt sometime past eleven, working bare chested, a dusting of dark brown curling hairs on his chest making him seem somehow even more pale than he was.

I was about to call it and head home, drawn by the promise of a joint and bad horror movies, when I heard a car veer off the main road and into the lot. I wiggled in my little hidey nook to get a better look, finding a silver sedan slowly rolling through the parking lot. I ducked my head as it passed Parker and Sons, but I could still make out the shapes of three figures inside.

Where the hell were they getting all these different cars from?

I mean, I had my own ideas, but their supply of borrowed vehicles seemed to be endless.

The car vanished around the edge of the lot, and I closed my eyes, hearing the faint sound of an engine rumbling somewhere in the distance. I was willing to bet they'd parked out behind that closed down pharmacy. That was where I would've parked.

The idling stopped.

I held my breath.

The *bang* of the door being kicked into the opposite wall rattled the building and rang in my ears.

I sank impossibly lower, drawing out my phone as I waited for the perfect shot.

"*Oh, Billy boy!*" Rook rasped, and three reapers spilled into the shop.

Dressed all in black, they appeared to almost blend into the shadows. The stark white of their *Scream* masks with their hollow black eyes and overexaggerated smiles making their heads seem to float in midair.

Dammit.

Unless they said something to give themselves away or removed the masks, any footage would be pretty much useless.

I ground my teeth as I switched my camera screen to record and nestled it against the corner of the metal trolley to get a clear and unwavering picture.

A clatter from the meat cooler and rushing footsteps.

The tallest of them, Corvus, threw his foot into the cooler door before Billy could lock them out, not even flinching as it thudded against his boot. Between their dark bodies, I saw Billy Parker fly backward, knocking into the hanging meat before slipping to the floor with a shout.

"Billy, Billy, Billy," tutted Rook, stepping past Corvus and popping his knuckles.

Grey entered last, and I guess luck was at least a little on my side because no one moved to close the cooler door behind them, offering me a fairly clear view of what went on inside.

"We warned you, Billy," Corvus drawled, his voice a detached rumble.

Billy put up a good fight as Rook stooped down to grab him off the floor. He squirmed, alternating between grunts and curses, but one good fist to the face and the drunken butcher was too dazed to fight anymore.

"Hold that hook," Rook said, his masked face tipping up to the curved piece of shining metal in the track on the roof. Grey obliged, gripping the topmost part of it to steady it as Rook lifted Billy with ease.

My stomach turned as he slid Billy onto the hook, the metal biting through the skin of his back. Through his muscle.

Billy screamed, an awful drawn-out sound that ended in a sob only to start again. Scream after scream until his throat was raw and he choked up bile. Until his back was coated in red and it began to pool on the stained tiles below his hanging feet. Until he stopped trying to reach the hook with wildly flailing arms, realizing he couldn't dislodge it himself no matter how hard he tried.

"You about done?" Corvus asked

He kicked a milk crate under Billy, enabling him to stand on his tip toes to alleviate some of the pressure no doubt shifting the bones of his shoulder blade. *Ugh.*

"P-please," Billy pleaded, his arms hanging in defeat. "Don't kill me."

"We're not going to kill you, Billy," Grey said, crossing his arms over his chest, making his fitted long-sleeve black t-shirt bulge around his biceps. My mouth went a little dry, and I chastised my aching cunt for wanting another taste of his cock. Even now. Even while I watched them *torture* someone, she still thirsted for him.

I mean, I knew I was fucked up, but...that had to be some next level shit. Maybe Aunt Humphrey was right; I needed therapy. Copious amounts of it.

"We explained this to you last time," Corvus droned. "That was strike one. This? This is strike two. Your last warning."

Snot dripped down Billy Parker's face, mingling with the drool leaking from his gaping mouth. "I won't..." he said, the words choking off on a pained intake of breath. "I won't ever touch them again, I swear."

Silence in the meat cooler.

"*I swear*," he repeated. "You've...you've made your point. Now please, *please* just let me down."

"Oh no," Rook said. "We're nowhere near finished."

If it were possible, Billy went even paler. His eyes, wide and round, terrified as he took in Rook.

"What was it you did to your little Ashley two nights ago?" Grey asked, his voice so cold, so different from the playful cocky tone I'd come to know as his. "Oh, right. You broke her arm."

"And to Stella?" Corvus asked. "Go ahead and tell me what you did to your five-year-old daughter."

Wait...*what?*

Billy began to sob quietly, hanging his head as my thoughts raced to catch up with exactly what I was witnessing here. This was clearly not what I thought it was. This wasn't gang business at all.

My chest burned, ignited by the accusations they were slinging at Billy. By his inability to deny them. If it were true, this coward of a man *broke his daughter's arm.* And apparently that wasn't all he did. Nor was it the first time.

My eyes burned and a muscle in my jaw twitched, remembering the time my mother hurt me. How it'd felt. The man at the train tracks. The feeling of helplessness after the initial shock subsided. Of being too small to do anything to stop it. Too weak.

"Say it!" Rook demanded, gripping him brutally by the arm and pulling downward, making the metal skewer in his back dig deeper. Billy whimpered, trying to pull away, and I hoped it fucking hurt.

"I…"

"Say it, motherfucker," Grey growled.

"I…I hit her."

"And then what?" Corvus prodded, his voice dangerously level.

"And then she fell," Billy croaked, his voice a hoarse mess of broken sounds. "She…she hit her head on the table and p-p-passed out."

"Go on, you piece of shit. *Then what?*"

"I…"

Rook gave Billy another sharp tug and his eyes bugged out of his skull as bloody foam gathered in the corners of his grimacing mouth.

"I locked her in her room," Billy blurted, the words overlapping so I wasn't even certain I heard him correctly. "For two d-d-days."

"Without any food," Grey finished for him in a snarl, his body going taut, his hands flexing at his sides.

Corvus stepped forward, but stopped, digging his hand into his back pocket as an audible buzzing broke the tepid silence.

"Hold that thought," he said, lifting the phone to his ear.

I held my breath as he left the meat cooler and walked toward the front of the shop, tugging off his mask. "Yeah," he said as he answered the call. "I'm a little busy at the—"

His words cut off as a garbled voice on the other end of the receiver interrupted him. I rushed to check the angle of the camera, to see if I caught him removing the mask, but he was just out of frame. I reached out to tilt the camera, but then he turned sharply toward me, pacing along the bank of refrigerated display cases. Fuck. I couldn't stick my hand out there without risking him seeing it. I'd have to pray he wandered back in view without that mask on.

"It's late, what are you doing calling me right...*shit*. All right. Yeah. Yeah, I have a sec. What is it?"

Corvus paced behind the counter, and I flattened myself against the side of the meat cooler, willing myself to be invisible.

"I told you, Max, I'm not interested. I can't be away that long."

The voice replied on the other end of the call, distinctly feminine despite the name, but I couldn't make out what they were saying.

"Well, I'm not most people, am I?" Corvus' voice was growing more irritated by the second, his steps quickening as he paced the short length of linoleum flooring behind

257

the register.

"Merch? I don't fucking know. I'll have Grey make something."

Corvus stopped suddenly, and I dared a peek around the edge of the display case to find him pinching the bridge of his nose as he inhaled. "I might have something new. Do you think we could...yeah, all right. I'll try to make it. Thanks, Max."

He hung up, and I whipped my head back around and closed my eyes as he lifted his gaze, praying I was fast enough. That the shadows were thick enough to keep me concealed.

Shit.

Fuck.

Fuck. Fuck. Fuck.

He cleared his throat, and I almost cracked a tooth for how hard I was clenching my damned teeth.

"All right," he said, sighing, and his heavy footfalls retreated, heading back to the cooler. Mask back in place. "Where were we?"

I blew out a breath, tucking my blade slowly back into the strap at my ankle.

"I think we were just about to show Billy here what happens when he doesn't heed our warnings," Grey replied, and I heard a sharp intake of air and looked through the shelves of the trolly to find Rook *smelling* the guy. He shuddered.

"Please…" Billy pleaded again, his voice distant now, heavier.

Corvus slapped Billy hard enough to start to draw him out of his stupor. "Hey. Pay attention."

Rook licked his lips.

Corvus slapped him again, and Billy slowly came around, his watery eyes widening in surprise like he was waking from a dream to find a nightmare waiting for him in real life.

"Pieces of shit like you aren't welcome in our town," Corvus said. "We see *everything*."

Well, not everything, I preened internally. They didn't see me barely fifteen feet away from them. Watching. *Recording.*

Billy's lower lip trembled.

"This is strike two," Grey added. "I think you know what happens if you get to strike three."

They let the threat hang in the air for a moment before Grey backed away from Billy to lean against the right wall of the cooler where I couldn't see him. Corvus backed up, too, leaning casually against the doorframe with his arms crossed over his chest. Blocking most of my view of Billy.

"What happened to you?" Corvus asked Billy.

"…w-what?"

"I said *what happened to you*?"

"I…I had an accident. I fell onto a hook."

"That's right." Rook answered him, and I could hear

his smile even if I couldn't see it behind his mask. "You also might've broken some bones. Maybe smashed your face into a table, too. Guess you should stop drinking at work."

"*Wait—*"

"Let's get this over with," Corvus said simply.

"No!" Billy screamed a second before a sickening *pop* and *crunch* tunneled into my ears. I knew what it was without having to see it. Rook had broken his arm, just like Billy had broken his daughter's. It's what I would've wanted to do, too.

An eye for an eye.

When the second break came and there was no end in sight, I carefully removed my phone from the shelf and stopped recording, gripping it tightly in my hand.

It would be almost useless. They were wearing masks. They didn't say each other's names. They would have been smart enough to take a vehicle not registered to them and even then, they would have carved a wide path outside of view of any surveillance cameras.

All I'd done here tonight was witness something I wished I fucking hadn't. I didn't want to feel this...connection.

And honestly? I wasn't sure what I'd do with the footage even if it had been usable. God*fucking*dammit.

I didn't flinch as Rook snapped more bones and Billy screamed and cried until Rook eventually knocked him unconscious. I listened, hating how much I wished I could hurt him, too. How the sounds of his agony had almost no effect on me.

A five and nine-year-old? They were too young. Too innocent to be subjected to that sort of abuse from someone who was supposed to love them.

I'd have just killed him, the thought came viciously to my mind and a sour taste coated my tongue, making me grimace and clench my fists.

People made mistakes. Hell, I'd made plenty, but I learned from them.

This fuckwad would continue to make mistakes. I could see it in his face. Hear it in his voice. Who was to say that he wouldn't kill one of his little girls the next time he was angry? Then it would be too late. Then *strike three* would only be vengeance instead of prevention.

I pressed my head between my knees as the Crows took a limp Billy down from the hook and left him on the floor in a pool of his own blood. My breaths came heavier. My pulse throbbed in my temples. Fingers twitching.

I worked hard to fight it, trying to stay calm. Stay quiet. Not let the darkness grab hold. Flashes of the man at the train tracks scorched into the back of my eyelids, and I forced my eyes open to erase them, sweat beading at my hairline.

A loud metallic *chink* rang out through the shop. Grey had snapped off the lever inside of the cooler and wiped it down for prints before tossing it to the floor. It scraped over the linoleum tiles and came to a clattering stop near my feet.

"What are you doing?" Corvus asked.

"Seeing how he likes being locked up," Grey replied stoically and closed the cooler door as he shouldered past Corvus.

"And if no one finds him?" Corvus asked, and I got the distinct sense that he was waiting to judge Grey's answer. That this was a test, and Corvus wanted to see if Grey would pass it.

"Then no one finds him," Grey replied and left, pushing through the back door of the shop to vanish into the night.

Corvus nodded quietly to himself. He passed.

"You hungry?" Rook asked. "I could really go for some McDicks right now."

"Seriously?"

Rook shrugged and Corvus snorted at him before the pair left to follow Grey out into the dark.

I couldn't be sure how long I stayed there, leaning against the metal, just breathing. Taking in everything I'd seen and heard.

A thousand questions swirled in the adrenal wasteland of my brain. What they were doing...did it make them any better than Billy?

They were murderers.

Fucking psychopaths.

None of them so much as balked as Rook broke Billy apart.

Neither did you, the darkest part of my mind whispered, and I swallowed hard, forcing my legs to push me back to standing. My back ached from crouching there for so long, and I took a minute to stretch it out.

A thud sounded, echoing in the butcher shop.

Then another.

"H-hello?" A weak voice called, muffled by thick steel and insulation. "Is anybody there?"

I judged whether I'd touched anything in the shop and did one last wipe of the front door to be safe. It was time to get the fuck out of here.

Another thud as Billy pounded a fist against the door. "Help!" he shouted. "Someone please!"

I groaned to myself, stopping near the door to the cooler. The handle was right there. I could just pop it open and vanish. I could free him.

But why in the absolute fuck would I do that?

Heat licked up my spine, and I took two steps toward the back door to leave before something made me stop. Invisible hands wrapped around my ankles like ghosts demanding proper justice.

I didn't even know what they looked like, his little girls, but I knew that they'd be better off without him. But was that enough?

What was I really considering here?

No one had seen me. I'd been careful. I'd triple check for prints.

What am I doing?

"P-please! I've been attacked! Please, someone open the door!"

"*Fuck*," I gritted out through my teeth, the flood of new adrenaline vaulting up through me in an eruption of rage.

I stalked back to the walk-in cooler and wrenched the door open. Billy poured out, falling onto the floor with a wet *slap.*

He twisted, fear in his swelling eyes as he took me in. A relieved gush of air passed his lips, and I wrinkled my nose at the acrid smell of beer and blood mingling in the air.

"Thank you," he sobbed, reaching his bloodied hand, the one that wasn't broken, toward my shoes. I stepped back. "*Thank you.*"

I bent, the dull side of my blade sliding along my fingers as I drew it from the strap.

He lifted his head and his eyes met mine.

Something registered there after a second. The relief smoothing the lines of his weathered face vanished. He stopped breathing.

"Who—"

A hard and quick arc of my blade.

A clean slice.

I left him there to die, dancing away from the spray of crimson as it rushed to leave his severed carotid. I was gone before Billy Parker even finished choking on his own blood.

And I felt...*incredible.*

Ava Jade

TWENTY-TWO

I slept like a baby after butcher butchering night.

Well, for the four hours I managed to sleep before the sounds of Becca moving around in our shared dorm woke me.

It'd been an entire week since then and only a couple days ago the stiffness and aching in my legs from the twenty-four-mile return trip to and from Parker and Sons finally leveled out to the normal daily burn. Really, I should've added two more miles to make it a murder marathon.

I kind of missed the ache if I was being honest.

It kept my mind off other things. Things I *shouldn't* be thinking about.

Billy Parker's murder hit the news just this

morning. They found his body two days ago and the fact his wife didn't report him missing and start an investigation sooner only served to cement I'd done the right thing. I didn't know what it meant that I slept better after killing a man. That I didn't lose my appetite. That I felt...*good*.

Not at all like the first time.

This time, I was certain there was nothing at Parker and Sons tying me to the murder. No prints, I'd wiped everything down that I touched. No camera footage, I was very careful to avoid the one camera in the plaza and honestly, I doubted it was even functional, judging by the antiquated look of it. There was nothing tying me to his death except for a very clean slit in a redneck bastard's throat.

And that could've been done by anybody. More likely the same people who caught his fishy ass on a hook to be flayed. Though, I was fairly certain they hadn't left any traces of themselves there, either.

I almost felt guilty when I finally secured the bug I'd been covertly trying to acquire on Monday night. And that same guilt ate at me when I planted it on Tuesday.

I *hated* that I felt guilty. I shouldn't. Not after the shit they'd pulled. Even if the self-proclaimed Queen of Briar Hall still hadn't attacked, I knew they weren't done toying with me. Once their meeting with the Aces and the other shit with the Mexicans was done, I'd be fair game again.

It was just like I'd planned. Easy in. Easy out. I didn't go inside the Crow's Nest to plant it. Not wanting to risk leaving so much as a stray hair behind to be found.

I'd had to settle for planting it just outside the kitchen window. It was strong enough to pick up conversations inside the house, albeit, not as clearly as I'd have liked. And the old wood siding gave me the perfect little knot to cram it into.

It wasn't top quality and the battery needed to be replaced every three days, but barring a trip back to Lennox to visit my usual contact, it was as good as I was going to get.

They had exactly three things planned that I was now aware of:

In three days, on the holiday Monday, they were meeting with the Aces whom Corvus didn't trust, but didn't think was at fault for the death of some guy named Randy.

In two days, Sunday, they would be making some kind of exchange with the Mexicans. I had to assume guns or drugs but couldn't be sure. They were all a little on edge about that one.

And tonight, in exactly three hours, at eleven, Rook would be up against some sorry sucker named Conor Jones in an illegal fight ring in the basement of a bar called Sanctum.

Two of those things, I was planning to attend as a

ghost. The fight and the Aces meet.

The thing with the Mexicans was too far. I could jack a car, but from the sound of it, it was in the middle of nowhere, so they'd easily spot a tail. And the ride would be too long for me to be able to get away with climbing into their trunk. An option I was considering for the Aces meet to avoid the thirty-mile round trip run to what they liked to refer to as no man's land. Which was basically just a fancy way of saying Spirit Lake, the all but abandoned village just east of Thorn Valley. The only place within a hundred-mile radius *not* claimed by a gang.

Talk about a useful bug, am I right?

Though knowing all of this paled in comparison to the fact that I was pretty sure Corvus would shit an actual brick if he knew I'd one-upped him and was eavesdropping on *everything.* The thought alone brought me so much joy I'd been living on cloud nine all week.

I'd gotten even *more* ahead on all my projects, academic and extracurricular. Becca and I had a new routine of evening horror movie watching and popcorn when she or I weren't out—which I actually enjoyed. Way more than I thought I ever would.

She seemed sad lately, and I didn't feel bold enough to ask her about it, so I simmered in silence hoping that one day whoever made her upset would cross my path so I could cheerfully gut them.

But all good things had to come to an end.

I lowered myself behind the burgundy SUV across the street from Pop's Midnight Cafe where the owner, a balding man in his late forties, would soon be exiting with his weekly cash deposit to drop off at the bank on his way home. Like he had done the last two Friday's before this one.

It paid to pay attention. Literally.

If I wanted to get into Sanctum, I needed cash. If it was what I thought it was, it would be pay to play. All attendees would need to place a bet before entry. A hefty sum of which would be raked by the house.

If I showed up with my last three hundred bucks, I'd be laughed out. If I showed up with the 8-10k I thought might be in that faded gray cash bag, I'd have a better chance of being let in.

I needed to see what I was up against. Watching Rook fight might give me an advantage if we ever came to blows. More than that, I wanted to see the man himself. Diesel St. Crow. I wanted to take a measure of him. See if he was made of the same things as his sons.

At least, that's what I was telling myself. It definitely *wasn't* because I wanted to see Rook beat Conor Jones to a bloody pulp. Not at all. And fucking *definitely* not because I haven't been able to stop thinking about all three of them since last Friday night.

Listening to the recordings on the bug only had me more confused. They talked about some show they had later this month, and I got the idea it was a concert. I *prayed* it wasn't the Primal Ethos one Becca was taking me to. That would be a surefire way to ruin my fun.

Oh, and Corvus cooks. Who would've thought? He also got up several times a night and wandered to within range of my bug by the kitchen for water and to grumble wordlessly to himself like a total lunatic.

I adjusted my wig, the short black bob had bangs and when it shifted, they tickled annoyingly at the skin just above my brows.

I groaned, hushing rapidly as the bells jingled and I peered around the edge of the SUV to see Mr. Jordan Hughes exiting with his big 'ol bag of cash. Right on schedule.

Fuck, he walked so slow it hurt to watch him. Made my skin itch.

Come on, fucker, hurry up. I don't have time for this.

Sanctum was across town and word on the street was that attendees were locked in when the show started. Unable to leave until it was over. Something about preventing a raid. If I didn't get there before eleven, I wasn't getting in at all.

I'd have to make this quick.

At this time of night, the streets were all but empty, but of course, because my luck was total shit, a patron exited the cafe right after my mark.

She went the opposite way, but would be quick to

turn around if there were signs or sounds of struggle.

Awesome.

So, plan B it was.

Mr. Hughes whistled to himself as he unlocked his car and slipped into the drivers' seat. He didn't even balk as I opened the passenger door and slid into the passenger seat opposite him other than to give me a confused look.

"Uh, miss, I think you have the wrong ca—"

I jabbed my blade against the base of his ribs, and he flinched away, eyes wide, hands raised, faded gray cash bag dropped onto the center armrest.

"Don't scream," I warned before his mouth even opened. "All it would take is one thrust and this will pierce your lung. If it does, there's about a fifty-fifty chance you'll live long enough to get to a hospital."

His face paled and his Adam's apple bobbed in his throat, but his wild, jerky eyes were narrowing. Fixing on me.

My blood boiled, and I pressed harder with my blade, just enough to nick him. A small blood offering to keep my darkness at bay. "Don't fucking look at me," I hissed. "*Drive.*"

The prosthetic nose, double layer of lip plumper, and colored contacts would be enough to protect me, at least here in the dark of his SUV. The nose at least, would have to be removed before I entered Sanctum. I ran out of Dermabond and this bitch was held on with a bit of school glue and a prayer.

"Let's go, dickface," I urged when he hesitated.

Mr. Hughes fumbled to dig his keys out of his jacket pocket and took three tries to get them in the ignition. Already the high was wearing off. This man was pathetic. Not even a challenge.

I sighed inwardly as he roughly turned the SUV away from the curb, making me jerk in the passenger seat. Idiot.

"Turn left," I ordered as he came to the next street corner, and I got an idea. Maybe I didn't have to walk *all* the way back across town after all. There was a dead-end road I'd found on a run a few days back near Sanctum. Well, near enough that it wouldn't take me that long to get there. Far enough that if Mr. Hughes woke up before I was finished, the cops wouldn't find me anywhere in the immediate area.

"What do you want?" Mr. Hughes asked, his voice the tone of a man trying his best to be brave and failing miserably.

I shifted and paper crinkled at my side. I noted the edge of a crayon picture sticking out between the seat and center console. It was upside down, but a name was visible as we passed under the last of the streetlamps before I guided my mark down the dead-end road. Bethany.

I already knew enough about him to have dismissed him as any sort of threat, but judging by the drawing, the ratty old booster in the backseat, and the wedding band on his ring finger, I doubly knew he wasn't going to fuck around.

Not if he was a good husband. Not if he was a good father.

Not if he wanted to go home to his family.

"Just keep driving," I replied, the leather glove on my left hand creaking as I gripped the blade tighter. How I'd missed them. They were faded black, well worn, and fitted to every curve and knuckle of my hands like a second skin. "We're almost there."

Mr. Hughes began to shake as we passed the *dead-end* sign and kept on going.

"Please," he said, the word a breathy plea. "I have a family. You...you don't have to do this."

I rolled my eyes. Fucking yawn.

"Park."

He did.

"Here's what's going to happen," I told him, slipping the faded gray bag onto my lap. "I'm going to take this, and you are going to forget that you saw me. You're going to say it was stolen out of your car. I'm sure your insurance will cover it."

He swallowed again, eyes shifting to the gray bag on my lap like he might make a play for it.

Try it, fucker.

Mr. Hughes didn't answer me, a knot forming between his brows.

"I'd hate for anything to happen to Bethany."

His head snapped up and a fire lit in his eyes. I'd struck a nerve. Good.

"I know where you work, Jordan Hughes. I know where you live. I know where you like to park and jerk off to amateur porn before going home to your wife. I know where darling Bethany goes to school."

His lips parted, a raw form of terror taking over his features. My thighs clenched, and I ground my teeth, a rush of power pulsing through my veins.

"Do we understand each other?" I asked after a second.

Hughes nodded and I flipped my blade away from his ribcage and lifted myself in the seat, using my full body weight to drive his face into the steering wheel. His sharp intake of breath was the only sound before a sharp blare of the horn. Then he was out. His body sagging against the wheel, arms hanging down.

The engine revved as his foot hammered down on the accelerator and I quickly shut off the engine and nudged his leg off the gas.

I slipped my blade away and unzipped the cash bag, flipping through the stacks of cash. They were nearly organized in bundles of fives, tens, twenties, fifties, and hundreds.

The smaller bills would be coming back to Briar Hall with me. The larger ones would be my bet.

I judged the sizes of the stacks, quickly tumbling through the bills for a rough count. About seven grand in larger bills.

I fucking hoped that would be enough.

"Thanks."

I gave Mr. Hughes a gentle pat on his arm and slid the money into the inside pockets of my oversized jacket. It cost me thirty bucks at the small Thorn Valley thrift shop, but it held all the cash easily. I'd find a place to stuff it and two of my three blades once I got closer to Sanctum. They'd undoubtedly be doing pat downs before entry, and I didn't want to be caught with big ass wads of small bills and knives.

I opened the door and stepped out into comparably chilly air, breathing it in to erase the lingering tang of his fear and stress-sweat clogging my nostrils.

"Here," I offered, digging a few tens out of the stack and tossing them onto the booster in the backseat. "Buy your kid a better booster seat, asshole."

Sanctum.

Not exactly a covert name for a pub owned by the Saints of Thorn Valley. But then again, I didn't think they really needed the anonymity. Hell, it seemed they strived for the opposite.

I was sure it helped officer Vick's pals know exactly

who not to mess with. Where not to step foot.

It didn't look like all that much on the outside. A heritage building at the edge of the strip, taking up the full corner lot. Three levels. Well, if you knew about the basement, anyway.

On the top floor, cherry red curtains hung in the windows, backlit with diffused light. I'd heard talk that there was a brothel of sorts up there, but hadn't confirmed it just yet. Couldn't go asking too many questions of the locals, especially when they were so clearly as enamored with their *Saintly* St. Crow and his merry band of misfits as they were with themselves.

I bypassed the burgundy painted front entry of the pub and went around the side of the building to the nondescript black service door near the parking lot behind the bar.

I felt naked in the skin-tight black dress I wore after getting rid of my larger jacket and the rest of the cash. But the long sleeve little number was easy to move in, made the girls look killer, and hopefully, would help me blend in. I knocked. Waited.

The door opened three seconds later and the burly bouncer gave me a once over.

It was five to eleven now. I knew I wasn't too late, but by the look on his face, he was going to turn me away.

"I think you're in the wrong place, sweetheart."

He began to close the door.

I tugged the cash from my thrifted designer purse and thrust out a palm to stop him.

He eyed the cash. "Don't call me sweetheart," I deadpanned. "You want my money or not?"

"Fighter?" he asked, his shoulders tensing as he frowned at me.

"Rook," I replied. I didn't even have to know a goddamned thing about his opponent to know where my money would be safest. If I could double it. The More the better.

But it still physically wounded me as Mr. Bouncer ushered me into the narrow space at the top of a set of stairs going down and took the wad of cash from my hands to feed it into a counter.

When it was done eating my spoils, he stuffed it into an envelope and wrote the amount on the front. "Name," he barked gruffly.

"AJ," I replied on a whim, kicking myself when it was too late to take it back. I had a cycle of names I usually used. All variations of Evangeline. That name had *so many* short form variations. Eve, Eva, Evie, Vanna, Angie, Lina, Gilly, the list went on and on. Made it easier to remember and if I forgot I could just say Evangeline and they would connect the dots themselves. *Voila.*

But *AJ?* Fucking, really?

I groaned inwardly, telling myself that AJ could stand for any number of things while mentally kicking myself.

He added the name beneath the amount and sealed the envelope before prying open a metal drop shoot in the wall and chucking it in.

The *shhhhh* of the paper sliding down the metal shaft made a weight settle in my belly.

Bye-bye, my sweets, I'll be seeing you and your cousins very soon, I promised each bill.

The bouncer looked me up and down, judging my ability to hide a weapon somehow beneath the skin-tight dress I was wearing. The heels, the ones Becca lent me the night at the docks, were strappy and wouldn't conceal anything, either.

"Spread," the bouncer decided, and I heard a few cheers erupt from deep below. I could hear the faint thud of music, too, but it was all so muffled up here, they must have invested a small fortune in soundproofing.

I lifted my arms and spread my legs as the guy completed a very thorough search. Above his head, I noted the blinking red light of a surveillance camera set into a nook on the ceiling. I wondered if they already knew I was here. I held no illusions that this disguise would fool the Crows, but if I managed to stay in the choked crowds of people I assumed would be surrounding the ring, I may skate by unnoticed.

"About finished?" I asked the burly fucker as his fingers trailed up my left thigh, hedging below the hem of my skirt. Another inch and he'd know exactly what I was hiding down there.

He frowned, but released me, snatching my small purse to look inside that, too. He grunted as he stepped out of my way and thrust the bag back at me.

I had a fake ID prepared, but it seemed my money was good enough to neglect the need for one even though I could smell the strong tang of mixed spirits and beer below.

"Good luck," he barked as I took the first step down into the bowels of Sanctum. I heard the deadbolt slide shut behind me and my heart skipped a beat, mouth going dry.

This was going to be one interesting night.

Rook

·TWENTY-THREE

"How is it?" Grey asked, finishing the wrap on my right hand. I flexed my fingers, making sure there was enough movement, but not so much that I'd easily break bones. I mean, I didn't mind a few breaks, but like Corvus and Grey liked to keep reminding me, if I broke the bones in my hands any more than I already had over the years I wouldn't be able to use them for shit when I got older.

Not to hold a gun.

Not to take a piss.

Not to jerk it when I woke from fever dreams of Ava Jade.

I hadn't dreamt a goddamned thing in years until now. I'd almost forgotten what it was like.

"Hey," Grey pressed. "You good?"

"Is he ready?" Corvus asked, storming back into our private area with a sour look on his face.

I lifted the dregs of my whiskey from the stool next to me and swallowed them down. Fight nights were the one time I let Corv regulate that shit. I'd had exactly four ounces of whiskey since we arrived an hour ago, and I wasn't allowed a drop more until *after* the fight. Something about not wanting to kill the other guy.

Personally? I thought it would make for an exceptional show.

"Yeah," Grey answered for me, and I knocked my glass back down onto the stool, glancing up through the dark hair covering my forehead to the clock.

Two minutes.

Heat swelled in my core, pouring steam into my muscles. I rolled my shoulders and twisted on my stool, stretching out my back muscles. I'd already gone through the rest of the stretching and pre-fight bullshit earlier, but my lower back was tight as fuck and I didn't want to risk it locking up in the ring.

"How's it looking?" I asked, shaking my head at Grey's offer of water.

"Better than we hoped. Conor Jones talked a big game. Won his last five consecutive fights. The bets are stacked against you, but not by much. A last-minute bet pushed it closer to even."

Which meant that when I won, the payout would be

greater for our proxies, and therefore, *for us.*

"Just put on a good show," Grey said, clapping me on the shoulder and giving a squeeze as he fixed me with a pointed stare.

"Don't I always?"

He snorted. "And don't kill him."

"No promises," I muttered, getting to my feet as the crowd outside began to grow louder than the thudding music. After I killed that one guy back in April, they were hesitant to let me fight again at all.

If the roar of the crowd out there was an indication, I'd say it helped.

Deep down, people were more fucked up than they liked to believe. Even the investment bankers and the mortgage brokers and the lawyers. They came here tonight not just because there was a fight and they could make some coin. They came because those dark parts of themselves craved chaos. Blood. The possibility of death.

The only difference between them and us was that they wouldn't admit it. They choked it down and snuffed it out. Pretended it wasn't there. Trauma hadn't destroyed the barriers their darkness hid behind, but it'd shattered ours. Setting us free.

Corvus gripped the thick black curtain, and I grimaced.

This was the part I didn't care for. Growling quietly to myself, I waited, bouncing from foot to foot, letting that unnamable thing inside of me slither to the surface. The rawest, most primal parts of myself awakening as a spark of adrenaline ignited them.

I shook my head, opening my mouth to allow Grey to shove the guard in. He gave my cheek a hard slap, and I let it ricochet in warm waves through my body, stoking the fire.

Fuck yeah.

I grinned over the mouthguard as the music changed, shifting to the entry song Grey chose for me. The distant echo of cheers accompanied the synth sounds as *Fire* blared over the speakers, and I stepped out.

I kept my head down as I stalked toward the ring, bristling as shouts and jeers assaulted my ears. As unfamiliar hands attempted to clap on to my back and arms, reaching, keeping me hemmed in on both sides. Stopped only by the look on my face and the weak half fence holding them back. I envisioned cutting each hand clean off at the wrist as I passed, which made it all bearable.

This was part of the show.

A part I endured as a means to an end, but when a meaty hand slapped against my cheek, my lid popped and I whirled, striking him once in the jaw. He stumbled and fell, making the surrounding crowd have to catch him.

Silence fell for an instant before the cheers erupted anew, louder and more wild than before as the unconscious man was forgotten, left to fall unceremoniously to the floor.

"Back the fuck up from the fence," Corvus snarled as he and Grey moved to form a protective barrier on either side of me. "I said *move* assholes."

Funny how these pissants thought my brothers were protecting me from the crowd and not the other way around. A smirk curled my lips as I stepped up the three short stairs and bent to slip through the two red ropes.

The spotlights always took some getting used to. So fucking obnoxiously bright. I squinted into the crowd of shouting, animated faces. Finding Diesel at the edge of the room, just next to the bar, his arms crossed. He nodded to me, and I grinned maniacally.

His fingers slyly came up to tap his jaw. Three times.

He wanted me to go at least three rounds before putting Conor down.

I nodded back. I'd try, but Diesel knew just as well as my brothers that I couldn't always control what happened once that bell rang.

The music shifted and Conor Jones entered from the other curtained off section of the wide, black-painted space. He pounded his fists together and lifted his chin, slapping the hands of the crowd on his way down to the ring. A swagger in his step. A showman.

Unlike me, Jones' body was entirely devoid of ink. A blank canvas. Unblemished. He looked like a baby. If babies had eight packs and a sick fade. Something in his clean-shaven face only heightened the illusion. The guy could've been sixteen or twenty-six. It was anybody's guess. Corvus would know, but I didn't care to ask.

He'd be prettier covered in purple and red. When I was finished.

Jones stepped into the ring and raised his arms, shouting into the crowd as they cheered for him.

A chant of *Con-or Jones, Con-or Jones, Co-nor Jones* began, and I held in a snicker. He brought some fans. Cute. I wondered if he spotted them the minimum bet, too. I knew his type. I wouldn't doubt it if he had. He'd be expecting a cut of his winnings, which he clearly thought he had in the bag.

We squared off, and I hesitated before bumping fists, letting him question the look in my eyes. His cocky grin faltered, recognizing that I was a predator. Or maybe that he was the prey.

Pinky positioned himself between us, getting ready to signal the start of the fight. That was basically all we had a ref for down here. There weren't really rules in the basement of Sanctum.

I glanced up one last time, looking for Grey and Corv. I found them in my corner, waiting for the end of the first round. Kit and water already in hand.

My lips parted. Breath catching as a sharp set of brown eyes met mine from the edge of the room. I'd know those eyes anywhere, even if they were tinted with false color. They'd been haunting my dreams for days.

It didn't matter that she was wearing a short black wig and heavy-handed makeup, there was no mistaking her. She shuffled uncomfortably, turning slightly and breaking eye contact.

Yeah.

It was her.

I'd know that ass anywhere.

Ava Jade had come to Sanctum. Ava Jade was going to watch my fight. I didn't know why I was surprised. I had no reason to be. Of course she could get in. Of course she could get the money for the minimum bet. I didn't think there was much she *couldn't* do.

The animal within preened like a motherfucking peacock, and I licked my lips, my focus back on my target. Blood buzzing in my ears.

Oh, I was going to make this good.

"Fight!" Pinky roared, dropping his hand swiftly between us before rushing to back up out of the crossfire. It was time for the beast to play. I lunged.

Ava Jade

TWENTY–FOUR

He saw me. I was sure of it.

Rook went at his opponent like a hurricane. A tatted hurricane with storm cloud eyes and a shock of black hair. And *fuck* if it wasn't the hottest thing I'd seen in my entire life.

His muscles rippled and flexed beneath the ink with each skillful blow. His focus was singular. Blind to the world around him as he danced and parried around Conor Jones, making him look a fool.

This man was born to fight.

Conor landed a blow to Rook's jaw, tearing his lip. Blood dribbled down his chin and splattered on the floor. He wasn't shocked though, I could tell he was grinning even with the mouth guard making it look more like a grimace. It was in his eyes. The high he was getting from not only inflicting pain, but receiving it as well.

I began a slow walk around the perimeter of Sanctum's underground club, getting different angles on the fight. I was certain of it on the next hit Conor landed; Rook had allowed it. It wasn't a lucky hit. Rook was letting the pasty-skinned fucker hit him *on purpose*. A slow grin spread over my lips, and I shook my head, unsure what to make of that.

I would have my work cut out for me with him. If Rook got close enough, I wouldn't be able to take him on my own. The admission stung. I ground my teeth, but it was the truth. It was why I'd come. I needed to know what I was up against.

Grey was a challenge, but I could take him if necessary.

Corvus... I had no fucking idea because I'd never seen him lift a finger. All he needed was his voice and the authority it commanded to get shit done. For all I knew, he could be a crap fighter. But I knew he packed heat, and I had no doubt about whether or not he knew how to use it. Learning to shoot would've been one of the first things Diesel St. Crow taught his adopted son.

Rook, though...seeing him now, he was not only dominating this fight, but also playing with his food like an animal toying with his kill before the final blow. I knew that if I had any chance with him, it would need to be at a distance.

I needed to brush up with my blades.

I'd practiced throwing all of *twice* since I arrived at Briar Hall. I'd need to keep that skill more honed than that if I stood a chance.

The first round came to an end and while Conor fell onto his stool and barely had the energy to lift his head to accept the straw his buddy offered him, Rook paced the ring. Only when Corvus climbed up and corralled him to his corner, did he go.

I paused my slow turn about the room and narrowed my eyes, watching Rook come back to himself. The faraway look in his eyes faded, and his heavy breaths subsided. He blinked, and it was like whatever possessed him in that ring was gone. He'd managed to beat back the beast within. Rook sagged a bit and pushed away the water, shouting something at Grey I couldn't hear over the crowd.

Grey's eyes narrowed, and his head turned on a swivel. Corvus' did, too.

Fuck.

I spun, finding a heavy dark curtain and slipping behind it. It was dark back here, but I could make out the shapes of heavy bags, weights, stools, and other equipment. Not a gym exactly, that would likely be under lock and key, but maybe a storage area.

I waited until the bell rang again and the second

round started before I leaned against the wall to peer out the slit at the edge of the curtain. The burning desire to watch Rook too much to deny.

My lower lip stung as I bit down on it, getting momentarily distracted by his ink. It covered him almost completely from his waist up. Two full sleeves stretching down to cover his hands. One of them stretched over to cover his right pec and creeped up the side of his neck. And his back...holy motherfucking shit. His back was fully covered in an angry crow captured mid-flight. Surrounded in expertly shaded clouds that appeared to be dripping blood instead of rain.

In the myriad of black lines and swirls and shapes, I could see stars, feathers, flowers, a portrait of a woman with long dark hair. And a roughly done tally grid running up the inside of his left forearm.

I could imagine what it was meant to keep track of.

He was a fucking masterpiece.

If he was a Saint, I might have to start praying.

No, Ava Jade.

Shit.

My stilted breath left my lips in a sigh, remembering why I was here. Why I needed to...

What did I need to do?

Blood burst from Conor's nose as Rook landed a vicious hit, his eyes slanted and wild as whatever *demon* inside of him took over once more.

I double checked to make sure no one could see me from my dark corner, hidden away behind the curtain, and licked my lips as an ache formed between my thighs. I twisted, leaning back against the cool wall to try to stifle the *need,* but it was too strong.

I hitched up my dress and braced my heel against the edge of a flat bench and tipped my head to the side to keep eyes on Rook through the slit at the edge of the curtain as he accepted a blow from his opponent and made a show of looking dazed when the sharpness in his stare told me he was anything but.

Moving my damp panties aside, I circled my slippery cunt, biting down hard as the sensation pulsed through my whole body, making my legs shake.

Holy shit.

Rook jabbed Conor in the ribs, and I *swear* I heard bone crack, even over the roar of the bloodthirsty crowd.

I moved my fingers faster, breaths coming hot and quick through my parted lips.

This is bad.

This is so fucking bad.

This is incredible.

Rook's dark eyes swung over the crowd between blows, catching on mine. A wicked curve drew up one corner of his bloodied lips and my lips parted in a silent surrender as my orgasm threatened to send me to my knees.

"Sparrow."

I froze, gasping as he pulled me from the wall. As my back met the solid warmth of his chest, his fingers curled around my throat, securing me to him. I blinked, my blade freed without thought from its sheath between my legs, the pointy end jabbing threateningly into his thigh.

"Let go," I gritted out, fury racing through me, tainting my still burning desire. Trying to figure out how he'd crept up on me from the shadows behind the curtain. Where and how he'd even gotten back there. "Let go or I'll cut your artery and leave you to bleed out back here on the fucking floor."

"If you were going to cut me, Sparrow, you'd have done it already."

My breath caught as he slid his other hand down my ribs, inching lower. I writhed against him, angry as fuck but also aching to finish what I'd started.

He guided my view back to the slit in the curtain with his thumb, squeezing my throat in a way that made me shiver. I caught sight of Rook striking like a cobra, his lithe body a weapon made of flesh.

"Watch." Corvus breathed against my neck. "Watch him all you like, but it's me you'll feel. It's *me* you'll come for."

His fingers grazed my inner thigh, and I squirmed, pressing more firmly on the blade, enough that I knew if I pushed any harder, it would slide right through his thick denim and into his flesh.

"Fuck you."

Corvus' fingers slid higher, brushing against my wet opening. His body shuddered against mine, and his breath came in a gush of heat against the back of my neck. "Go ahead, then," he said, his voice low and teasing. A rumble against my spine. "Tell me to stop."

I opened my mouth, but no words came out. The scent of him, like leather and lead was seeping into my nerve-endings, making them misfire. The truth I wouldn't dare utter hid within the confines of my lips. Unable to be spoken.

I don't want him to stop.

From my periphery, I watched as he lifted his damp middle digit to his mouth and slid it over his tongue, sucking off my sweetness.

"Mmmm."

An ache spread low through my belly, and I tried to look away from Corvus' finger in between his lips, away from Rook. Tried to force the insatiable need to dissipate, but Corvus only tightened his grip on my neck, prodding my line of sight back to his brother.

"Watch," he commanded, emboldened by the fact that I hadn't refused him. He had no idea that his force was only turning me on even more, or maybe he did know. Maybe this Crow knew exactly what he was doing.

When he slid that same middle finger and one more

inside of my throbbing cunt, my back arched, and my mouth popped open on a moan. My grip on my blade faltering.

I wouldn't come, I decided as he began to pump his fingers into me, circling my wet clit with his thumb. I would *not* come for him.

"That's it," he cooed roughly against my cheek, and my head fell back as he did some fuckery with his fingers that was seriously going to make me fall apart.

No.

"Stop fighting it," he growled, speeding the movements of his fingers. "You *will* come for me, Sparrow."

"*No*," I managed through gritted teeth. "I won't."

Somehow, the round changed from second to third, and the sound of the bell ringing again sent Rook flying into action. Different this time. He wasn't holding back anymore. His movements were reflexive, not practiced. He was a beast caged in human flesh as he dragged Conor Jones around that ring, pummeling him like he was nothing more than a sack of meat and bones.

"Yes," he rasped. "*You will.*"

"*Fuck*," I managed past the stopper in my throat, trying so hard not to let on what both of them were doing to me.

Rook landed the perfect blow to Conor's jaw, and his eyes went blank as he stumbled back, dazed and trying to regain his wits. Covered in blood from his temples down to his chest.

The chanting changed. They were no longer shouting for Conor, they shouted for Rook.

Rook, Rook, Rook.

"Finish him!" I heard Grey roar above the cacophony of voices.

Rook stepped up, and I cried out, my core tightening to beyond anything I could control. I squirmed in Corvus' grip, and he fought me the whole way, forcing me to come just like he promised he would.

No.

His merciless thrusts and rough circling of his thumb came impossibly faster, finger fucking me to within an inch of my life as Rook took the final swing.

I came hard on Corvus' fingers as Conor Jones hit the mat and Rook was declared the winner to a roaring crowd. My blade hit the cement floor with a clatter as I rode the wave of my orgasm, my knees weak and shaking.

He withdrew his fingers, and I spun away, but his fist around my throat remained, and he pushed me to the wall, his mouth finding mine in a cruel, bruising kiss. His hard length pressing against my belly.

The sound of my own moan broke me free of the trance he had me in, and I chalked it up to low O2 levels.

I thrust my arm up and knocked his away, freeing my throat while I used my other to grip him and pull, twisting us until *he* was the one backed up against the wall with my forearm across his throat. Shock registered in his cold eyes for an instant before his gaze leveled out into a wicked sort of triumph.

I pushed hard against his windpipe as I shoved myself away, making him cough to clear the ache from his throat.

He laughed ominously to himself as I collected my blade from the floor and pulled my dress down to cover the evidence of what he'd just done. What I'd just *allowed* him to do. My face turning a shade of red that I hoped the shadows concealed.

"Hope you got what you came for, Sparrow."

"Go fuck a goat, Corvus."

The bastard laughed some more as I pushed through the curtain and back out to the chaos of the main floor. I shoved my way through the throng of wealthy drunks to leave, feeling Rook's eyes on me all the way to the exit.

Rook

TWENTY–FIVE

I'm not sure what possessed me as I raced from the stage, heading straight for the cash room to smash my bloody fist on the door. Corvus was nowhere to be found, and Grey was right on my heels, barking at the crowd looking to congratulate me to step back.

I pounded harder, faster, until the lock disengaged and I shoved through, knocking the glasses off Jimmy's face. "Rook? The fuck you—"

"Who'd she bet on?" I asked, as if Jimmy would fucking know. "The girl. The girl with the short dark hair and tight black dress."

Jimmy's eyes crinkled with confusion as he righted his glasses.

"Move," I growled, shoving past him into the

counting area, searching through the baskets of envelopes and cash on the table. Money spilled, and I could hear Grey shouting behind me, but I didn't give a flying fuck. If I didn't hurry, I wasn't going to catch her.

I needed to know.

If she got into Sanctum, it meant she'd placed a bet.

She must've…

I flicked back to an envelope I'd just passed, yanking it out of the *paid* basket. It said AJ on the front. Ava Jade. It had to be hers. She bet seven thousand…on *me.* I opened it, a slow smile turning up one corner of my mouth, straining the cut there.

Christ. My cock twitched in my pants, hardening as I choked on a laugh and shoved back through Jimmy, only pausing when Grey stood in the doorway to block my exit. A snarl tearing from my mouth.

"What the fuck is going on over here?" I heard Diesel roar, and I clenched my teeth, staring down Grey as Diesel tried to shove through the crowd toward the cash room.

"Move, Grey." I enunciated the words slowly as I leveled my stare on him. The blood dripping into my eyes stained my vision with a crimson tint, and my inner beast perked up like a bull.

Grey's nostrils flared, but he moved, knowing there would be no stopping me. "Brother," he said in a hard whisper as I passed, a warning in his voice to match the worried knot between his brows.

"I just want a minute," I cut back at him. "Stall them."

His jaw flexed as he looked away, and my neck heated, right eye twitching as I tore myself away from my brother and the cash room, launching myself up the stairs.

"Which way did she go?" I asked in a growl as I passed Diesel's newest recruit, the bouncer whose name I could never remember.

I shoved through the door and glanced back to see the big oaf pointing down the street to the right. "That way," he said. "Think she took a left on Churchill."

I nodded and began to run, my ankle protesting each step from a rough kick by my opponent. The cool air licked at the sweat and blood still clinging to my skin, making the cut on my lip and the gash above my right brow sting.

An odd scent, like rotting limes, permeated the air, and my nose wrinkled as I rushed past it onto Churchill, slowing to a quiet jog. The street was silent as the grave. A few small shops clustered near the main street gave way to a residential area of apartment buildings and a few older homes. Most lights were snuffed out for the night, save for a small handful of oven lights and late-night TV screens.

I stalked down the streets, the damp *slap* of my bare feet on the rough pavement the only sound aside from my breaths and the thudding of my black heart.

I could feel eyes on me, watching, and pursed my lips to contain a grin.

"Come out, come out, wherever you are," I called into the dark, licking the blood from my lip. "You forgot something."

Waving the envelope, I followed my gut, letting that *other* sense lead me toward the side of one of the more rundown apartments. I glanced down the narrow gap and caught a jerk of movement near the end.

Got you.

I sprinted down the side of the building, cut glass biting into my heel, making me snarl as I rounded the corner and stopped dead, my shoulders expanding and heaving with each slow pant.

Ava Jade waited there, a large black lump of fabric at her feet, her blade raised. Fire in her eyes. The delivery area was devoid of trucks tonight, leaving it wide open save for a bank of trash bins. Only one streetlamp illuminated the lot, and she stood just outside of it. Her blade glinted in the light. A threat that I'd take as a promise.

I licked my lips.

"Where are the others?" she demanded, her gaze jerking to the alley I'd just come from before checking her six.

"Not here," I shrugged, tapping the cash filled envelope on my palm. "Thought you might want this."

Her cheekbones flared, giving her away.

"How kind," she replied, her voice dripping sarcasm.

I stepped forward, and she stepped back.

I cocked my head, stepping in and to the left. She stepped back and to the right.

Smart.

She'd seen what I could do, and clearly she knew she wouldn't be a match. Judging by the way she was holding that blade, though, she knew how to throw it. I was willing to bet she was a crack shot, too.

"You don't seem very grateful."

"You don't seem like the considerate type," she lobbied back, still eyeing the alley and glancing down at her blade. Checking the reflection? I shivered.

"You don't know me."

"I don't want to."

"*Liar.*"

Her face heated, jaw tightening with anger. If it were possible, she looked even more beautiful when she was angry. Almost as good as she looked when she was covered in blood.

I dangled the envelope from my two fingers. "Come on," I challenged her. "Just come get it."

She scoffed, giving her head a slight shake, but I could see it, the instant she made the decision. Her eyes snapping to the envelope. She *did* want it. I could imagine what she might've done to get the money in the first place, and now she'd doubled it, betting on *me*.

It was a lot of cash to kiss goodbye.

"I won't bite," I told her, taking another step forward. She didn't retreat, her gaze jerking from my face to the cash and back again.

"*Liar,*" she hissed, turning my own word against me.

I smiled, all teeth, giving her a glimpse of my monster.

Conor Jones balked when I let him see, but Ava Jade...her darkness smiled back.

I saw in her what I'd only seen in three other people in my entire life. It made me stop. Take stock. The intense need to know every dark corner of her mind took root in my mind, festering.

Without ceremony, Ava Jade lifted her shoulders and closed the gap between us in eleven long strides, stopping just out of my reach. Her dress was wrinkled, and her wig was slightly askew. She noticed me looking and tugged it off, tossing it on the asphalt as she shook her hair out of the spiral she had it contained in. It swirled around her shoulders in a wild mane of darkest auburn and something in my chest cracked.

Her lips popped open when she noticed the scar on my collarbone. Her eyes narrowed as she followed the line of it down, finding other scars to match it, and different sorts hidden within the ink. I didn't cover them because I was ashamed, I covered them to avoid this. The look of pity from others. The disgust.

I braced for it, but it didn't come. Her eyes jerked back

up to meet mine and she betrayed no emotion at all except a sort of calm understanding that did things to me I wouldn't dare speak of.

Ava Jade made a valiant grab for the envelope, but I lifted it out of her reach, catching her wrist with my opposite hand. She had her blade to my throat faster than I could blink. I rolled my hips, soaking in my hunger for her.

"You saw my cards," I whispered, lowering my head so our faces were only inches apart. "It's only fair that I see yours."

Her eyes widened a second before I twisted away from her blade and pulled hard on her wrist, sending her stumbling to catch her footing.

I stuffed the envelope of cash in the front of my shorts, against my slowly building erection. Ava Jade whirled on me, her upper lip curling.

I beckoned her forward with a curl of my fingers.

She rolled my challenge around in her mouth before glancing down at her blade. She gripped it tightly and reeled her arm back for a sniper-like throw. I closed my eyes. Waiting for it to impale somewhere vital, but the *thunk* of it came and I felt nothing.

When I opened my eyes, her blade was embedded in the pockmarked wood the streetlamp beam. She attacked while I was turned, and the breath whooshed from my lungs as I went down, my legs swept out from

307

under me. My ribs and temple cracking against the pavement, a ringing forming in my ears.

Damn.

I was up and ready before she could launch her next assault, blocking a throat jab and a knee meant for the family jewels. Ducking from a punch that, if delivered in just the right place, might've been my end.

Fucking hell.

She roared her fury as she came at me again and again, and I blocked her, waiting for my opening. She went for a jab at my lower back, and I was too slow to block it. Pain exploded through my abdomen, making me clench my teeth.

When she went in for another hit, misjudging my level of pain, I narrowly dodged it, yanking her arm to get her off balance. She fell, and I was on top of her in a second, using the full force of my body weight to pin her to the pavement.

She struggled, cursing and writhing, trying uselessly to find any opening to get free, but my weight was greater than hers. Her legs were locked down. Her arms pinned. My cock against her belly.

She was trapped.

I saw the moment she realized it, too, her breaths coming faster. Panicked.

No.

Her face went white as a sheet, her body trembling,

but it was her eyes that I couldn't stop staring into.

I knew that look.

Distant. An echo of past trauma lighting her up from within with blind terror.

Without thinking, I fell back, jostling to my feet in my rush to get off. The scent of pure fear putrefying in my lungs. The need to take it back wrestling with my still pounding need to dominate. To destroy.

"*Shit,*" Grey shouted as the sounds of two sets of footfalls reached me through the ringing still growing in volume in my ears. "What did you do?"

"Fuck," came Corvus' grunt, and I let him pull me back another step away from her.

Ava Jade slapped Grey's hand away as she got to her feet, unable to look at any of us. "Don't fucking touch me," she growled, shoving him hard in the chest. Making his eyes narrow.

She stormed away, snatching up the bundle of black fabric and retrieving her blade from the wooden post.

"Wait," I said before I could stop myself, reaching down the front of my shorts for her winnings, but by the time I looked up, she was already gone. The bramble at the edge of the lot shifting from her ghost.

I lurched forward but was stopped by a firm grip on my shoulder. Corvus. I bared my teeth, feeling too many things I didn't want to fucking feel.

"Leave it, man," he said. "Just leave it."

I shrugged him off and pegged the envelope to his chest, forcing him to take it.

"I need a fucking drink."

Ava Jade

TWENTY-SIX

I used the back door, like I always did, creeping into the silent lemon-scented halls of Briar Hall. Pro tip? No one ever checked to make sure that one was locked, and slipping a plug into the lock slot on my way out had always worked. Though I thought I could climb up to my window using the weathered brick facade and climbing vines if I ever needed to.

A violent buzzing almost had me tripping over my own feet, and I cursed in the dark as I rooted around in the lining of the oversized jacket for my cell, expecting a text from Becca.

Instead, the screen lit green with a text from another *problem* I didn't fucking need right now.

Unknown: You should have killed the dark one while you had the chance, but now I see I'll have to do it for you.

Nobody touches what's mine.

Rage flared back to life in my veins like liquid fire and I saw red, my thumbs jabbing the keypad to the point of cracking glass.

Ava Jade: I belong to no one, asshole. Text me again, and I'll find you and gut you like the animal you are. Fuck. Off.

The reply was immediate.

Unknown: That's my girl.

I closed my eyes and took a deep breath in before flicking over the screen to get the unknown phone number, I committed it to memory before blocking it. Even if it wouldn't help, since whatever piece of shit this was liked to change phones every few days, at least it would shut him up for tonight. I had enough on my goddamned mind as it was.

Safe to say it wasn't Corvus, though, or any of the Crows as I'd once thought, unless this was an attempt at misdirection, which was also entirely plausible.

Groaning, I stuffed the phone back into my jacket and pushed the hair from my face, deciding to stuff away the added stress in a back corner of my mind. Ignore it. At least for now.

I could analyze later. I could find whoever it was and pour bleach in their eyeballs and chop off their thumbs *later*.

Removing my heels, I padded up the narrow back staircase the janitors used, avoiding the main floor and second floor cameras. I fumbled with the keys once at the door, my hands still infuriatingly unsteady after what happened.

I swallowed past the dry lump in my throat, cursing my weakness, as I finally sheathed the key in the lock and twisted. The door opened out of my hand before I could even push. The darkened shape of a disheveled Becca filled the entry.

"Hey," she said, bag of M&M's in hand. "Thought that was—"

She paused mid-sentence, backing up a step to flip on the hall light. I lifted an arm to shield my eyes, wincing.

"Girl, what the fuck happened?" she demanded, hustling me inside and shutting the door behind me.

I tossed my jacket and the small clutch swaddled within it to the floor and ran my palms over my face, sighing as I dragged my tired feet to the couch. Fear Street was paused with a still-image of a screaming female face filling the entirety of the sixty-inch screen.

Becca shut it off and my own reflection appeared in the black, not looking much better than the girl that'd been there before. She rooted around under the magazine covered coffee table until the rattle of her metal tin rang out around us.

"Here," she said, passing me a joint. "You look like you could use it."

I put it to my lips gratefully, leaning forward on the

sofa as she flicked on her torch lighter. I inhaled deeply, my tensed muscles relaxing already as I blew out a cloud of pot smoke.

I passed her the joint and glanced up in search of smoke alarms.

"I disabled those months ago," she said without my need to ask. "I usually just smoke outside, but fuck it, they won't say shit to me anyway."

She took a long drag and went to pass it back, but I shook my head. The edge had been taken off, any more and I wouldn't be able to stay as sharp as I needed to be.

"So, you going to tell me what the hell happened, or…?"

I sighed heavily, letting my head fall back against the cushions.

"I mean, you don't have to, I just—"

"It's fine," I interrupted her. It might be nice to talk about it, and even though I'd only known Becca for a few weeks now, I really felt like I could trust her. But feeling like I could and *knowing* I could were two different things. There were some things she could know. Others, not so much. Not yet.

"I went to Sanctum tonight," I admitted, trying to suss out how much I wanted to share. "Rook was fighting there, in the basement."

"I've heard of that place," Becca mused. "I think my dad actually went there once for a match, before the Saints started buying up all the properties in Thorn Valley and pushed him out further South."

She snuffed out her joint and tucked her legs up under her on the sofa, getting comfortable. "If Rook was the one fighting, why do *you* look like shit?"

"Thanks," I scoffed, bringing two fingers up to pinch the bridge of my nose. There was a nasty headache forming behind my eyes, and it was just adding insult to injury. "I fought, too," I told her. "Afterward. With Rook. In the street."

"What?" she gushed, leaning in. When I chanced a look in her direction, her brown eyes were wide with worry. "Why? Oh my god, are they coming after you?"

Becca's gaze flicked fearfully to the door.

"No, I don't think so."

She cocked her head. "*Okay*, I don't think I'm following. What exactly is going on?"

I met her stare, curious if she would be able to see the truth in my eyes. The one I didn't want to admit. Not even to myself.

She gasped, her hand going to her mouth. "Shit," she said on a breath. "You want them, don't you? And they've made no secret about wanting to claim you."

I looked away, and she stiffened next to me.

Becca blew out a breath. I couldn't look at her as I worked my jaw, unable to confirm or deny her suspicions. I wanted to dick punch them as much as I wanted to fuck them, but that was just semantics.

"Fuck, babe. That's…"

"Insane?"

"*Hot.*"

I twisted back around, my face screwing up into a scowl. "*What?*"

She shrugged. "I don't know, I mean, they're dangerous. Fucking total psychos. Criminals. But…"

"But what?"

"But they are three of the most powerful men in this city. They are *definitely* the hottest guys in this school. Girl! You could have your own reverse harem! And I *know* you can handle them. I mean, I've had some pretty vivid dreams about *handling* them myself."

My stomach soured.

She laughed, oblivious to my green-eyed monster trying to lay claim to property that was definitely *not* hers.

She stopped laughing abruptly, her eyes gleaming. "Oh fuck! Bri would absolutely *shit* if you ever fucked Grey."

I winced.

"Oh my god *you fucked Grey*?"

"A little bit."

She shoved me, pulling a blanket into her lap to get comfortable. "Tell me *everything*."

So, I did. At least the parts I could. About my confusing split feelings and how I wasn't sure yet if I wanted to fuck them or bury them. How I might just do both. It didn't change anything though.

Tomorrow night when they went to meet with the Aces, I was going to be there. I *would* buy my freedom by whatever means necessary, whether or not I dreamed of Corvus's hands on my body tonight. Or Grey's cock thrusting into my pussy. Or Rook's dark eyes, his bloodstained face. The power behind his punch.

...the moment I thought he was going to kiss me when he lifted that envelope out of my reach. How my traitorous heart nearly stopped.

None of that mattered because they made their stance clear. To them, it was either me on my knees or hell on earth at Briar Hall. That shit wasn't going to fly. Not as long as I was still breathing.

It was time to trap some Crows.

Corvus

The Rover chewed gravel as Grey pulled out of the driveway and bumped onto the road leading down past Briar Hall and into Thorn Valley. The tension in the front seat enough to form a physical weight on my chest. Meanwhile, Rook picked something out of his teeth with a switchblade in the back, lounging over the entire bank of seats like we were headed to a fucking picnic instead of a meet with our would-be enemies.

Sometimes I envied him. His ease in high-tension situations. He'd always been more at home in chaos than in calm. It was immobility, idleness, that was his kryptonite. My jaw flexed as I thumbed a quick message to Dies.

Corvus: On our way.

His reply was immediate.

Diesel: ETA 12.

We'd hang back if we looked like we'd arrive before him, better to pull in all together. And since Diesel refused to ride with us, this was the best we had. Dies would park near the old warehouse, but not right at it. Just in case anyone fucked with the Rover. Having two getaway vehicles wasn't the worst idea, but I didn't like the idea of him riding alone.

I wished he'd at least brought Pinkie or Cash. Or, hell, both of them, but I could understand the reason he didn't, too. Diesel had control over his men, but vengeance could sometimes outweigh sense when push came to shove. I couldn't say I wouldn't go absolutely fucking feral if anything happened to my brothers or Diesel. Heads would roll. And I wouldn't be waiting to find out for certain who was at fault and who wasn't.

My back stiffened as the phantom scent of Ava Jade passed under my nose, my lips parting to taste it. I concealed a soft groan with a clearing of my throat as I shut my eyes, cock twitching in my jeans as last night's encounter replayed in my mind. Fuck, she'd smelled so good. Fresh and soft like spring moss and sandalwood, but also sharp, like some kind of strong herb. A poison that lingered in my memory longer
than anything else.

Damn.

I shook my head, trying to dislodge the ghost of her from my thoughts. I needed to focus.

"Five minutes," Grey warned as we turned off Freemont Street and onto Clove Drive, leaving Thorn Valley.

I polished off the last of my coffee, setting the metal mug down with a thud back into the cupholder. *Still*, the scent of her lingered, distracting me. Like a stain left branded on the inside of my skull.

The feel of her tight little cunt squeezing my fingers, hungry for me even though she tried so hard to fight it.

The moment she lost that fight.

Her expression as she came, her muscled body hard and soft in all the right places.

I didn't sleep at all last night.

Not even for a fucking second.

I was afraid of what I'd see when I shut my eyes.

"*Fuck*," I muttered, inching my window down for some fresh air. Praying it would wash away the stain of her long enough for me to focus on *this*. On tonight.

"What's eating you?" Rook asked from the backseat.

A snarl curled my upper lip. What was eating me? Rook had been smug as fuck since we left the Crow's Nest, like he had a secret he was happy to keep all to himself. It made me wonder, not for the first time, what happened between him and Ava Jade in the street last night.

"We're here," Grey said.

I sat up straighter, squinting out into the gloom. The sleepy town was all but uninhabited these days, but here, just outside of it, it really was no man's land.

An old industrial area that housed only rickety old buildings and warehouses left to desiccate on a pockmarked gray paved road. Grey rolled to a slow crawl up the street. The area we wanted was at the very end. Another half a mile up the road into the dark.

"Where's Diesel?"

As if on cue, headlights bounded behind us, and I drew my weapon, finger on the safety. Rook did the same and Grey lifted his from the back of his pants to lie flat on his lap. We had a few higher-powered weapons already hidden strategically at the meet point. Just in case. But if their plan was to box us in on the road, this was all we had.

The uneven canter of my pulse steadied, settling into the focused rhythm of a hunter. My vision sharpened, and I blew out a slow breath, watching the approach of the car until I recognized the distinct shape of the headlights. Saw a flash of red paint.

"It's him," I said. "keep going."

"Anything on cams?" Grey asked, and Rook tapped on a small tablet screen in the back, bringing up the feed of the area. It showed a view of the rear yard of the largest warehouse, where the meeting would take place. Diesel had the camera well hidden, and it hadn't sent a notification of movement, so I had to assume the Aces hadn't arrived yet.

"No, nothing," Rook replied, and I heard the swish of liquid in metal as he took a nip from his flask.

"Hey," I warned. "Not too much."

"Fuck off, Corv. I'm fine."

Heat licked across my back, but I didn't push him. He'd been in a way since last night. I wasn't sure if he slept, either.

That girl was going to get us all killed.

Destroy us from the inside.

She was everything I worried she would be and then some. And yet, I couldn't imagine letting her escape our reach. If she ran, I knew my beast would hunt her. Drag her back. Make her mine.

"Let me see," I growled, twisting an arm to the backseat for the tablet, scraping her from my bones.

He dropped it into my palm and leaned back, draping an arm over the seatbacks, letting his hand hang down into the trunk space.

The screen showed a wide-angled view of the lot behind the old warehouse at the very end of the road. Stacks of old tires lined the edge nearest the tree line, wrapping around the bulk of the yard. Stacked haphazardly, some piles having fallen over, leaving an obstacle course of tires strewn over the dirt and gravel.

An old bobcat and some other equipment withered in

the yard. Broken and rusted. The bobcat closest to the southern side was where our extra firepower was hidden. It was where we'd approach the yard and make our stand and would provide the best cover and quickest escape should we need to use it. Meanwhile, the Aces would be mostly hedged in by the mountains of old tires on the other side.

They wouldn't like it, but if they had nothing to hide and wanted to clear their names from Diesel St. Crow's shit-list, then they wouldn't have a problem with it.

Dies veered off to park near the front of the warehouse while we went off road, bouncing over a cement piling and onto the overgrown grass between two warehouses, driving right to the yard at the back.

Grey spun the Rover around in a sharp U, letting the back end fishtail out so we were parked just ten or so meters from where the meet would take place, the Rover positioned for a fast and easy exit.

"Good here?" Grey asked to confirm, and I gave him a nod. He could've had a career as a professional driver if *the life* hadn't claimed him first. As it was, I wouldn't trust another soul in that seat. Not even myself.

"Shit." I hopped out of the Rover and gripped my gun with both hands, glaring as the unmistakable shape of Diesel rounded the edge of the warehouse, walking toward us alone. "What the fuck, Dies, you were supposed to wait for us to come get you."

"It's fine," he said with a wave of his hand, his face coming into view as he stepped from the shadows and into the moonlight. "They aren't here yet."

I grit my teeth but didn't argue. It was no use with him.

He stalked past me, running a hand over his beard, rings glinting in the light.

"You set up a spotlight?" I asked as he went to double-check the bobcat, showing us where the guns were hidden in the rusted metal bucket.

He nodded. "It's on a timer. Should be on any—"

The light clicked on, expanding to shed its glow over the yard.

"—second," Dies finished. "It's not as bright as I thought, *shit*."

"It's fine," I assured him. We could do this just as well in the dark, but the light would keep anyone from trying to draw on us while concealed in the shadows. Plus, Diesel liked to look in the eyes of those he met with. He said the truth was always written there, no matter what words fell from their mouths.

Rook and Grey did a quick sweep of the neighboring warehouse yard, keeping tight, guns up and ready.

"Clear," Grey announced as they made their way back, Rook tossing something up and catching it in his palm. I thought it was a rock, but as they came back into the light, I cursed.

"Rook, we said no fucking grenades."

He wrinkled his brow at me like he had no idea what I was talking about.

"Don't look at me like that. We talked about this."

"It's just one," he argued, tossing it up again and catching it. The pull-pin rattling.

Diesel laughed, clapping Rook on the shoulder as he came to stand with us, and my jaw flexed, frustration rolling down my back. A crooked grin pulled at one corner of Rook's mouth, but it faded when he lifted his gaze back to me.

"Killjoy," he muttered and pocketed the grenade, lifting a cigarette to his lips.

Unbelievable.

The unmistakable sound of a vehicle's approach filtered into my ears, and I lifted a hand, signaling for silence as I listened.

"They're coming," I told them. "One car. A van maybe. A max of maybe eight Aces."

"Just like we thought," Diesel replied, drawing his weapon to click the safety off only to return it back to the sling across his chest beneath his leather jacket. "Get into position, boys."

We did the same, readying our weapons and getting into position near the old bobcat, but not directly behind it. Close enough that we could dive for the automatic rifles in a pinch.

Headlight passed by the gap between warehouses and the roll of tires stopped on the other side, out of sight.

I cursed Diesel's lack of foresight in not installing a cam on the roadside, too. I'd have liked even a thirty-second advantage of knowing how many there were before they made their way to the yard.

Diesel seemed to notice his mistake, too, a frown turning down the edge of his mouth for an instant before his all-business mask was tacked back into place. The unfeeling face of the founding Saint.

The crunch of boots over dry dirt sounded at the opposite end of the warehouse as the Aces made their way down the alley toward the yard.

Movement in my periphery drew my attention for a heartbeat and I stilled, my hand twitching toward my gun, my mind racing with possibilities of an ambush. My brows lowered as I registered what it was. A reflection in the crooked mirror on the rusted-out bobcat, reflecting the image of the Rover parked at our backs.

The breath was robbed from my lungs as the shadow of legs appeared beneath the chassis.

Shit.

The softest click of a door closing told me the fucker was *inside* the Rover. Maybe the whole time.

I hedged closer to Dies, ready to give him an elbow and a signal to the threat at our backs when she crept out from behind the sleek black SUV and darted for the tree line.

No.

Fury and dread coiled in my chest, burning and sinking and heavy.

My little sparrow didn't make a sound as she flew to the trees, concealing herself in their darkness. My eyes jerked to the guys, to Dies, to the Aces piling into the yard across from us.

No one else noticed her.

There was jack shit I could do.

If she was discovered spying, she'd be killed. Or at the very least interrogated to within an inch of her life. My pulse throbbed in my temple and the muscles of my neck stiffened, burning.

Stupid fucking woman.

What the hell was she thinking?

I should have known. *Her smell.* Her scent had been all over the goddamned Rover, and I chalked it up to another sleepless night. Convinced myself she was driving me insane when all the while the little viper was hidden away in the trunk.

Stupid.

So *so* dangerously stupid.

Diesel elbowed me, and I blinked, refocusing my attention to where it should be. Squarely at the seven men standing opposite us in the yard.

"Welcome," Diesel said, lifting his arms, the warm

welcome serving the dual purpose of showing them that he wasn't holding his weapon and telling them that he wouldn't use it so long as they didn't give him a reason to. "I think we all know why we're here, so let's get to it, shall we?"

Ava Jade

TWENTY-EIGHT

I forced the air to enter and exit my lungs in slow, quiet breaths, clinging to the base of an old redwood for cover as I watched the exchange unfold.

Four against seven.

I didn't like their odds, but Diesel St. Crow and his sons didn't seem bothered by them in the slightest. In fact, with the exclusion of Corvus who looked wound tighter than a top, they all looked calmer than they had right to be.

Rook especially. I eyed him suspiciously. The fucker had draped his arm over the seat and his fingers brushed into my hair. Like an idiot, I shied away, moving away from his touch. Unless he was more drunk than he was letting on, there was no way he hadn't figured out there was something back there that shouldn't have been. But if he'd known, then why not say something?

Why not call the whole thing off?

Turn around and take care of their unwanted passenger?

It didn't make any sense to me.

He didn't make any sense to me...and yet, he didn't have to. I felt like I knew him on a level where *sense* didn't have to play any part at all.

"Welcome," Diesel called into the chasm of devoid space between their two gangs. "I think we all know why we're here, so let's get to it, shall we?"

I dug out my phone and flicked to the video screen, tapping record.

I hadn't had a chance to spot the man himself last night at the fight and now, seeing him for the first time, I could see why he was their leader.

Formidable. Tall and thick through the shoulders with hooded eyes that cut like a shard of ice. A tapered beard and strong jaw. But it wasn't his looks alone that made him exude power. It was something in his stance. A relaxed power. A predator's grace. The unfeeling, unflinching mask of his expression gave not even an inkling of what he might be thinking beneath it.

If I was a weaker person, I'd cower at the mere sight of him. It was said many had, but he only served to pique my interest further, and I watched him closely, trying to figure him out.

A man across the yard stepped forward, putting himself a few paces ahead of the others. It was clear this was their leader, though he didn't have the same atmosphere about him as Diesel.

I'd done a bit of digging, well, as much as I could without drawing unwanted attention, to know that his name was Leonard Boniface. Aka Lenny Ace.

Shorter than I thought he would be. Younger, too. With coiffed brown hair and a clean-shaven, gaunt face. In a black t-shirt, bulky with what was unmistakably a bulletproof vest beneath, with two silver-handled pistols proudly strapped over his chest, lying flat against his ribcage.

He was the original Aces leader's nephew. Took up the position when his uncle died a couple years back under *suspicious* circumstances. As an outsider, it was easy to see how the death wasn't an accident. That it was very likely Lenny Ace himself that did it, but his gang brothers didn't seem to mind. They all stood in a neat row behind him, ready to give their lives for whatever their leader deemed a fair price.

"We heard about your man," Lenny replied. "Sorry for your loss."

Diesel cocked his head at Lenny, and a moment of silence stretched on between them. Long enough to make me squirm internally, my pulse picking up speed with anticipation.

"Appreciate it," Diesel replied finally. "Though I'll admit we were under the impression you might've had a hand in it."

A tick made Lenny's jaw jump. From my vantage point set a ways back from mid-field, I could see it easily, but I wondered if Diesel could. If his sons were paying close enough attention because that man was definitely *lying*.

He may not have pulled the trigger himself, but he knew something. I was certain of it.

I glanced to the Crows, finding Grey and Rook watching intently, studying Lenny and his entourage as closely as Diesel seemed to be. But Corvus...Corvus' eyes skimmed their faces. Unseeing. His brows were pinched tight and there was a distance in his eyes like he was a million miles from here. It wasn't what I expected from him and made my insides chill.

What was he doing?

Why wasn't he paying attention?

"Us?" Lenny asked, a brow lifting. "What made you—"

"The 'A' carved into Randy's chest. Your gang tag. The same one you paint over your territory."

Lenny's jaw ticked again.

This wasn't good.

"Now," Diesel continued, raising a hand in a calm

gesture, not allowing Lenny to rebuke him. "I'm not saying it was by your command, but perhaps one of your men went a little rogue. It happens. You understand, Lenny, that blood must be paid for the life that was taken. Think carefully before you speak again."

The thinly veiled threat hung in the air like a promise and a thrill went through me, making me shiver despite the warm black pullover I wore.

The thrill quickly morphing to something else as I spotted one of the Aces slip a gun from the back of his jeans and press it to the side of his thigh. His black hair was slicked back, giving a fully unobstructed view of his face. The way his upper lip was twitching into a snarl.

He was at the very end, closest to me. The light from the battery-powered spotlight hung off the back of the rusted metal warehouse wall didn't quite reach him. The only one who might've been able to catch his movement, or the glint of his gun in the moonlight, was Corvus, and he was clearly distracted as fuck.

Look, I wanted to shout. *Pay attention, you fucking idiot.*

I had to reposition my phone, having lowered it while I, myself, was distracted by everything they seemed to be missing.

"I can assure you, Diesel," Lenny replied after a moment. "None of my men would have acted so recklessly. They wouldn't dare go against my orders."

...unlike yours... Lenny seemed to be implying and a

small fissure formed in Diesel's perfectly crafted facade. That struck a nerve. So the king didn't have full control over all of his men, then. Though I doubted any gang leader did. It came with the territory, didn't it?

There was clearly a history between these two, one I wasn't privy to.

The man with the greasy black hair fixed his sights on Corvus and my lips parted in wordless alarm as his thumb pushed the safety off.

Oh god.

Why wasn't anyone noticing?

I raced to check all the other Aces, checking to see if they were readying weapons, too, but none seemed to be. Just this one. The one at the end looking like he had an ax to grind.

Fuck.

Fuck. Fuck. Fucking fuck.

"You wouldn't lie to me would you, Lenny?" Diesel asked, his tone one he might use on a child who'd misbehaved. Trying to tease out the truth with the promise of accepting it without punishment.

Something told me Diesel would, too. If Lenny admitted one of his men had acted without his permission, Diesel would have demanded that life in exchange for Randy's and no others.

A fair trade if you asked me.

People had to pay for their mistakes or else they'd just

keep making them.

Blood for blood.

It was the one adage of theirs I could get behind.

But Lenny wasn't going to budge, I could tell by the way he was standing. Defensively. Chin raised.

It had to be this clown at the end, the one still looking at Corvus like he might want to carve out his eyes. Maybe?

Ugh.

If Corvus would just fucking *look* then...

The Ace's hand moved to rest beside the trigger and I could *feel* his readiness from here. Like a strain in the air I was breathing. Making it harder to inhale. Thicker.

He's going to shoot him.

"No," Lenny told Diesel. "I wouldn't lie to you."

"You know I don't like being lied to."

"And you know the Aces own their shit. I'm telling you we had nothing to do with it."

Diesel bristled. "Very well. If you had nothing to do with it, then might you know who *does*?"

Lenny opened his mouth to reply, but I wasn't paying attention to him anymore. My body flooded with heat, flushing my cheeks as a fresh wave of adrenaline pulsed through me, narrowing my focus.

Don't do it, I mouthed, eyes fixed on the guy with his sights set on Corvus. I slipped a blade from my ankle and held it loosely in my palm, turning to flatten my back against the rough bark of the tree, positioning myself. My phone was forgotten, slipped into my pocket with the video still recording.

I hesitated, my hand jerking with my own indecision.

If Corvus was killed, there was a good chance my problems would be over.

With Corvus killed, the remaining three Saints would stand even less of a chance against the seven Aces.

Once the first shot was fired, and the first man fell, I had no doubt it would be a bloodbath.

If I let that greasy motherfucker shoot him, I could be kissing my problems goodbye. I could delete the videos, slip out of here and go back to a boring life of books and a future of freedom.

I tested the weight of my blade, lifting it over my shoulder, pinching the edge of it, at war with myself. My pulse pounded in my temples until all I could hear was the rush of blood in my ears, making every other sound distant and garbled.

I couldn't hear what Diesel and Lenny were saying, not really. I couldn't even hear my own breathing, though I knew it would be shallow and slow, measured as I lifted from my knees, my sweater catching on the bark as I uncurled to my full height.

Sweat beaded at my brow.

All you have to do is let it happen, I told myself. *Just close your eyes and let nature take its course.*

My stomach turned, and I swallowed back acid, my

teeth grinding.

The man with the black hair bared his teeth, and Grey noticed, squinting at him, but he couldn't see what was hidden at the guy's side. It was too late.

I saw the moment the Ace made his decision, jerking forward, his arm snapping up like a whip, his gun trained on Corvus.

My heart stopped.

I threw.

The bone-chilling *pop* of gunfire ricocheted through me, the sound coming only a split second before the Ace's shriek of agony. My blade speared through the meat of his palm. His gun thudded uselessly on the ground.

The shot went wide, and I sighed loudly, my breath leaving me in a painful gush when I found Corvus alive.

Guns raised all around.

Grey and Rook were fast enough to grab what looked like fully automatic rifles from the bucket of an old bobcat. Corvus and Diesel had their guns drawn, too. Safeties clicked off. Hammers were drawn back. Fingers rested on or next to triggers.

I waited for the bloodbath with bated breath, but it didn't come. The standoff held until Lenny broke it. They must've known that one more bullet would spell all of their deaths.

"Shut the fuck up, Carl!" he snarled, shouting at the hunched form of the black-haired man clutching his hand to his chest and whining obnoxiously loud. He was lucky I didn't aim for his thick skull. If I'd had the time to, I would've. As it was, the best option I could think of was to make him drop the gun or at least alter the trajectory of his shot.

Lenny side-stepped, keeping his sights trained on Diesel as he kicked Carl's gun far out of his reach. "Idiot," he hissed and then chanced a look into the trees. I ducked down, crouching in tight to the tree again, trying to shrink into the shadows, cursing myself for not beginning the quiet retreat straight away. For being too damn curious.

"What the fuck was that?" Lenny demanded. "Who do you have out there?"

Diesel's face betrayed nothing as his lightning-quick eyes flitted toward the trees and away again.

Corvus held his gun high, but his face visibly paled and his chest heaved.

Rook smirked, and my spine tingled when I realized he had a grenade clenched in his left hand while the rifle was butted to his shoulder and held with his right.

Grey was a study in mute power. His sights fixed on the injured Ace and nowhere else. Murder in his eyes.

"It's not ours," Diesel admitted, though I was willing to bet he hated owning to it. An honest man, I'd give him that. I wondered if he thought the next blade might be meant for him.

"Not yours?" Lenny hissed. "Then who the fuck—"

"Get out of here," Diesel barked right back. "We'll handle it."

I froze, drawing out another blade as I tried to soundlessly back away from the gun-toting gangsters in the yard before me.

Lenny squinted at Diesel, confused, but the Ace's leader backed up, gesturing to his men to get their fallen man and move out. I wouldn't question it either if someone gave me a get out of jail free card.

"Not him," Diesel said in a cold monotone, his gun still trained on Lenny's head as his eyes flicked to the injured Ace. "He tried to kill my son. The reason for which I'm sure you will fucking explain to me at a later date. But for now, I'll accept his life as payment for his *mistake.*"

Lenny's Adam's apple bobbed.

"Boss?" Another Ace pressed, torn between helping his buddy Carl and leaving like he was told to.

I lost sight of them as I crept backward, remaining crouched as I began my slow retreat.

They are coming for you, my darkness whispered, unspooling to her full power in my gut. *Any minute now. If you don't get away, your heroic display there will have been for nothing. It'll be them or you. Blades versus bullets.*

Time to find out if all that running was worth it.

I may not be faster, but I would bet my left kidney I could run *longer.* Go farther.

Then what, idiot? That's your blade in that asshole's hand.

The Crows will recognize it. They'll know it was you, even if you do get away.

Stupid didn't even begin to cover what I'd just done.

"Leave him," I heard Lenny order, and a cry of protest came from Carl before a gunshot rang out in the night, marking the start of my sprint.

I jumped to my feet and ran like hell. Flying over dirt and rock and tree roots. Honing in on those other senses. The ones that only flourished under extreme pressure. Relying on reflex and the strength of my body alone.

The feel of the blade clenched in my fist gave me the extra dose of fortitude I needed to keep pushing when the sounds of them giving chase reached my ears.

My legs pushed me impossibly fast until I was soaring through the darkened trees like an arrow shot from a bow.

The dirt and tree roots gave way to rockier terrain and the ground underfoot turned upward, the earth and grass giving way to a rockface slick with moss. I had no idea where I was going or where this path would lead me, but I didn't like the look of the long incline ahead. The trees were more sparse here, and thinner. There would be nowhere to hide if...

A shot blasted apart a thin tree to my right, the splinters of it exploding into my path. If I hadn't been running with quick, jerky movement in a zigzag, it would've hit me, I had no doubt. My heart shriveled in my chest, imaging one of the Crows on the other end of the bullet.

Corvus shouted to stop, but another shot was fired, this one narrowly missing me. The bullet tucked itself into the stone at my right with a *crack!*

The inclining stone sloped down sharply to my left and when I thought I had enough cover, I dared the fall, jumping down to skid on my heels all the way back down to level ground. My ankle twinged with pain, but I didn't let it stop me, pushing forward.

With the tree cover, they wouldn't be able to see me from above, but more importantly, they wouldn't be able to get a clean shot on me. I growled inwardly as the pain in my ankle grew, forcing me to slow despite the adrenaline still pushing me onward.

I wouldn't be able to go much farther.

Fuck my life.

Rocks slid and tumbled as they made their way down the incline after me.

I would be shot like a fish in a barrel if I didn't hide or run, and since the latter seemed to be out for the moment, I crouched low and made for the deepened shadows of a fallen tree. It was held up by the rock face, and I folded myself into its dead, scratching branches, sandwiching myself in between stone and insect infected wood.

Cobwebs tickled my neck and face, but I didn't let

myself think of all the things that might be crawling in between layers of my clothes right now. It wasn't important. Not even a little. I drew my last two blades, promising them I'd retrieve their brother from the dead guy in the yard if I made it out of this alive.

There were four Saints in these trees, and they all had guns.

If I had all four of my blades and the ability to throw them, I might've stood half a chance, but now, with only two, my only chance would be to stay hidden. To not be found.

I held my breath as their footfalls grew louder, until I could hear their heavy breaths.

Please, I sent a plea to whatever gods could hear me. *Please keep going.*

"Diesel," Corvus said, and I shuddered, closing my eyes against an assault of mixed emotions.

His father hushed him violently and all sound ceased. They were listening for me. I gave them nothing to hear.

"You hear that?" Diesel asked after a moment.

"I don't hear anything," Grey replied.

"Exactly," Diesel said in a husky whisper. "They stopped running. Whoever it is, they're hiding somewhere."

"Dies, come on," Corvus said, his voice taking on a tone I didn't recognize. What was up with him tonight? "They're gone. Let's just—"

"Spread out," Diesel barked, cutting Corvus off. "Rook and Grey, that way. Corv, you're with me. We'll find this son of a bitch."

They spread out, and I evened out my breathing, not moving a muscle as I caught sight of two silhouettes approaching. Grey and Rook.

Rook broke off from Grey and headed further away to the right, bent low with a mischievous grin on his face, his gun raised. This was all just a massive game of hide and seek to him. Unlike the others, he didn't seem bothered by the fact that the person they were hunting had blades, and maybe even a gun. Or maybe he'd already put it together.

The thought struck a nerve. Rook knew I was here.

What would he do if he found me?

But it wasn't him I had to worry about as he moved further and further away, it was Grey, who was carving a path almost straight for me.

"Clear!" Corvus shouted from somewhere far off in the distance.

"Clear!" came Diesel's brusque voice, closer than I'd have liked.

"Clear!" Rook.

Grey stooped low, tipping his head to the side as he examined the hollow between the tree and the stone. I held my blade high, but my hand trembled as
he crept closer.

345

Don't make me kill you...

He darted forward, yanking a branch out of the way, handgun raised.

I could have thrown. I could have stopped him. I didn't.

I stood there in full view, blade at the ready if he looked like he might fire.

He didn't.

Grey's lips parted in silent horror as he took me in, his gun lowering.

"Grey!" Diesel snarled from somewhere far too close.

Grey blinked, stepping back and releasing the branch. His eyes didn't leave mine as he hollered back. "Clear!"

Then he was gone.

I sighed, my breath tripping from my lips, broken as I let the relief cascade over me. My breaths loud in my own ears, but they'd already moved on. I didn't think I could hear them anymore.

Never let your guard down, that was rule number one that Dad taught me when he took me on our first job. When he bought me my blades after a good win at the private casino. Rule number fucking one, and for just a second, I forgot.

I didn't even see him coming. His hand curled around my forearm and dragged me from my hiding place, tossing me to the ground as though I weighed no more than a sack of potatoes.

My shoulder and the side of my face knocked into the hard dirt, and I scrambled to get to my feet in the dark, shaken but regaining my balance quickly.

I lifted my blade, ready to throw it straight into the heart of Diesel St. Crow before he could lift his weapon to take aim.

"Sparrow, don't!"

Corvus' shout shattered my resolve, but I held there, blade at the edge of my fingers, ready to throw as I heard their footsteps running toward us. In a second, I'd be surrounded.

In a second, it would be too late to do anything.

I'd lost my chance.

Diesel's blisteringly cold stare bored into me like a spike of ice as he trained his gun on my face, but I showed him no fear. I always knew I'd meet my end by the bite of a bullet or the slice of a blade. I'd just hoped it would come later. Much later.

"You know this girl?"

Grey

TWENTY-NINE

AJ wouldn't allow us to disarm her, and Diesel didn't push for it, so we didn't either. She stood between Rook and Corvus, with me at her back, letting us corral her back the way we'd come. She limped slightly, but she was doing a good job of hiding it.

What the fuck was she doing here?

Did she have a death wish?

My pulse thrummed uncomfortably behind my ribcage, making my stomach twist. This wasn't good. Already, my mind raced with possibilities, options that might end with her somehow still alive. We had a shadow once. A guy who thought he'd strike it rich blackmailing the Saints. Diesel found him, too.

He never saw daylight again.

Our father might be called Saint, but he was merciless when it came to protecting his found family. His brothers and his sons.

That guy was a threat, and now AJ was, too.

"In the warehouse," Diesel snarled from up ahead as the yard came back into view through the trees. The spotlight dying with the battery so there was only a diffused glow over the tires and the dead guy lying among them.

"You're a fucking idiot," Corvus muttered, and I realized he was talking to AJ. I'd picked up on it earlier, how neither of my brothers seemed at all surprised to see her here. I had to wonder if they were in on it. Or had seen her somehow before I had.

"Yup," AJ replied, popping her lips on the 'p,' like she didn't care at all that she might be chum for the sharks before sunrise. "Saved your ass though. You're welcome, asshole."

Corvus visibly stiffened, but said nothing as Diesel slammed a palm against the door to the warehouse, shoving it open, the rusted hinges screeching in protest.

We escorted AJ through, and her shoulders tensed, immediately on edge, the blades in her hands twitching.

I left the door open, squinting into the dark to find Diesel hunting through the place, throwing random bits of scrap into a barrel. He dumped gasoline over the mess and flicked on his lighter, igniting a bit of stray paper before tossing it into the metal drum.

Fire roared as the pile of scrap wood ignited, illuminating enough of the space to see that the warehouse was devoid of anything more than some withering old wooden pallets and a sagging desk in the corner.

"Who are you?" he demanded, coming at AJ with a look in his eyes that made my guts twist.

When she didn't answer or so much as flinch when he stopped just short of her, he turned his fury on Corvus. "Well?" he pressed. "Who the fuck is she?"

"Ava Jade Mason," Corvus replied, and only then did AJ betray any discomfort. I wouldn't like Diesel St. Crow to know my name either if he wasn't my family. Especially not if he was looking at me the way he was looking at AJ right now.

"Who do you work for?" Diesel asked her, his nostrils flaring. "Who sent you?"

She locked her lips tight.

"*I asked you a question.*"

"She isn't with a gang," Rook replied with ease, leaning back on a stack of pallets like we were at a casual bonfire.

Diesel's steely gaze moved to Rook, studying his second eldest son before bringing his sights back to AJ. "Check her," he ordered.

I moved in to do it before Corvus could, unsure of why. "Lift your arms for me, AJ," I murmured, low enough that Diesel would have a hard time catching it over the roar, pop, and hiss of the flames in the metal drum.

My back warmed from the fire as AJ grudgingly lifted her arms, her knuckles white from her grip on her blades. I patted her down.

"Be thorough," Diesel commanded, and I re-doubled my efforts, careful to caress every inch of her body. The curve of her breasts. Between her legs.

"No wire," I announced, but as my fingers dipped into her pockets I found something else and winced. Her phone.

Diesel would've seen the shape of it sagging in the pocket of her baggy pullover, so I drew it out. "Phone," I announced.

"Check it."

I did, flipping the screen to her first. "Password?"

"Fingerprint," she replied without a lick of trepidation, but her face betrayed what her voice wouldn't as it paled when I pressed the digit to the fingerprint reader.

I flicked through the main screen as Diesel waited, his trigger finger twitching.

Bile rose up the back of my throat as I flipped through to videos and found not one, but two.

The dots connected in my mind, seeing Billy Parker trussed up like a pig in his cooler. We'd heard he was found dead, now we knew why.

She'd killed him.

But she'd also saved the video.

I wasn't sure what that meant.

And the other video was of tonight. I didn't watch more than a few seconds of either before deleting them, my mouth going dry.

"Well?" Diesel prodded.

"Nothing," I gritted out, giving AJ a loaded look as I handed her phone back to her. I didn't let go straight away when her fingers curled around it, making her have to tug it out of my grasp. If she survived tonight, she had some fucking explaining to do.

I wasn't even sure why I deleted the evidence of her crimes. Why the fuck was I trying to save someone who so clearly was trying to blackmail us?

Were you not blackmailing her first? The traitorous thought echoed back to me, bouncing off the recesses of my skull.

Something told me there was more to it than what it appeared to be.

"Then she's collateral," Diesel snarled, raising his gun.

I blocked his shot, lurching into the line of his bullet at the same time Corvus made a move to disarm him.

"*Don't,*" Rook growled, and all eyes turned to him, no longer lounging easily against the pallets but standing like a hulking shadow, his arms tense at his sides, shoulders heaving. "No one touches her."

"Just what the fuck is going on here?" Diesel shouted, his carefully constructed mask crumbling as betrayal flashed across his eyes. It cut deep to see it, making me shudder, but I didn't budge. I wouldn't.

What the fuck was wrong with me?

"Dies," I managed, able to keep my voice level despite the chaos raging within. "A word?"

Corvus whirled on me, his brows drawn as if to ask what the fuck I was playing at.

If he wouldn't do it, then I would. AJ was worth at least *trying*, wasn't she?

Diesel glanced between the three of us, calculating. Studying.

His upper lip curled, and he dropped his gun, stepping back with a hiss. "Don't let her out of your sight," he spat at Corvus and Rook as he shouldered through them both and vanished back out into the night.

"What are you doing?" Corvus asked as I turned to follow him, giving AJ's arm a squeeze, an apology unspoken on my lips.

"What we should have done from the start."

"What?" Diesel snapped as I walked out of the warehouse, going to where he was pacing near the Rover. "You want to tell me what the hell is going on, Son, because I'm two seconds shy of—"

"We know her," I admitted. "She goes to Briar Hall."

Diesel's breathing evened out at the level tone of my voice, or maybe it was something in my face. But he softened, running a palm over his beard with a heavy sigh.

"I don't know why she followed us, but I do know that she's the only reason Corvus isn't the one lying dead in the yard."

Diesel stilled. He didn't like that.

"And we both know what would've happened if that motherfucker killed Corv."

It would have been anarchy. We'd have been lucky not to lose another. Or all of us...

"What are you saying, Son?" he asked, clearly exasperated as he shuffled, dropping his head to take a long slow breath. "You saying she's friendly? Hmm? Is that it? That she came here, what? As...as unsanctioned backup?"

I frowned, shook my head. I didn't know what I was saying exactly, but I needed to drive this point home. "She saved our asses, Dies."

"You saying you trust this girl? This *outsider*?"

I flexed my jaw. "Yes."

"And your brothers?"

"They trust her, too."

Not any further than they could throw her, but that wasn't the point right now. The point was saving her life like she'd just saved my brother's, and possibly all of ours.

"We owe her a debt of life," I pushed, speaking in terms he would understand. The unwritten code of the life.

Diesel's lips pressed into a taut line as he considered that. "She's a liability. She's seen what went down here tonight. The girl can't go free."

"No," I agreed. "But maybe there's another option."

"Speak it, then."

"We bring her in." I spoke the words quickly, my stomach dropping at the implication of them. It was what I'd been saying since the beginning, since I looked at her, *really* looked, and saw someone my soul recognized. That'd only happened three other times in my life. I had to trust it.

"Let her take the trial," I continued when Diesel looked at me like I might be losing my mind. "If she survives, she'll be in so deep that she'll never be able to use anything she's seen against us without burying herself, too. If she doesn't..."

I let that hang between us for a second, knowing he might like that option better.

"...then I guess you won't have anything to worry about."

"You're serious."

I nodded, and he turned pacing away only to return again, rolling my suggestion around behind the dam of his lips. Eyes unfocused.

"She's a girl," he argued.

"It's been done before. Mom was a Saint."

He bristled, and I realized belatedly it was the wrong thing to say. Comparing AJ to his dead wife.

I waited, unable to take it back now that it was said, but when the silence stretched too long and something inside me felt pulled so tight it was near snapping, I continued.

"You saw how good she is with a blade. She can fight. Sly as a fox, too. She could be useful."

He looked at me, his stare darting between my eyes as though he might find some truth there I was saying out loud.

"Do you have feelings for this girl?"

"No."

"Don't lie to me."

I clenched my teeth.

"I've never asked you for anything," I said, using the last tool in my arsenal. It was the truth. I'd always done what I was told. Everything I was trained to do. I was a good soldier. A good brother. A good son. I didn't push for anything, because in my limited experience, when you pushed, sometimes the person would never come back. But I was pushing now. I would push for her.

It was what was owed.

"I am asking for this. *For her*."

The hurt in his stare almost broke me, but I hid the

pain well. Stood taller instead.

"So be it," he said, his gaze turning dark as he stalked past me, unable to look me in the eyes anymore.

"She doesn't leave your sight. Not for a second. Not until the trial begins," he called back, and I stood there, mute and numb until I heard the sound of his engine roaring to life and his tires peeling away from the warehouse, carrying him home.

Ava Jade

THIRTY

After Grey returned, they escorted me to the Rover and closed me inside. I could hear snippets of their heated conversation through the bulletproof glass, but not enough to piece together what was going on.

Grey sat with me in the car while Corvus and Rook cleaned up Carl's body. The air permeated with anger and things unsaid.

It must've been hours before they finally returned from the dark of the trees, coated in dirt streaked sweat.

I thought of running again, but with my ankle still in bad shape, I knew I wouldn't get far. The only other option I saw was to slit Grey's throat and make a stealthy getaway instead of a rapid one while the others were busy disposing of the evidence of Diesel's kill, but…

I couldn't.

Just like I couldn't let that greaseball shoot Corvus.

I stewed in silence, angry at myself and trying to work through the puzzle of my thoughts, only bothering to speak once Rook slid into the seat beside me and Corvus hopped into the front seat.

"I'll fight back," I warned, crossing my arms over my chest as icy dread pooled in my stomach. I could take one of them. *Maybe,* I could take two. But all three? I could fight, but I knew what the outcome would be.

Rook lifted a brow at me, and Grey swiveled in the front seat, his face drawn. Corvus didn't bother to turn, sitting stoically in the passenger seat to stare out into the growing dawn.

"Just make it quick, would you?" I requested, sinking into the seat as Grey turned back to the front and started the engine, pulling slowly back onto the road.

They didn't speak to me the entire drive back to the Crow's Nest. Rook twisted his lip ring round and round with his teeth, his dark gaze slipping to me and away, only to return again a few moments later.

He kept his distance, lounging in the seat closest to the opposite window, knee bouncing behind Corvus' seat.

Somewhere around the halfway point, Grey turned on the radio, drowning out the tense silence with the early morning show from the local radio station.

The reality of my situation didn't seem to truly hit me

until we bumped off smooth pavement and onto gravel and the Crow's Nest came into view. But it wasn't what I couldn't stop staring at. The small shed at the edge of the property, half hidden by trees as the first rays of dawn lit the metal roof made my stomach plummet to my toes.

I was *this close.*

This close to freedom.

Why couldn't I have just bowed like a good girl and done what I was told.

Oh yeah, because I wasn't a good girl. I didn't bow. And I did whatever the fuck I wanted *whenever* the fuck I wanted.

The real question was, why couldn't I be someone else?

Someone else wouldn't be about to die in a tiny ass woodshed, their body parts hacked up and hid over three different states.

Fuck.

I gripped my knives, letting the darkness come, beckoning it.

I could kill them.

Maybe not before, but this was different. It was kill or be killed.

"We need to talk," Grey said as he shut off the engine, sighing.

Corvus muttered something I didn't catch to himself as he shoved out the passenger side door and slammed it, stalking into the house.

Rook whistled low, a smirk playing at the edge of his lips as he opened his door. "Want a whiskey?" he offered. "You're going to need it."

What?

"We aren't going to kill you, AJ," came Grey's exasperated voice from the front seat as he withdrew the keys and stepped out himself, shutting his door as he opened mine. I shied away, lifting a blade.

He looked between it and me, a tightness around his eyes. "And you aren't going to kill us, either," he challenged as I caught sight of Rook in my periphery, going into the house, too. "I think you made that pretty clear tonight."

"If you aren't going to kill me, then why the fuck am I here?"

He bent his head, pinching the bridge of his nose, making his dirty blond hair fall forward, shining with streaks of purest gold in the soft early morning light.

"Don't make this harder than it has to be. Either you come willingly on my word that you won't be harmed, or I call my brothers back out here and we drag you inside. Your choice."

I rolled my eyes and stepped out, forcing Grey to move out of my way or be hit. He shut the door behind me. "Good choice."

"The only reason I'm going in there is because Rook

said there's whiskey, and I'm hungry enough to eat a whole fucking turkey," I grumbled, knowing how I must sound but unable to stop myself.

"If you say so."

"Fuck you."

His hand closed around my wrist, and I lashed out, slicing his forearm as he tossed me against the door of the Rover. Grey bared his teeth as he moved to box me in, the blade between us the only thing keeping him from closing the last few inches of the gap. Blood dripped in a slow stream from his arm, but he didn't seem to mind. Didn't even seem to feel it.

Fury burned in his eyes. A deep, pained thing that hurt to look at.

"Do you have any idea what I just risked to save you?" he demanded, his anger so hot that I could feel it soaking into my skin. Making the small hairs on the back of my neck raise. "What we'll *all* risk to keep you alive?"

"What are you talking about?"

"And after you were trying to...to what? Blackmail us?" he continued, drawing back with a dark laugh. "I saw the videos, AJ. I know what you did. What you were doing—"

"You gave me no fucking choice!" I shouted, my own fury rising to meet his, the icy dream in my belly turning quickly to acid.

"Yeah, you gave me no choice, either," he scoffed.

"Just remember that."

"What's going on out there?" Rook called lazily from the front door, sipping a short glass of amber liquid. "Come inside so we can all join the fun."

I growled in frustration, shouldering past Grey toward the front door. I snatched the whiskey right from Rook's hand and tossed it back in one long burning swallow before shoving the glass back at him and going inside.

They wanted to talk. *Fine. Let's talk.*

I knew the basic layout of the house since I'd been stalking it on and off for weeks, and I took an easy left from the hall in the entry, through to the kitchen, where there was a whiskey bottle open on the counter. I snatched it up and kept going, through the kitchen to the right into the living room.

Corvus was already there, sitting on the couch, the dirt streaks gone from his face and hands. His dirty jacket missing, leaving him in only a black shirt, dark wash jeans, and sock feet. It felt strange to see him so comfortable. I didn't think there was a place on earth where he wouldn't be ready for an attack at all times.

He lifted his head, and upon seeing me, threw the item he'd been twirling in his fingers at me. My lips parted in surprise as I caught it, the blade cutting into the pads of my thumb and forefinger. The blade that'd been embedded in Carl's meaty hand.

"You're welcome," he grunted, fixing me with a deadly stare.

I tucked it into my ankle sheath with its brother, keeping one at the ready in my palm just in case. "Yeah, well you still owe me one."

He shook his head.

Grey and Rook entered behind me. I fell into the only armchair in the room, forcing the others to all share the sofa on the other side of the long, narrow coffee table. It acted as a line in the sandy carpet, and I didn't intend to cross it again until it was time to leave.

I took a swig of the whiskey, then leaned forward to set it down on the table, noticing Rook eyeing the bottle.

He grabbed it, taking a pull straight from the bottleneck, too, and licked his lips.

Grey leaned forward between his two brothers, elbows on knees as he regarded me coldly.

"I've told them what I found on your phone," he began and already I was on edge, my fist tightening on the blade, regretting the whiskey already starting to nibble at my reflexes and senses.

"There are no secrets between us," he continued, though already I knew that was a lie. Maybe they didn't keep the important shit from each other, but I knew damn well that Corvus had no idea Grey and I fucked. I didn't think he'd like that after his possessive touch and words on fight night.

I waited for him to go on, and when he didn't, my irritability skyrocketed, fueled by whiskey and exhaustion. "How nice for you," I said with a false smile, my voice dripping sarcasm. "Do you also pick daisies on Saturdays and wish upon shooting stars?"

A tick in Grey's jaw was the only giveaway that my comment annoyed him, but I'd take it.

"This isn't a fucking joke," Corvus butt in, his eyes on fire. "Do you know what would've happened if Grey didn't stick his neck out for you?"

"Do *you* know what would've happened if I didn't throw that blade?" I countered, my voice rising in volume.

"Would you shut the fuck up for one second and listen?"

"*Corv*," Grey warned, and earned himself a snarl from his brother.

Corvus got to his feet and paced down to the edge of the coffee table. I thought he might leave, but he turned around, his jaw flexing, and sat back down.

I wasn't sure I'd ever seen him this worked up. I didn't think he *got* this worked up. It made me want to poke him some more, see how long it took before he snapped.

"What does he mean?" I asked Grey, instead, tabling the idea of provoking Corvus, at least for the moment. I didn't like the way they were looking at me. How they seemed to be hesitating to tell me something. "About you sticking your neck out for me?"

"Diesel wanted you dead, AJ," he said. "The instant you threw that blade, you became a liability. A threat."

"But I also saved his precious son," I pointed out. *"Who I wouldn't have needed to save if he was paying any attention at all."*

"Maybe I could've paid more attention if I didn't see your ass creeping out of the back of the Rover."

"Enough," Grey hissed, and Rook snorted, taking another swig of his drink, seeming to be having way too much fun just sitting there watching this conversation happen.

Corvus' nostrils flared, but he fell silent, content to sit there and glare at the carpet.

"AJ," Grey hedged, drawing my attention back to him. "I asked Diesel to bring you in."

"You did what?!"

"I asked him to let you take the trial."

I was on my feet, the burst of shock hauling me up like marionette strings, making me move. "He didn't agree to that."

Diesel St. Crow wouldn't agree to that, would he?

Grey's eyes slid from my face. "He did. I've never asked him for anything. Not ever. I asked him to spare you and let you take the trial. If you pass, you'll be in so deep there's nothing you could do to hurt him, or us, without also burying yourself."

I barked a laugh at the ludicrousness of what he was saying. This wasn't happening.

"And if I fail?" I asked, my tone light, joking. As if I were really going to take the trial to become a motherfucking Saint.

"You die," Corvus said, detached, his hard stare seeming to penetrate deep into my soul.

I flinched as though slapped. A trap door opened beneath my feet, and I was plummeting, searching for anything to hold on to. To pull myself out.

"I won't do it."

"Then you'll die, anyway," Rook interjected, finally speaking up, unlike the others, there was no apology in his eyes, no ire, either. Just amusement. Fucking bastard.

"Then I'll run."

"Diesel won't let you get away."

My heart beat out a discordant rhythm in my chest, fluttering like a caged bird. I worked to catch my breath, cursing myself for the hundredth time for not being able to be that *someone else*. A girl who could be controlled.

"Sparrow," Corvus urged and something in his stature changed. It made the lead in my bones turn to quicksand, melt into glass. Shatter. "You don't have a choice."

ACKNOWLEDGMENTS

The crazy idea for this story wrapped its callused fingers around my throat and demanded to be written, and I'll be honest, I wasn't sure I had it in me at first. It was so unlike anything I'd ever written before. So, I have to thank my readers for pushing me to go for it. From the moment I posted that first chapter in The Lair, you were there for it, cheering me on. I am eternally grateful for that support. I don't think I've ever felt more connected to a story or its characters as I have with Ava Jade and the Crows.

This book may not have been possible without the support of my fiancée, Matthew Bishop. Thank you for taking time off work and doing more than your fair share around the house while I made strange faces at my computer screen all day. Thank you for listening to me rant and complain and gush about these characters while listening to my Crooked Crows playlist on repeat. You are the real MVP.

I doubt this book would be half as awesome without the help of my incredible alpha readers. Casey, Sam, Claire, Frankie, Courtney, Kim, and Amanda, you were all vital to the process of bringing Ava Jade's story into the world. Thank you for all your input, feedback, and support. Most of all, thank you for falling in love with these characters and this story. Without you cheering me on, the finish line would've been much harder to reach.

Jennifer, you total fucking champ. Thank you for always making my words sparkle, and for dealing with last minute changes and my batshit crazy schedule. I couldn't ask for a better editor.

Dez, thank you for the drop-dead gorgeous cover. That shit is hot at fuck.

Papa, for believing in me without question and always reading my books. If you read this one (even though I specifically asked you not to), maybe do us both a favor and pretend you didn't? Oh, and stop now. It just gets darker and dirtier from here on out.

I also need to thank my author friends for being there, especially the ladies of the DARC, you know who you are. And I can't forget my Sprint Syndicate bitches, without whom I would have procrastinated the shit out of writing this book. Thank you for being there at all hours of the day and night, ready to write along with me and keep me honest.

Last, but certainly not least, I want to thank the advance reviewers, PR companies, and everyone who has helped or will help to share Crooked Crows. Without you, I would be nothing but a blimp on the radar of publishing. I see you, and I love the shit out of each and every one of you.

Printed in Great Britain
by Amazon